WHAT IT'S ABOUT...

Jake Priest learned at an early age to take anything he could get and never look back. With the help of his foster sister Bea, and the catchy song she wrote, he finally gets a stroke of luck and becomes the hottest new entertainer in the industry. He's always felt a little guilty for using Bea's song as his ticket to fame, but after years of hiding her talent, Bea's finally crafting musical masterpieces again. Jake credits one woman with inspiring her to do it.

When that woman, Octavia Rothschild, shoved Beatrice Cipriani into the limelight, she really had no idea that Bea would try and drag her on stage too. Octavia's finding the attention uncomfortable. Ever since an accident that left prominent burns on one side of her face, Octavia has attracted too much attention, none of it good.

And now the studio's insisting that Octavia perform one of Bea's songs with Jake Priest. The label's wild for the kind of publicity a duet would create, even if Jake's famously impossible to deal with. Only, the more time Jake spends with Octavia, the more he's drawn to her voice and her unique beauty.

But Jake's shady past was only contained, not erased.

When Jake's father finally walks out of prison, the first person he wants to see is his newly rich and famous son. And good old dad has some demands—and some secrets—that may just change everything. Can Jake and Octavia heal from past trauma in time to deal with everything the world's about to throw at them?

FILTHY RICH

B. E. BAKER

For my darling cousin Katie

You've always been stunningly beautiful both inside and out. For the monsters in the world, I apologize. I just want you to know that so many more of us see you for the gorgeous and unique beauty you are. You have always inspired me... and so many others.
SHINE ON.

PROLOGUE: JAKE

Every single person on earth has a story, but most of them don't like what they've written for themselves. A con man's only real job is to discover the story a person *wishes* was theirs and give it to them. Or at least, make the person believe that they're giving it to them. People will pay everything they have and they'll betray everyone they love to live the story of their heart.

Even if it's a lie.

That's why con artists are still around. My dad taught me that if people weren't lying to themselves, we couldn't lie to them either. That's why it's important to evaluate someone to make sure they're an easy mark. Finding that person's the most important part, and making sure they're someone whose story you can provide.

I've heard people get all up in arms. "You're stealing from them. You're criminals." But entertainers have been doing the very same thing for years. When we plonk our money down for a story about how the poor, disheveled girl gets the prince? We're paying for a lie. It's just that they're bilking you out of a few bucks for a few hours.

Con artists provide a more immersive experience that they'll never ever forget. You could even say we're teaching them an important lesson their parents should have taught: be careful what you wish for. If the same people would stop being victims and accept the life they had, we'd have no marks. At the end of the day, it's their fault.

We're just giving them what they want.

Learning all of that from the time I could talk taught me to be one of the best actors in Hollywood. Unlike most of my peers, I know the camera's always rolling. In every interaction, in every meeting, I'm always playing a part.

I can't ever forget who I'm supposed to be in that moment.

But sometimes, in the quiet moments, I wonder who Jake Priest really is. If I wasn't acting, if I wasn't working an angle, if I wasn't selling someone a lie. . .who would I be?

Is it even someone I'd like?

CHAPTER 1
OCTAVIA

Everyone makes mistakes.

I've heard that cliché my entire life. And largely, I'm sure it's true. But my life's goal has been never to make any mistakes. I try my best in every situation to make the right choice the very first time.

But there's one notable exception.

I did something really terrible once, a few months ago. As a judge in a contest, I scored the best person the very worst. I did it specifically so that she'd lose, even though she clearly deserved to win. Her talent was, to someone who was actually trained in the subject, crystal clear. I shouldn't have done it, but in that moment, I had no choice.

Had she won, she might have turned out just like me.

And having an epic dream coupled with real talent. . . but hiding it. . . is about the worst thing in the world.

I don't have a choice, but she did, so I forced her to try.

Unlike me, Beatrice Cipriani's face was pristine—flawless. Mine is the opposite of that. Even if I pursued my dream of becoming a popstar full throttle, there's no way it would ever happen. Like a plane with a broken turbine, a train with rocks in the engine, or a sprinter with a leaky heart valve, I'm doomed from the start.

My failure was decided many years ago when a cheap plastic wig caught fire and stuck itself to my face, neck, and shoulder. My body healed the damage, but the scars. . .those are permanent.

There are many dreams a girl with a terribly burned face could pursue. If I wanted to paint masterpieces, my face might even be a fascination. If I loved designing video games, I'd be just fine. A show jumper? Horses don't care what you look like, or at least, I don't think they do. If my talent lay with crafting unique stories, I could use a cartoon profile photo and no one would ever have to know.

To do those things, I'd probably need a bigger brain.

My one true asset in life is my voice, and people have to look at you for nearly every iteration of success as a singer. Thanks to that fateful day and that cheap, miserable wig, exactly no one wants to look at me. That's why I'm stuck singing jingles, so no one has to look at me.

I can't blame people—I don't want to look at myself either.

It's interesting that symmetry is the standard of beauty, because that's the one thing I can never achieve. Ironically, that darn wig plastered itself down my face in very nearly a straight line. The straight line down the center of my face neatly highlights my *lack* of symmetry. It didn't help that my body seemed to hate all the treatments—not that it's totally the doctors' fault. I hated the bindings and wraps and wasn't the most compliant patient. The one graft that took well was the one that repaired the burn on my chin. Only a hairline scar remains there now, connecting my lower lip to my jawline, the other side of the graft concealed just below the edge of my face.

The other grafts we tried didn't go well at all, and it shows.

When we gave up on medical intervention, I had to accept my situation. After that, my vocal talent kind of hurt. So watching someone else with the raw talent to do what I couldn't blow it on jingles? I just couldn't help her settle for second best. That's why, as a judge for the Jello jingle, I voted Beatrice Cipriani down. If I'd known what she'd do next, I'd have let her win. She could have hidden away with me at our jingle agency, a co-worker and a new friend for life.

I hated the idea of her dying inside a little more every day as she wasted her life on commercials, but that darn girl's been almost worse than the wig, which at least had the decency to stop torturing me once the doctors pried it away from my body, taking my ruined skin along with it.

No, Bea just clings on, torturing me in new ways every day.

She is talented, though. She's probably more talented than anyone I've ever met. In fact, just this morning she came up with yet another song, one that the studio's *dying* to get down. "It'll be perfect for the kiss scene," I finally agree. "It hits just the right tone, and that melody."

"I think it should be piano only," Bea says. "They made us add drums, bass, and guitar to everything else, but this one has to be soft, understated, and flowing. *Only* piano can get that right."

Our guitarist, Morgan, is already opening her mouth to argue.

"Ah, ah, ah," Eddy says. "We promised her one song that's just piano in the contract, and the first kiss is a good place for it."

Morgan's eyes flash, but she says nothing. She's a bit of a

diva, but she can really play guitar, so I try not to hold it against her. Most artists can't get out of their own way.

"They're filming this right now," Eddy says. "The kiss scene, I mean. So when I said you nailed the music, they asked you to come watch. Jake thought it might help you get the tone right or tweak the words or something." Eddy shrugs. "He said it's part of your process."

"I already read the scene," Bea grumbles. "Why do I need to go watch him being all weird and fake?"

"Does he look fake to you?" That surprises me. He seems exactly the same in person as he does on screen.

I might be a bit of a Jake Priest fangirl in the privacy of my own home. As long as Bea never finds out, or worse, *Jake*, it should be fine. How could anyone not have a harmless crush on someone like him? Between his huge dimples and his big, shiny teeth. . . It's like he was made for the big screen. His well-defined muscles don't hurt, either. I always assumed that people like him would be just awful in person, but he's not. He's funny, personable, and kind, and he would do anything for his sister. That goes a long way with me, because I'm an only child, and I always wanted a sibling.

"Not so much fake as just. . .hollow. I can't really describe it. The part of him that makes him Jake just. . ." She shrugs. "It's like it's not there when he's acting. It's annoying enough to me that I don't really like watching his movies." She grimaces. "If any of you repeat a single word of that, I'll chop you up into small pieces and feed you to that stray dog that keeps lurking just out of reach behind the hotel."

Watching Bea try to act threatening is cute. It's like a rabbit brandishing a long twig. My lip twitches, but Morgan outright laughs. "Yeah, we'll be sure to keep that one a secret. Can't have you hacking us up."

"Okay, let's go." Eddy gestures at the door.

There's a studio van idling on the curb. I sigh, like I'm annoyed, but really, I'm a little shaky with excitement. We'll be on set with Jake Priest and Patrice Jouveau. Honestly, if I had to pick someone to date the practically-perfect-Jake-Priest, it would be her. They both have wide, cartoon eyes. They both have beautifully symmetrical faces. They both have a presence about them, and they both pull some real fandoms.

There's been a *lot* of chatter online about this movie, mostly because we're all wondering whether the universe might explode when they touch. Two perfect people in one small space. . .finally having their first kiss.

I can't help my shiver.

"Are you cold?" Bea asks. "I have a sweater."

Even though it's technically fall, it's a perfect seventy-two degrees in LA, like it is eight or nine months out of the year, pretty much. "I'm fine."

Bea, however, is always cold. She puts the frumpy sweater on like she couldn't care less how she looks on the set of a glamorous, Hollywood film. Then again, she has a beautiful face, and a gorgeous fiancé who adores her, so she probably *doesn't* care.

Even if I was so frozen that my arms and legs would barely move, even if I was actively turning blue, I wouldn't wear that chunky, ratty old sweater. But then again, when you have one glaring flaw that everyone you meet gawks at, you can't risk even tiny faux pas.

I watch in partial awe as the scenery rolls past.

Massive mansions.

Dolled up women in designer dresses and monstrous heels.

Palm trees, rippling waves, and a cloudless blue sky for miles in all directions. It's pretty surreal to be here. New York weather's fickle and usually at least a little glum. We also don't have beaches like this—not anywhere. And our women have *waaaay* less silicon in their bodies and a lot less sun-kissed gold on their skin.

As we finally pull into the lot and park, my heart accelerates.

Can I manage to be just another person in the crowd? Or will everyone notice my face, stare, murmur, point, hiss, and jeer? It's usually about fifty-fifty odds which way it will go. Sometimes people avert their eyes, like I have some kind of gruesome injury they don't want to see, but honestly, that's better than the unkind remarks, the rude questions, or the protective words and gestures they make to move people away from me.

A gorgeous monstrosity.

Bea named me well.

I've been waiting, ever since this madness began, for my face to ruin everything for me, for Bea, for Jake, and for the movie, in that order. It's just a matter of time before it happens, but no matter how many times I've warned Bea, she ignores me.

I can't tell whether she's oblivious or willfully ignorant.

Either way, she's remarkably consistent. The very second we reach the viewing area behind the cameras, Bea waves, catching Jake's eye immediately.

He was leaning against a boardroom table in a tux—the way they construct these sets is impressive to me. The furniture looks like it costs more than the set design. Jake in a tux is. . .distractingly handsome. I'm sure it was for the scene, but he was managing to look truly, genuinely bored, which was impressive, because not two feet away, Patrice Jouveau's standing in a floor length evening gown, slit almost up to her hip bone. Her makeup's pristine, her luminous face adorably vulnerable.

Her lips—it's clear they knew this was the kiss scene. They're full, pink, and glistening. I almost want to kiss them, and I have zero interest in women.

"You'll have to go again," someone's saying.

But Jake shakes his head. "Let's take five." He's smiling now, as he strides toward us. "My sister's here."

"Oh, your sister who's doing sound, right?" Patrice smiles as she follows Jake our direction. "I can't wait to meet her."

"Not sound," Jake says. "The sound*track*."

Patrice's face barely wrinkles as she frowns. "Sound. Soundtrack." She shakes her head, like he's being an idiot. "Right."

"Sound is all the effects for the movie." Jake glares. "The soundtrack is art."

"No, I know, and you're totally right. I said it wrong." Patrice's smile looks forced, but I can't blame her. I'd be annoyed if someone corrected me so harshly for one little slip in front of people I'd never met.

"I hear today's the first kiss," Bea says. "Pretty exciting."

"Not really," Jake mutters. "Should be as awkward as ever."

Patrice laughs. "As if."

"As if what?" Bea's frowning now, and her entire forehead wrinkles when she does.

"As if it could possibly be awkward with the two stars in Hollywood who are the most famous for their excellent kissing." Patrice blinks and stares at Bea. "You know, you look *nothing* like Jake." She blinks again. "Honestly, you look Asian."

Jake laughs. "You have a keen eye." He shakes his head. "Adopted sister."

"Oh." Patrice arches one carefully groomed eyebrow. "So you're not really related at all. You could—" She cuts off and huffs.

It's slight, but Jake's nostrils flare. "That's—"

"You're right," Bea says. "We aren't *really* related at all." She steps closer to him. "In fact, now that you mention it, we *could* get married. I had never realized that." Her eyes widen and her hands paw his chest. "Oh, my darling Jake."

Jake starts laughing and shoves her off.

Patrice looks horrified.

I can't help a small snort.

"Bea's fiancé's one of the film's investors," Eddy says from behind me. "I don't think she has any plans to start dating her brother—genetically connected or not."

"I'm sure she didn't mean to imply that adopted siblings aren't real siblings," I say. "You probably just misunderstood."

Patrice's face swivels my direction. "And who are you?" She looks quite unhappy, though I'm not sure why. I was defending her.

"This is our main talent," Bea says. "She's my best friend, too, Octavia Rothschild."

She's never called me that—her best friend. My heart expands, like a very dry sponge drawing in water. I can't help my smile.

"You've never heard anyone with a voice as beautiful as hers," Jake says.

Patrice grimaces. "Or a face quite so ugly."

Her words are like the hit of a habanero pepper, the sting from a slap, and the crack of a broken bone.

Unexpected.

Painful.

Debilitating.

"That's not true at all," Bea's eyes flash, "and it was horribly mean. You should apologize immediately."

"I think her words are more a reflection of her ugliness than anything else," Jake says, so quietly, so casually, that I almost don't register their meaning. "An apology from her's worthless anyway. Don't bother asking."

Patrice's big, beautiful eyes widen, and she blinks. "I—I'm so sorry. I shouldn't have said that. It was rude, and of course, not true. I was just so shocked. I haven't seen anything like the burns on your face before, and. . ." Her face has flushed quite red.

"It's fine," I say. "Don't worry about it."

"I can see why they said you and I would be filming the scenes for the music videos," she whispers. "Because who would want to look at. . ." She sniffs.

A muscle in Jake's jaw tightens and releases. For a moment, I worry that he'll criticize her again, making a big scene. It would be the exact wrong thing to do, of course, since it would only draw more attention to me.

Thankfully, he doesn't.

"Looks like we're out of time," Jake mutters. "Come on, *Patty*. Let's go get this scene over with."

"Yes," Patrice says. "Of course. Work first. Play later."

If the sides of Jake's eyes tighten and the slant of his lips is a little hard, well, I don't know him that well. Maybe I'm misinterpreting it.

"I can see why he hates her," Bea whispers. "She's horrible."

"Wait, he hates her?" Morgan has leaned so close that she's inches from toppling over on Bea. "Because I'd pee on her Cheerios with a smile on my face, and we just met."

Bea chuckles. "He didn't know her when they chose her

for this part, but he said she's arrogant, irritating, and obtuse."

I'd say those are all accurate descriptions.

"Well, you couldn't pay me enough to kiss her." Morgan scowls. "I'd be worried my lips would wither and fall off."

That makes me laugh, and the camera crew, as well as Patrice and one of the set guys, all glare.

Jake, however, looks amused. He catches my eye and winks.

After that, I feel a little better. It helps to know he doesn't like Patrice the Poop. If I hadn't just noticed, and if Bea hadn't told me, I wouldn't be able to tell he disliked Patrice at all. When he slams one hand beside her head, his eyes fixed on hers, his teeth biting his lip, my heart hammers in my chest. And then when his head drops slowly, so painfully slowly toward her mouth, I forget to breathe. He's a really good actor, and I'm not the only one to notice. Bea, Morgan, and even Eddy are all watching intently.

Even without our soundtrack, this scene's going to be epic.

When they finally kiss, I can't help a small sigh.

But the second the director yells cut, Jake drops her like a burning coal and pivots on his heel. "We good?"

"One take?" The director whistles. "Let's make sure we got it from every angle first."

Jake nods, walking back toward us.

"How long will you need the song to run?" Bea asks, the second he reaches us. "Because it looks like the scene's about three minutes, and I think the song's only going to be two and a half, but we could do a reprise, or we could add another verse."

"I'd have to hear it to say," Jake says. "But you know we want the swell to happen right as the kiss does."

Bea nods. "Right, so maybe not a reprise."

Jake shrugs. "Loses some impact, really. We could also segue from--"

Eddy clears his throat. "This isn't really your job, you know."

"But it is mine," Bea says. "And he knows more about music for movies than I do, so he offered to help."

"Fine, but you're not going to convince Jane to credit you for the soundtrack." Eddy's smiling, or I'd be worried he was serious.

"We should go to karaoke tonight," Bea says. "I hear they have a new place not far from our hotel that just opened called Seoul Town."

Jake cringes. "Soul town?"

"Not like my heart and soul," Bea says. "Like Seoul, Korea. It's like the karaoke places in Korea instead of the big bars here where everyone takes turns getting a song and performs for a hundred people. These are a bunch of smaller rooms where they have a screen, sofas, and props. It's for small groups and parties, and we could sing this song a variety of ways to try it out."

"But they won't have the music," I say. "We can't practice—"

"Are you saying you can't sing *a cappella*?" Bea looks smug. "I find that hard to believe."

"We could record a few different versions before we go," Morgan says. "One with a guitar and one without, for instance." She side-eyes Bea. "People could weigh in on what sounds better."

Bea's shoulders straighten. "Eddy promised me—"

"Calm down," Jake says. "You're worse than a movie star."

"Hardly," Bea says. "And you should be in favor of preserving the artistic integrity of the project."

"I like the karaoke idea," I say. "You get so caught up on the piano that you sometimes make a lot of changes to things that don't even need them. I think we should try it a few different ways, and record them, and then you can listen to them in the morning."

"Actually that's not a bad idea." Jake shakes his head. "I can see it now, the news headline. *Bizarre artist drags piano into local karaoke club, scraping floors and smashing doorways in order to write new song for hit movie—*"

"Did someone say karaoke? Because I think we're done now." Patrice half-smiles. "I'd love to come sing through the options for you, since Jake and I will be the ones singing for the album."

"Since. . .what?" Jake asks.

Eddy coughs. "Well, we meant to talk to you about it, but some of the investors thought it might be good publicity to have Patrice do the vocals for the music video, and then when her agent told us she could sing, we thought maybe she could be the headliner for the album. We'd still have Octavia singing backups, of course, and she'll be credited on the album."

They want to ditch the major liability for a sure thing.

They'd be stupid *not* to do that.

I'm just wondering why it took them so long to think of it.

CHAPTER 2
JAKE

Dear Jake,

Cowbirds aren't the only parasitic breed, you know. They're not even the most famous. No, that distinction goes to the cuckoo. In fact, that's the root of the word "cuckold." A man is a cuckold if he's caring for a woman, paying for her clothes and home, and she's stepping out with another man.

All I'm saying is, watch out.

You may be cared for in that nest, and you may mistakenly come to care for the birds caring for you, but never forget that you're not the only one who's pulling on their time and sympathies. Make sure you're the loudest, the most effective, and the best-fed.

I'm glad to hear that you're playing your role well. I know because those holier-than-thou foster parents of yours wrote me a letter. The more I read, the prouder I got. They told me what a good boy you are, how kind, how smart, and how talented.

17

You've sure got them fooled.

So just keep on keeping on. I have some big plans for when I get out of here, and trust me. We'll repay them for what they did to us. Don't worry—in addition to tricking them into raising my chick, in addition to you taking everything you can from them, I have something even better planned.

Have you ever known me to fail? Not in the long run.

I'm proud of you—just don't forget you're not their good boy. Not really. You're a cowbird, and I won't be stuck in here forever. That's a promise.

-Dad

"So who's driving to karaoke later?" Precious Patty actually looks at me, as if I'd let her ride with me.

"Please tell me Regina George is kidding," the guitarist mutters.

The understated snark makes me smile, but it's momentary, because Eddy seems to be serious about the vocals. "Obviously you can't change significant album details now," I say. "You already signed all the contracts. Patrice is doing the videos, and that's enough."

"It's because I'm just that awesome," Precious Patty says. "I offered to do it for free, so they don't need to change anything. I'm doing it out of the goodness of my heart." She tosses her head. "I'll do all the work and she'll still get paid—no breach."

"But we already recorded most of the songs." Bea looks like she's seconds from a full-on explosion.

Before she can say a word, Octavia grabs Bea's wrist and

shakes her head. "Let's just talk about it later. This isn't the place."

Bea's head snaps sideways. "What?"

"Not here." Octavia shakes her head tightly, her eyes narrowing.

She doesn't want to make a big scene here, on set. It's the grown-up, mature way to handle things, which I respect, but I doubt it's going to work with Bea.

Only, my sister's brow furrows, and she sighs. "Fine."

Fine?

Really?

I've never seen my sister stand down like that. It's as if. . .is Octavia the boss between the two of them? Is she the one who cares less? The one willing to walk away? I didn't realize that until this moment.

"I can drive, if I need to," Precious Patty says. "I have my Land Rover. I can even fit. . ." She glances at Octavia. "Whoever."

"I'll take Octavia," I say. Because there's no way she's riding with Patty.

"Oh, it's fine," Octavia says. "I'm sure I can ride in the van with—"

"No, you'll come with me," I say. "We have some things to discuss."

"What could you possibly need to talk about?" Precious Patty asks.

"Fine," Octavia says. "It's fine." She walks toward me.

Bea might rip Patty's head off if they ride together, but it would be far worse for Octavia. She'd sit silently while stupid Patty is awful over and over.

Bea smiles as if she understands. "Yes, you two go together, and we'll find our way over too. We can all talk once we're there." I'm pretty sure she'll be calling Easton the very second we walk out the door. Her future husband's as good as anyone I've met at manipulating, wheeling, and dealing. I'm sure he can get this worked out.

Only, as we reach my car—I only have one car in California, my white Mercedes—my phone dings. I set my alerts to ping whenever I have any official emails from the network or studio people. This one announces the official change for music on the movie soundtrack from Octavia Rothschild to Patrice Jouveau, and the tone's excited.

That straight up ticks me off.

"Everything okay?" Octavia asks.

I toss my head to tell her it's unlocked.

Once we've both closed our doors, I shake my head. "Not exactly. It looks like we were the last to find out about this switch. If I had to guess, I'd say they pushed it through without any of us knowing for a reason."

"Easton would be upset too," she says. "But you guys shouldn't worry about this. I've been concerned about my involvement and the impact it might have on the project since the start."

My hands tighten on the steering wheel. "It's messed up, Octavia. You know it is."

She shrugs. "It's not. They're just being smart. They aren't sure what the public reaction might be to me, and Patrice is a sure thing."

I want to tear the steering wheel off and throw it out the window. Or better yet, at the production team, with Eddy standing in the front. He's met her. He knows her. She's not a meaningless name on paper to him. "He should have gone to bat for you on this."

"Who?" Octavia asks. "Eddy?" She blinks. "Or do you mean Easton?"

"I'm sure Easton had no idea." I sigh. "But Eddy knew. I thought I could trust him, but I guess not."

"It's not Eddy you should blame," she says. "They want this film to be a success, and the soundtrack album is early marketing." She drops her hand on my arm, and my entire body reacts. Like a live wire spraying sparks.

My head snaps toward her. Until now, she'd been looking out the window, hiding the left—burned—side of her face from me. Now she's turned toward me. "If people were braver, if they gave us a chance to do the right thing, we might surprise you."

"Or the production team might lose their shirt." She squeezes my arm. "After a lifetime of being let down by the American public in virtually every public space, I can tell you that they made the right call. If I'm not upset, you shouldn't be either."

Except, I still am.

She can't just tell me not to be upset and expect that to work. If it was that easy, big pharma would sell a lot fewer anxiety meds, among other things. "I'm sure once you've heard Patrice sing a few of our songs, the recorded files for which Eddy assures us are being emailed, you'll feel better." She drops her hand back into her lap.

I hate that she's resigned to this sort of thing, as if people's stupid reactions to her perfectly lovely face is just her cross to bear.

"There's nothing wrong with it, you know." That came out wrong. "Your face, I mean," I say. "In fact, it's beautiful."

"My face. . .is beautiful?" Her lip's twitching. "Gee, thanks, Dad."

Being compared to her dad's not a good sign. "What I meant is that when Patty said your face was ugly. . ." My knuckles have gone white on the steering wheel. "I've never hit a woman, but I thought about how that rule really matters today. I thought hard."

She snorts. "Don't bother doing anything like that for me. As you said, that sort of comment tells me more about her than it does about me. I have mirrors. I know exactly how I look, and believe me when I say she's not the first and she won't be the last to say something similar."

I *hate* that. I hate it so much.

As we drive in near-silence to the address for the Seoul Town Karaoke place, I can't help thinking that she must *not* know how she looks. If she did, would she simply say it's the 'way the world is'?

"What do you know about Van Gogh?" I ask.

Octavia's eyes narrow. "Is this some kind of test?"

I laugh. "Not at all, but it's something I've been thinking about. Van Gogh died young, and I know he has a bad public image, even now. The man clearly suffered from some mental health issues, depression at the very least. They say he valued himself so little that he always ruined things he made that others praised. But his story. . ." I don't want to upset her, but I think she's seeing things all wrong.

"I know his story." She's remarkably composed for someone who just got attacked by a movie star on a set in a work environment and then found out she'd been wrongly removed from a contracted job. "He was a minister turned painter, and he was a failure during his lifetime," she says. "He sold a handful of paintings, all sold by his brother Theo. Though some other artists found his work to be impressive, no one of means seemed to agree with them. He cut off his ear —theories abound as to why—and only after his death did the value of his paintings soar, probably because he was an off-putting personality in real life."

"That's mostly true, but you're missing a few things." I

can't help my smile. "Van Gogh only painted for six years, dying before he could do more. He painted the things he did with great skill and speed—an unknown speed, really. He could paint something like a sunset in the forty-five minutes it took the sun to actually set. No other painter at the time could accomplish such a feat—actually, I'd guess the number of painters in any time that could do it is small."

"That's fascinating," she admits, a small smile on the edge of her mouth. I like that she's not turning away.

Sadly, my GPS dings to tell me that the stupid Seoul Town place is right around the corner. "Like someone else I know, he had almost a freak-of-nature level talent." No time to be subtle. "His skill was undeniable. You remember that he wasn't famous in his lifetime, but if he'd given the world a chance to recognize his talent, he could have been."

"Are you suggesting that I *don't* cut off my ear as planned?"

"It's a funny phrase, cutting off your nose to spite your face. Maybe it should be ear."

"I mean, I don't think—"

"I've almost made my point." I glance over to make sure she's not upset I cut her off. "Vincent was famous just a few years after he died. I don't think it was because he was off-putting, *per se*. I think it's because his style, his bold colors, and his common-man subjects were a change from the usual. He needed to have more faith in humanity, that they would see and appreciate his brilliance."

Octavia's smile is actually bright—stunning. "It's harder to have faith in something that has been consistently disproven, Jake. But there are some people who give me hope, people like you and your sister, so thanks for that."

"I'm not good at saying things—usually I have brilliant writers who arrange my words—but what I'm trying to say is that you think your face makes you a liability. You think it's something you should apologize for, and you're wrong. You have a beautiful face. I could look at it all day."

She blushes then, and I realize that only the unburned part of her face blushes. The rest of it stays whitish. As if she knows exactly what I'll see, she ducks her head, shifting so her hair falls across the front of her face.

"I'm not just saying that," I say. "If you give people a chance, they'll notice your special beauty, too."

She quirks an eyebrow. "My special beauty?"

"Okay, so I may not be Mel Gibson in *Braveheart*, but I'm trying to get you to fight. If Van Gogh had kept fighting, we might have so many more epic paintings that they'd be in every Holiday Inn across America."

"I'm not about to commit suicide, but I don't want my songs played in every elevator in the country either." Her smile's wry.

"It's not a perfect analogy." I hate how wrong this is all coming out. "But what I mean is—"

"I think I know what you mean, but Jake, this movie soundtrack isn't an end," she says. "It's a beginning. I just started working with Bea, and—"

"But it's a big chance," I say. "It's the kind of start that can change everything. I know that, because one of Bea's songs changed my life."

"I heard that." She compresses her lips. "Well, I'll be curious to see if they even care what we think. . ." She looks up at me and meets my eyes. "Please don't go cutting off your ear to spite, well, anything. You have nice ears, and that would be a true tragedy."

I'm chuckling as we get out of the car.

"Did you two talk about whatever it was you needed to discuss privately?" Precious Patty's glaring.

"How did you get here so fast?" Octavia asks. "Jake drives *fast*, and didn't you have to change clothes before you left?"

Patty shrugs. "My driver knows LA."

"Well, we're both very happy you made it," I say. "We can't wait to listen to you sing the songs you're trying to steal from Octavia."

Patty frowns. "You know, this wasn't even my idea." She tosses her hair. "We can talk about it more inside." She glances to the left and beams at the people who are pointing and snapping photos of us as we pass.

Once we reach the entrance, a member of the staff's waiting for us. "We have a private VIP karaoke room this way." The hostess is smiling, and Patty follows her with her nose up, like she thinks she's royalty or something.

"I'm going to apologize in advance," I whisper to Octavia. "But there's no way I can let this go—especially because of her. If you think she really had nothing to do with this change, you're wrong. Precious Patty is a complete diva, and-_"

"Precious. . ." Octavia laughs. This time, it's big enough that her entire face changes, and I love it. Yes, her skin is different. Yes, it moves differently than most faces I've seen, but it's also really stunning, like it was sculpted by a master. I wish she could see that. I wish people in the world hadn't treated her so badly for so long that it skewed her perception of what beauty actually is.

People liking roses isn't what makes them beautiful.

No matter what anyone thinks, they are beautiful.

And there are an awful lot of lesser-known flowers that are *more* beautiful.

"Shh," I mock-shush her as we enter the room. "Can't let her hear."

"Who?" Patty looks up from the booklet on the coffee

table. The room has a large, u-shaped sofa, and there are several booklets on the massive coffee table in front of it. I'm assuming they have the different song selections that Seoul Town offers.

Luckily, before I have to clarify anything, Bea, Morgan, Q, and Everett blow into the room like a hurricane. Eddy somehow peeled off, but at least the whole band's here. "I gave the front desk the music files Eddy sent." Bea's eyes are glinting. "But the guys and I were talking." She glances at Morgan. "Well, the guys, the girl, and I."

Morgan rolls her eyes. "Just say the guys. Doesn't hurt my feelings."

"Anyway," Bea says. "We think you should let today be an audition." She folds her arms. "If you can't sing the songs well, the whole production will suffer. So today, after you sing, we'll decide if you can take Octavia's place."

Patty looks upset. "But you aren't the ones who make that decision."

"But you must want what's best for the movie, and you could surely go back to your agent and beg off." Bea glares. "Right?"

Patty smiles. "It won't be necessary. You'll see."

"I guess we will," Bea says. "Because in more than twenty years, I've never heard a voice like Octavia's."

"This isn't an opera." Patty glares.

She starts with the title track, but just before it begins, she turns to Octavia, thrusting the mic in her direction. "You should sing it first—gorgeous monster, right?" She purses her lips. "Once I've heard you in person, I'm sure I'll have a better idea of how to sing it."

"Sure." Octavia takes the mic.

Bea restarts the music, since we blew past her opening. "Alright, prepare yourself."

But nothing can really prepare someone to hear Octavia's voice. She hasn't warmed up. She hasn't prepared, and it doesn't even matter. It really is opera quality, but richer, warmer, and brighter than what I'm accustomed to thinking of opera as being. The word shrill couldn't ever be used to describe her.

It's also clear that Bea wrote this song *just* for her. When she reaches the transition, my heart flip-flops inside my body. I should be watching Patty to see whether we're getting through to her, but I can't tear my eyes away from Octavia.

The world is full of beauty.
The world is full of peace.
The world is full of light and joy,
that almost never cease.
You made me lots of promises.
You made them all come true.
I can hardly imagine living in,
a world devoid of you.

The song has changed, slightly, some of it through the work they've done together, and some for the movie, but the impact hasn't lessened at all. When, at the end, the focus shifts and moves to the listener, to their culpability in the ugly parts of the world we all share, I finally force myself to look at Patty.

She's glaring, her expression flat.

I shouldn't have hoped that someone as emotionally tone-deaf as her could possibly understand why she can't take these songs specifically from Octavia. But when she snatches the mic from Octavia, and begins to sing the same song...

It's blue eye shadow on a baby. It's a bloodstain on white marble. It's an actor wearing athletic gear on the red carpet.

It's just *wrong*.

Every single person can hear it.

Except Patty, the person who could repair this mess with one text.

The sad part is that her voice isn't bad. She might actually break out with something like this. I'm sure that's all she cares about. It's a stunning song—a stunning list of songs— and someone greedy and self-centered like Patty might willfully refuse to see how she's all wrong for it.

But every single person in the band knows it.

In her heart, Patty must feel it, too. If she has a heart.

I realize, though, that it's not going to matter. And all my hopes of getting a video of her sounding like a wounded bird are gone. Precious Patty has clearly had years of voice lessons —she sounds like everyone else on the radio.

Which is probably what the studio wants.

It also means we're totally screwed.

That's why I do something stupid after I get back home to my apartment that night, something I probably shouldn't do. I post on social media account about the change.

On set today—studio made a big mistake, replacing Octavia Rothschild with my talented co-star, Patrice Jouveau. She has a nice voice, but it's not right for the music for this movie. I hope the studio will reconsider. Once you all hear Octavia, I'm sure you'll agree.

I tag the movie's social media account, and I link it to the YouTube clips of Octavia's contest performance with Bea.

In my entire career, I've never spoken out against a studio decision, even when they made terrible ones. I'm smart enough not to bite the hand that puts dollar bills in my savings account, and I'm savvy enough to handle any disagreements in other, more constructive ways.

But this isn't about me.

It's for Octavia, someone who will absolutely never

defend herself, not over something like this. I could tell in the car—heck, I could tell the moment we met. Before I have time to second-guess myself, I plug my phone in, shut off the lights, and go to sleep.

For once, I don't have a single nightmare. Maybe that's my reward for doing the right thing.

CHAPTER 3
OCTAVIA

I was seven years old when I was cast as Dorothy in *The Wizard of Oz.*

My mom, whom I expected to be overjoyed, was very, very angry. In fact, when I came home and told her the news, she kicked the wall so hard that it left a small hole.

When Dad came home from work that day, she told him I caused the damage by throwing a video game controller—I didn't even play video games. At the time, I thought she was upset because she'd have to take me to so many rehearsals—Dorothy had to be at every one.

Now I'm not sure why she was so angry.

People are funny, with their conflicting hopes, dreams, and fears. I can't imagine ever being upset about my own child's success, but maybe the world changes you. Maybe once I have a child, watching my kid do what I've failed at will upset me.

Mom loves to sing, but her voice has never been more than serviceable. Instead of being happy when my ability was praised, the older I got, the more my ability seemed to upset her.

Until a wig stuck to my face and caused my burns.

While I was recovering, she got me singing lessons. In some ways, that might have been the single most critical event of my life. It's what took me from having a decent voice to having a phenomenal one. Thanks to my disfigurement, I no longer got cast for any musicals, so my mom didn't get upset that I was doing better than her. I never showed her up again. How could I? I was just the poor, sad little burned girl with the lovely voice.

It's all I've ever been since that day.

People call me hideous or a monster.

When they meet me, all they see is my face. They always focus on the very visible manifestation of the worst moment of my life. In fact, when Eddy confirmed that Patrice Jouveau would be singing for the album alongside Jake Priest, I felt relieved. There's no way that doing something so visible, something so *exposed* wouldn't result in a million comments, interactions, and incidents just like the one where Patrice called me ugly. I know their reactions say more about them than they do about me. That's the whole point of the song, after all. But it still stings.

Every single time.

No one wants to be called ugly.

When I wake up, the morning after getting the news that I wouldn't be performing for the movie album after all, I start to pack my bags. I definitely won't miss living out of a suitcase. Being here in Hollywood has been an amazing experience in many ways. But being in a place that's all about appearances is even harder when you look different.

I'm more than ready to get home.

I've nearly packed everything when I hear a banging on the hotel front door. I'm absolutely sure it's Bea. She literally never remembers to take her key when she goes out. I'm still wearing my pajamas, plaid button down and pants, but I whip the door open without a second thought.

Bea storms past, but then she pivots and glares at my plaid pants. "Girl, why aren't you ready? You can't mean to go in that."

Maybe she did notice.

"Go where?" My eyebrows rise. "If I'm not going to be recording, I don't need to go. . ." Unless. . . Does the studio still want me to do the voice, while Patrice is just the face?

"Um, we're going in to the recording studio, duh. Have you not checked social at all?" She smacks her head. "I forget sometimes that your Instagram account has one photo—a bouquet of lilies—and you never check it." She whips out her phone. "Look."

I'm a little confused, but I pull it up. "Did I post something last night? Or did you?" But there's nothing. I didn't post, and neither did she. "What exactly am I supposed to be—"

"I didn't think anyone could be worse at this than me. Gimme." She grabs my phone and holds it in front of me like she's doing a tutorial. "You tap here, and you see where people have tagged *you*."

I frown. "But why would—"

But there are dozens of tags—more than dozens. Hundreds.

"What is all that?"

"Well, I've been tagging you in clips and album recording news, from our new band account, but forget that. Look at this one." She purses her lips, taps something, and swivels the phone.

The video isn't very sharp, but it's clearly me. The camera zooms in on my face, and across the top, there's fixed text.

WHO'S THE REAL MONSTER? YOU DECIDE.

It's a clip from when we visited the set yesterday. Jake has just jogged over to say hello.

"My sister's here," he says. His voice sounds a little tinny, which means this video isn't the best—was it something that was just rolling on set?

"Oh, your sister who's doing sound, right?" Patrice practically saunters over next to him. "I can't wait to meet her."

"Not sound," Jake's saying, just as he did in my memory. "The *soundtrack.*"

Patrice scowls, but it quickly disappears. "Sound. Soundtrack." I didn't even notice in the moment that she waved her hand so dismissively through the air. "Right."

"Sound is all the effects for the movie." Jake glares. "The soundtrack is art."

"No, I know, and you're totally right. I said it wrong."

"I hear today's the first kiss," Bea says. "Pretty exciting."

"Not really." Jake arches one eyebrow. "Should be as awkward as ever."

Patrice's laughter is high-pitched. Almost unhinged. "As if." It's strange watching this as a bystander, and not being there in the moment. It feels. . .different, probably because I'm not awed by famous people's presences.

Though, I do remember what's coming. "How long does this video roll?"

"Long enough." Bea's nodding slowly. "Keep watching."

My talking made me miss some of it, but Patrice is just saying, "Honestly, you look Asian."

Jake's laughter sounds a little ruder than I remember. "You have a keen eye." He shakes his head. "Adopted sister."

"Oh." Patrice arches one carefully groomed eyebrow. "So you're not really related at all. You could—" It's even more blatant with the way she's glaring at Bea that she was implying they could date. I get it—Bea's really pretty. If I were

Patrice, and if I had an interest in dating my co-star, I'd see Bea as a threat. She's someone he cares about, someone he likes a lot, and someone so gorgeous.

I wouldn't try to undermine the other woman, but I'm not Patrice.

Jake opens his mouth, but before he can respond, Bea cuts him off. "You're right. We aren't really related at all." She steps closer to her brother. "In fact, now that you mention it, we could get married. I had never realized that." She turns and stares up at him, pressing her hand to his chest. "Oh, my darling Jake."

Jake's laughing, but he shoves her away.

It's still funny the second time, but Patrice looks upset. I don't recall snorting, but the noise definitely attracts Patrice's notice.

"Bea's fiancé's one of the film's investors." Eddy's speaking, but with the angle, I can't see him, since he was right behind me. The fact that I can hear him makes me think someone smart tinkered with the sound to make it clearer, crisper, and cleaner.

Who posted this?

It's the first time I've wondered.

Before I can give it much more thought, I'm talking on screen again—defending Bea and trying to excuse Patrice. "You probably just misunderstood."

Patrice straight up glares at me. "And who are you?"

Again, like I did yesterday, I can't help wondering why it upset her to have me step in and excuse her silly inference.

"This is our main talent." Bea never hesitates to defend me. "She's my best friend, too, Octavia Rothschild."

It hits me in the feels again, hearing her call me her best friend. I'm sure it was another method of defense, since we've barely known each other a few months, but it still feels nice to hear. I'm smiling brightly, which is probably what pushed Patrice into it. My burned skin pulls funny when I smile. It makes a lot of people uncomfortable.

"You've never heard anyone with a voice as beautiful as hers." I forgot Jake said that, too.

But this I remember—Patrice's eyes spark as she says, "Or a face quite so ugly."

The video cuts then, and there's just a blue screen with the words VOTE FOR WHO'S UGLY IN THE COMMENTS.

Only, in the comments, there's only one option: Patrice Jouveau.

That's when I grab my phone and look at the account—it only has this one post, and the title of the account is PATRICEJOUVEAUSUCKS.

An anonymous hater? At least from an anonymous source, very few people probably saw it. . .except when I check the views, it's already in the millions. Tens of millions. And the comments. . .there are so many comments.

This is bad.

This is very bad.

CHAPTER 4
JAKE

Dear Dad:

I'm glad you had that Quintin guy reach out. They check every single email I send you officially, I'm sure, so it was hard to say anything useful at all. You always manage to find the right people. I'm sure you'll be free in no time.

I did want to tell you all the ways I've already taken advantage of the Fansee family. They really are easy marks. I have to assume they had no idea what they were doing when they got you caught. They're not smart enough to have done it intentionally.

Since coming here, they've been buying me lots of clothes and shoes, and they're paying for acting club and the plays for theater. They treat me just like every other stray they've brought in, and believe me, the other kids are just as stupid as they are.

The worst one is Bea, who seems to think she's going to save me—I'm convinced they must go to meetings and pat each other on the back for how they're saving a bunch of irredeemable kids. Can you even imagine being that dumb?

But maybe you don't need to target them when you get out, because trust me, I'm already bleeding them dry. They just have that little hotel, and I'm not sure it's very profitable. You'd be better off searching for richer marks in the time you have. These guys have made themselves into victims, and they have a bunch of leeches already attached. I can't wait for you to get out so you can break me out of here, and when you do, let's get out of here as fast as we can.

Love,

Jake

I'm mid-stretch after waking when I remember what I did. It's in my contract that I won't say anything disparaging about the film, its executives, or the other actors. Anything that might harm any of them is grounds for disciplinary action—a court can literally put a price tag on the damage I've done and fine me for it.

I don't regret it.

But I'd be a moron not to be nervous.

I didn't attack Patrice, but I did kind of attack the executives for their decision. They're the ones who are the *most* likely to sue. We're too far into filming for them to replace me, I think. They'd lose their shirts if they did.

But if this film tanks because I criticized them, they could make it very hard for me to line up my next project.

I'm really going to be kicking myself if I'm stuck filming infomercials for the next decade because of my white knight moment. If my dad were here, he'd be shouting at my naïveté. Clearly my years with do-gooders like Bea, Seren, and Dave have warped my brain. I finally force myself to pick up my phone, and it's bad.

114 text messages.

16 missed calls.

I knew there would be fallout, but why are six of them from Bea? Is she calling to thank me for standing up for her friend? She sent me a link.

When I click on it, I can't help my sideways smile.

Someone—a very smart, very sneaky, and probably well-connected someone—yoinked the studio feed and posted it online with just the right hashtags. I really, *reeally* doubt it was Octavia. She rolled over and accepted the pronouncement. She almost looked relieved not to be doing such a high-profile job.

No, it wasn't her. I'm sure of it.

But who *did* post the video?

I search the comments for clues, hoping the original poster replied to something. Of course, there are always plenty of trolls online. I often wonder just what sort of human would make a comment with the ugly, rude, and completely moronic trash I regularly see. The handful of comments about Patrice being right, saying that Octavia *is* ugly make me squeeze my phone a little too hard.

But for every comment like that, there are ten more defending Octavia.

Posting this was a calculated gamble, and it was clearly put up by someone who had something to lose from Patrice taking over. There aren't many people in that category. The studio was making the safe play—selling out the new for the sure-thing. I get why they'd do it, being a group of conservative businessmen, mostly.

The studio will be upset by this, and I realize, slowly because it's early, that I'm probably their number one suspect. Bea was upset, and she's my sister. Once Easton complained, which I'm sure he did, they'd know her position on it if they had any doubts. Then when they checked my social media. . .they'd see my position.

In support of my suspicion, I notice that Eddy, our executive director, called me four times. Adam, the producer, called me five. Even Frances called me—the woman who makes finance and budget cuts—and I only have her number saved as a courtesy. She's never called me about anything else. I get memos and information from her via email, but for her to call. . .

It must be really bad.

I call Adam first. I know him best, and he understands how I feel about Bea and by extension, Octavia.

"This is bad, Jake. You posted that, and then you ducked our calls?"

"My post was even-handed, considering how you handled the so-called plan to cut Octavia out. You signed a contract with her and Bea."

"They'll still be paid," Adam says. "Eddy says you knew that."

"All I said was that trading Octavia for Patrice was a mistake. I didn't insult you guys or Patrice."

He grunts.

"And you should know—I have no idea who leaked that video."

"You're saying it *wasn't* you?" Adam grunts again. "And I should believe that. . .why?"

"If I'd been smart enough to think about leaking that video," I say, "why on earth would I also post on my social, drawing a blinking line right to me?"

"So you could ask me that very question?"

"Yeah." I can't help my chuckle. "Not that smart."

When he grunts a third time, I wonder whether he's sitting on the toilet. "I wish I could believe that." He hangs up.

That could've gone better, but it also could've been worse. No threats. No swearing. No demands, either. He's probably not sure what to demand now, because with the number of views on that video, it's surely been duet-ed, stitched, and remade about a zillion times. There's no shutting it down at this point.

And it's a real video—not spliced.

Anyone who has met Patrice in real life, even for a moment, will immediately realize she's a horrible person. So who's smarter than me and willing to stand up for Octavia, but not brave enough to attach their name to it? I'd like to buy them a drink. Could it be my sister? She wouldn't have wanted to implicate me, but she would have wanted justice for Octavia. She also would have been plenty smart enough. With Easton's help, she could have doctored the video.

I call her.

"Did you do it?" Her first words basically tell me it wasn't her.

"Well, shoot," I say. "I was hoping it was you."

"The studio's released a statement," Bea says. "Two

minutes ago. They say they never had a switch planned, and that Octavia currently has and *always has* had their full support."

I can't help my smile. "Well, that's the first good news since yesterday. They're running scared."

"They want proof it was you," Bea says. "They may have been forced to keep Octavia in for vocals, but they'll want someone's head to roll for having their hand forced."

"I hope they don't find out who it was," I say. "Because you're right. They'll kill them."

"Same."

"Did you see the email?"

"Bea, I've been up for ten minutes," I say. "I watched the video, called Adam back, and then I called you. What email?" I drag myself across the apartment and start a pot of coffee. Even with the adrenaline, my eyes are burning, and my head feels fuzzy. I am *so* not a morning person.

"They want you to come in early this morning," Bea says. "You're doing the music video with Octavia, not Patty."

"They're cutting her for the video—what about the movie?"

"I think she's safe there," Bea says, "if she agrees to do some damage control. She's already released some crap about how the video was spliced and the whole thing was taken out of context."

I can't help rolling my eyes, not that Bea can see.

"Losing the music video's her hand slap, I guess," she says.

"They have to prove they don't think I'm ugly." The words are so faint I can barely hear them.

"You're with Octavia now?"

"Duh," Bea says. "She's really not excited about doing the music video."

"Do you think there's any chance *she* posted the video?" I whisper.

Bea laughs. "Not a single one."

"Then who do you think it was?"

"I'm not sure I can tell someone who blasts all their thoughts on social media." I know just the expression she has right now. Smug condescension.

That means she saw my post.

"In case I haven't said it yet," Bea's whispering now. "Thank you. I love you for that."

It warms my heart a little bit to hear it. I'm not sure why I care, but I can't help myself from asking, "Did, um." I clear my throat. "Did Octavia see it?"

"See what? The video?"

"Never mind," I say. "How long do I have to get ready?"

"They want you there for blocking in an hour and ten minutes," Bea says. "Octavia's doing her hair."

"Didn't you tell her that professionals will do that for her on set?"

"She's not keen on anyone else messing with her hair and makeup, but I did mention it," Bea says.

"Well, I'll see you in a few, I guess," I say.

Usually I roll in for prep with wet hair and whatever t-shirt I happen to grab off the pile, but I find myself doing my hair, at least a bit, before we go. We're only blocking for the video, after all. That means they may *not* do anything. I'd hate to look like an idiot, you know, in front of whoever might be there.

Not any particular person, but just, whoever.

I have an image to uphold, and after my post, it can't hurt to look my best. Inexplicably, Patrice is there when I arrive, waiting. She's sort of fiddling with the ring on her left hand, almost as if she's nervous.

When I head for the set, she moves to intercept me.

I brace myself for whatever favor she'll be asking this time. "Hey, Jake." Her forced smile sets my teeth on edge.

I bob my head, my lips compressed tightly.

"I saw your post—I thought it was so well done. You were careful not to imply that *I* had anything to do with the studio's decision, and you even complimented my singing."

I force a smile. "Why are you here?" I tilt my head. "We're blocking for the video you aren't stealing now."

"I was never—" She inhales sharply and nods. "No, I know. I do."

I lift both eyebrows.

"But—I guess I wanted to check in with you and make sure you'd support me."

"Support you?" I can't do it. I can't force a smile right now. A blank stare's the best I can manage. "Yesterday, you called a good friend of mine—a talented genius friend of mine—*ugly*. To her face."

She coughs.

"You're one of the most beautiful women in America in terms of your face and general figure, and you've made quite the career on that. The fact that you felt the need to call names—of anyone—is truly. . ." I shake my head. "It's appalling, really. I didn't want your agency to sue me, so I didn't say everything I felt, and I had no idea that video was going to be exposed. But Patrice, if you think I'm going to somehow intercede with the public or even with the Devil himself on your behalf, you're delusional."

All the blood has drained from her face. "You're such a hypocrite, Jake. You're better looking than everyone else just like I am, and I was just saying what everyone else was thinking."

"Don't try and pretend your twisted brain bears any

resemblance to everyone else's," I say. "I think Octavia's one of the prettiest people I have ever met, and not only her appearance. She's been through something painful, something miserable, and now everyone she meets points it out. I'm guessing you didn't even think what it must have felt like for her to have been burned like that. To you, the reminder's ugly."

Patrice drops her voice, like she can't risk a repeat of yesterday. "To literally everyone, it's ugly."

"I think it shows how strong she is. Have you ever heard of raku pottery?" I arch one eyebrow. "I'm thinking you're not much of a pottery person."

"What?" Patrice huffs. "What does that have to do with—"

"Raku's a style that began in Japan, and the word means 'happiness in the accident.' They plunge the fired pieces into water, and then they set the outside of them on fire, letting various things, like paper or sawdust, burn on the exterior. It makes for different and varied colors and textures, and it's my very favorite style of pottery, because it's *not* always the same."

"You're saying she's pretty *because* she's different?" Patrice bunches up her nose.

"I'm saying she's pretty." I snort. "Period." I step closer and narrow my eyes. "You just can't see it, because in addition to being ugly inside, you're too stupid to have an eye for real beauty."

"Okay." Patrice shakes her head. "Now who's delusional?" She tosses her hair. "I'm just here to apologize so I can get it on video and move on from this dumpster fire."

"Great timing, then." Octavia's voice is both loud and clear from the far side of the room.

I spin around as fast as Patrice, hoping she hasn't been

there long. I'm not sure she'd appreciate me comparing her face to clay that's been set on fire.

"Oh," Patrice says. "I didn't realize—"

"It's fine." Octavia's smile is tight. I've noticed that she usually smiles small enough that the shift doesn't pull on the burn. I wonder whether she's practiced in the mirror just how big she can smile without interference. I bet she has.

Patrice looks pretty flustered, but she recovers quickly, gesturing at the guy wearing slacks, a white polo shirt, and thick-rimmed black glasses beside her. He surreptitiously whips out a camera and taps on it.

As if she's filming, Patrice steps forward with halting steps. "I am so, so sorry for yesterday." She sighs. "When your whole job depends on your face, you start to obsess about it, and all the insecurity I felt about myself had to go somewhere." She shakes her head slowly. "Then two days ago, I was super nervous about the scene, so I binged a whole Twinkie. That made me break out for yesterday's shoot, and I thought my agent was going to spank me, I swear. It's so hard doing what we do." She turns back toward me and bites her lip.

Does she think she's cute? Ugh. She's revolting.

"Anyway, I was so insecure about my breakout and all the makeup they had to use to cover it up that I went crazy yesterday. Add to it that I just started my period today—" She coughs. "I hope you can forgive me for saying what I was thinking about myself to you. Clearly you're true beauty." She smiles and bats her eyes. "That scar shows you have both bravery and strength, and I'm so in awe of the person you are."

She stole my words to save herself.

Precious Patty is a truly terrible person.

Octavia dips her head a bit and says, "Of course. No

offense taken. All's forgiven." She smiles big enough that it does pull on her burn, and then she extends her hand. "Friends?"

Patrice's eyes widen, and then she blinks. "Of course." She holds her hand out slowly, and I can't tell whether she's shocked or put off. Either way, once the handshake's done, the guy taps on the phone, and Patrice yanks her hand back. "Sorry. I don't shake very often."

Octavia shrugs. "If I'd known, I'd never have suggested it." Something about the way she says it has me pulling up "patrice jouveau phobias" on the search bar of my phone.

What do you know? A dozen hits where Patrice refuses to shake someone's hand. It makes me laugh out loud. I guess Octavia took the injunction to *know thy enemy* to heart.

"What's funny?" Patty's frowning.

"Nothing. We'd better get moving," I say. "We're due for the blocking in. . ." I glance at my watch. "Three minutes ago." I hold out my arm, and Octavia walks toward me like we're old friends.

It makes me smile for real.

As we duck into the section of the set that's prepped for the title track, I can't help glancing over my shoulder. Good old Patty's grimacing something fierce, and my smile broadens.

Sometimes when I reach the set for blocking, they already have tape on the floor and movements in mind. Other times, they're literally spitballing places we could stand and things we could do on the day we show up to film. I'm expecting it to be closer to the latter, since they just changed to Patrice and then back to Octavia without warning.

I'm shocked when I look down and see bright blue tape. "I hear this is your first time doing anything like this." A woman with eyebrows so thick they look like bushy caterpillars shifting up and down smiles and gestures toward Octavia. "Welcome."

"Uh, yeah," Octavia says. "At least, it's the first time in a very long time. I was in community theater productions for five or six years as a child."

"I think you'll find this is a little different than that." The woman slides an arm around Octavia's shoulders like they're buddies already.

Octavia flinches and slowly shifts away. "I'm happy to have someone to show me what to do, then."

Caterpillars, unconcerned, is still smiling broadly. "That's just the attitude we want." She points. "So we'll start out here, and when you start singing, I want you standing like this." She angles her body to show Octavia.

"Will I actually be singing for the filming?"

The woman nods. "Just exactly like you will for the sound recording. We'll remaster the sound and do touchups in the studio, of course, but it needs to be real for that to work."

The first few minutes goes really smoothly. We nearly have the whole thing blocked when I realize something.

"Is the main camera there?" I point.

"It is," Caterpillars says. "But as I'm sure you're familiar, there will be satellite cameras we can pull from for any shot we choose."

I go over the movements in my head, most of which I liked well enough. "It's a song about her pain," I say. "And that mirrors the pain my character feels when he's abandoned, finds a place, and yet again has to leave."

The woman nods. "Exactly."

"You know Octavia's most obvious pain comes from her burns, so why do you have her turned this way in nearly every shot?" I angle my body. "It feels like you're trying to keep her burns out of the video."

Caterpillars frowns. "We want the focus—"

"Who's your boss?" I fold my arms. "I want to talk to him or her, and I want to explain the whole point of this, because I think they're missing it. How can the world see how beautiful she is if we're constantly closing off their chance to really see her?"

Oh, boy. Caterpillars is ticked. "Actually, Mr. Priest—"

"No." I can't help my nostrils flaring. "Just go get your boss. Clearly you're not going to help me. You don't get it."

A small hand drops on my forearm and I look down and realize it's Octavia's.

"I asked her to change the blocking to be like that." Her voice is small, her expression composed. "They agreed, only because I insisted."

Well, shoot. "You—why?"

Octavia's smile's small. "I'm glad you find my face to be 'accidentally beautiful.'" Her air quotes are a painful reminder of what I said to Patrice about her reminding me of pottery. "But for most people, it's hard to look at it. I want very much for this album to be a success." She pauses. "I think you do too."

CHAPTER 5
OCTAVIA

Fighting things is exhausting.

When you watch television shows like *Avatar: The Last Airbender* as a kid, small children can master powers to fight against the injustices of their world. It always got me all jazzed up to do the same. When I was older, I planned to do the very same.

But given enough time, the unsteady roads wear down tire treads.

With enough sand, the hardest of rocks are polished smooth.

And after enough snide comments, even the fieriest hearts burn out.

Sometimes all I want is one day without needing to fight. I just want to walk out into the world and be small enough, normal enough, and average *enough* that the world doesn't notice me.

I do appreciate the people who are raring to fight for me.

It just never changes anything, and I've been worn down over the years until I realize that the one being battered the most forcefully by all the lessons taught is always me.

Nothing makes a noticeable difference, and I can't fight things forever. The world will go on being exactly as it has ever been, so what I really need is to find a way to make a place for myself, a place that isn't all sharp edges and bared teeth.

Jake means well.

Bea means well.

Whoever posted that video means well, too, I'm sure.

It's just not a defense I want or need.

I know exactly how I look, and I'm acutely aware of how it impacts my future and my present. I've lived it for years, now.

"Are you ready? The studio wants you and Jake there soon, and today it's recording, no blocking. You can't be late." Bea's tapping her foot again. I swear, the woman hardly puts on any makeup at all, so she's ready in three minutes.

"Not all of us have the face of a porcelain doll," I say. "I'll be ready in five more minutes."

"You look great now," Bea says, "but I wasn't actually trying to rush you. Just checking in."

"I'm just doing one more coat of mascara, and then—"

Bea drops her hands on the small tabletop. "Hold up. I was serious that I wasn't rushing you, but this is nuts. Are you actually nervous right now?"

My hand jerks and I spread mascara across my whole eyelid. I suppress my frustration and exhale. "I am, yes."

"You've been a performer your whole life," she says. "And you're finally getting the chance to do it again, on a massive scale. Isn't it kind of a dream-come-true?"

I'm wiping off my entire eye's worth of makeup, but that doesn't stop me from laughing. "I did perform as a child, but this has never been my dream."

Bea drags a chair next to me. "Are you serious? I thought you were Eliza in *My Fair Lady* as a kid."

"So. . .about that. I actually didn't even audition."

"You have to tell me about this. I totally thought you were obsessed with acting as a child."

I shake my head. "I've always loved singing. I could sing all day and all night and be happy. I should've been born as a nightingale." I can't help my smirk. I pause to redo my eyeliner. "But my mother has always wanted to be an actor." I frown. "She *is* an actress."

"Okay." Bea bobs her head. "And?"

"After having me, she couldn't really afford a babysitter—she didn't have any roles that paid yet. So she would take me with her to auditions, and when she got parts, she'd haul me to the practices too."

"A baby?"

"Luckily I was a happy baby." I shrugged. "And as I grew, I went as a toddler. I basically grew up on the sets of plays, commercials—you name it."

"And?"

"Well, as I got older, I would watch what they did, and I listened, and I learned. So when Mom went to audition for *My Fair Lady,* she heard the cast was mostly going to be children, but she was desperate. The director of the local production was taking a sabbatical to spend more time with her child she had ignored, and she was heading back to Broadway after doing this one local production. Mom was sure if she could just be discovered by the woman, she'd finally get her role—the one she deserved. She'd break out."

"Wasn't it a production for the children?"

"It was, but a few characters were going to be played by adults, and one of those was Mrs. Higgins, the professor's mother."

"Okay, but your mom didn't break out."

"Right as her individual audition ended, someone called

the applicants over to learn some moves for the racetrack scene. I overheard the director talking to the assistant, and they said she was terrible, and wouldn't be a good fit for Mrs. Higgins."

"That's a lot for a kid to deal with." Bea frowns. "But how did you wind up—"

"I argued with them. I told them that Mom could change whatever they wanted, if only they gave her some notes. I told them they were wrong about her, and that she just needed a chance." I wince.

"And?"

"I guess I reminded them of Eliza, popping off about injustice. They asked me to read a few scenes and we'd keep talking about how my mother would make a great Mrs. Higgins."

"But really they wanted you."

I shrug. "Then they asked me if I could show them how my mom would sing a few songs. I told them she was a way better singer than I was, but I did it." I grimace. "You can see where this is going. They ended up picking me for Eliza even though I hadn't auditioned. Mom. . .she—"

"Oh, I bet your mom was giddy." Bea's eyes are dancing. "Even if she didn't get the part, she could live vicariously through you."

"Not exactly." I can still see Mom's eyes flashing, her lips thin and tight. "She was. . .unenthusiastic. She tried to talk the director into finding someone else, but I insisted on taking the role."

The furrowed brow is back. "But if you didn't want to do it--"

"I'd made a deal with the director," I say. "I told him that I'd take the role, but only if he cast my mother as Mrs. Higgins." I shrugged. "I couldn't exactly tell Mom that I'd bargained for the first decent role she'd been offered in years. She'd have been. . .disappointed. So I kept my mouth shut and gritted my teeth and prepared to act my little heart out."

"You'd never done a play before that?"

"I did a few plays at school," I say, "but they upset my mom, so I avoided them after that. Mostly I did choir. Singing's my thing, not acting."

"When you sing you get up on stage and act some, so just channel that and today should be a breeze," she says. "When you get nervous, remind yourself that you're just singing."

I roll my eyes. "While a million cameras record my face, my body, and my interactions with Jake."

Bea smirks. "Better you than me."

"Gee, thanks," I say.

"But seriously," Bea says. "You really do have a face, a body, and a voice for film. You look *amazing*." She points at my eye. "You should probably redo the mascara though. Right now you look a little like Twiggy on that side, by comparison."

She's probably referencing some old movie or something —I swear, Bea would fit right in if she had been born in the early nineteen hundreds. I have been slowly trying to watch a few of the old movies she loves with her at night, because she makes a lot of references I just don't get. I've learned it's better not to let on that I have no idea what she's talking about, or I'm in for an hour-long recap.

As we're traveling to the set, this time to actually record, I can't help my knee from bouncing.

Bea drops a hand on it. "As someone who acutely understands your reticence to do this," she says, "let me just say. . .let Jake do the hard parts. When you get stressed out, just look my way, smile, and sing."

"Is that what you do? You just sing and smile?" I arch an

eyebrow. "Because you and Jake aren't related, you know. *You* could be in the video."

"I could if I sounded like you—but think about the PR they can get from this, once people hear your voice and see you together? You're already trending."

"Me and Jake?" I roll my eyes. "Please."

"Please, what?"

"The world's prettiest man and the world's ugliest woman?"

Bea slaps her hand against the glass in the cab. "You aren't ugly. Stop saying that. I forbid you to say it ever again."

The cab stops. I yank the door handle and climb out. "Just because I'm not saying something doesn't mean it's not true."

Before she has a chance to argue with me, I trot toward the entrance and check in with hair and makeup. They insist on touching things up, always, but they don't make many changes, thankfully. After more than ten years of doing my makeup, I've gotten pretty good at it. All the makeup tutorials in the world don't really make you an expert on balancing the skin of a severe burn with regular skin—life experience and two different colors of foundation help, though.

We all become experts at things when they become necessary.

Usually not a moment sooner.

"Your hair is just breathtaking," the woman—Cecilia, I think?—gushes again. "I swear, I can't believe you don't get it colored. People kill for this rich, mahogany color."

"Thanks." Though I'm not so delusional that I think it's different than just plain old brown.

Well-intentioned people go one of two ways when they meet me. They become super complimentary of everything, or they avoid talking about my appearance entirely. I'm not sure which is more awkward, but I know the people who are paying me loads of compliments are really trying, and that means something.

"Octavia?" Eddy's standing in the doorway. "They're ready for you."

Now if only I was ready for them.

"Right." I stand and brush the nonexistent lint off my pants. "I did want to clarify." I gesture at my outfit. "Do I really need to be wearing all white, basically?" The white slacks feel like butter, and the white blouse is silky and gorgeous, but it's strange. "Am I some kind of sacrifice for a dragon?"

Eddy's lip twitches. "Not as far as I know."

"Because I'd rather go in prepared if I am. At least give me a knife to hide behind my back."

"It's because you're light and he's dark. You're the beauty and he's the monster." A woman steps out from behind Eddy. "I'm Jane Wellford, and you, my dear, need no introduction."

"I do have a uniquely recognizable visage," I say.

The woman has a dark brown, perfectly coiffed bob. A smile plays with the corners of her mouth just before she says, "It's not your *visage* that interests me, though it seems to have created quite the furor online."

"No?"

"It's your voice. The second I heard it, I greenlit the request to use two nobodies for the soundtrack. If you knew who else we were considering, you'd know what it meant that I chose you. Now that you have the chance, I want you to take it. Go out there and be light and beauty." She lifts her chin a hair. "Got it?"

Her strange sort-of pep talk actually helps. I can't tell whether she's a fan or a hater, but either way, the intense way she's studying me is invigorating. I square my shoulders and walk past Eddy and Jane and toward the area marked as set eighteen. Before doubts can sneak back in, I push through the door. Standing in the center of the set, surrounded by at least five or six different women, is Jake Priest. He looks like he's a king holding court or something.

Golden hair falls just so across his brow, shining under the stage lights. His brilliant, large blue eyes, dimples, and broad shoulders are visible even when occluded by the gaggle of flirting women.

"She'll be here any minute, and I need to be—" As if something alerted him to my presence, he turns, his eyes meeting mine. When he smiles, it's like a light was flipped on. The room brightens.

It's outrageous that people online are linking us romantically. There couldn't be a more mismatched pair than Jake and me, so I need to focus and get these music videos out of the way before the crazy ideas make me unhappy with my real life.

"Ready to get started?" Jake actually looks. . .excited? Which I do not understand at all.

"Sure," I say, only now noticing that he's wearing all black to my white. "This—" I gesture between our outfits. "It's funny."

"Is it?" He quirks a brow. "I kind of like it."

The girls are whispering, and I wonder what they're doing here until I realize they're all in grey. They're our backup singers. Of course they are. Six perfect faces, all of them here to help us stand out.

"This set." Jane steps past me into the smallish room and waves. "We decided to mirror the meet cute scene of the movie."

"Meet cute?" Jake arches one eyebrow. "I'm not sure you can call a courtroom cute, and I'm not sure you can really say that anything about their first meeting is cute."

"That's what I like about it. They're diametrically opposed from the start. So in the movie, when they meet, grabbing disgusting courtroom coffee from the cart outside, they have no idea they're on opposite sides. It's not until Helene carries the coffee into the same courtroom. . .and hands it to her father that Tom realizes. . .she's here with the prosecution."

"So the courtroom. . ." I glance around. "And the coffee?"

"Everything in a courtroom is black and white," Jane says. "So we're doing the shots in black and white, except for the two of you, and you're dressed in black and white too. That means your faces will really stand out." She beams. "I think it's brilliant. We might do the same thing for the introductory scene."

"Might?" I ask. "Haven't you filmed it yet?"

Jane shakes her head. "Time passes between the—"

"Her hair's shorter, so we're doing the opening scenes last," Eddy says. "Now, let's get to the places we blocked."

Yesterday, the set was still being built. I wasn't sure quite what it was. Our blocking had more to do with where we stood and how we'd be angled when we sang our lines. Today, in costume, with benches and a podium. . .it feels a lot more real.

When everyone vacates and the lights click on, I know what's going to happen. I'm prepared for the whirring of the fan, and the introductory music. I even remember the modifications we made to the song for the movie soundtrack.

But having Jake staring right at me, like he's fascinated with me, like he can't look away. . .it's. . .he's clearly a very gifted actor. It feels real. I remind myself that literally no one has ever looked at me that way, not in my entire life.

But I miss my cue, and then lots of people are looking at me.

"Okay, let's do that again—did you hear it?" Eddy asks. "Do we need to get you headphones or turn up the sound?"

"I heard—" my voice cracks and I want to die. I cough to clear my throat. "I did hear it. Sorry."

"It's a lot," Eddy says. "Let's take it again."

This time, Jake's still staring at me, but I'm listening, and I come in right on time.

The world is full of beauty.

The world is full of peace.

Jake reaches up and tucks my hair behind my ear on the right side of my face. He bites his lip as he smiles at me, and then he picks up perfectly when it's his turn.

The world is full of light and joy,

That almost never cease.

When I take over again, he drops his hand on my hand, his fingers encircling my wrist. It's warm, and it's strong, and if my voice wobbles a little as I sing the next lines, well, at least they're replacing this sound with one from the studio.

You made me lots of promises.

You made them all come true.

We sing the last lines together, our voices blending much better than I anticipated.

I can hardly imagine living in

A world devoid of you.

I'd never thought of this as a love song, not until this moment.

During the musical segue, the backup singers spring out from a side door. It's a little corny, or at least, it feels that way right now, but maybe they have some kind of plan for editing them that's less dumb than the six of them dancing around us like wannabe gremlins in grey monochrome outfits. Jake does, right on cue, release my hand and walk away, but it's his eyes that get me. He furrows his brow, and for all the world, it looks like walking away from me is killing him.

As I sing the opening lines, the backup singers are essentially just humming a harmony. I wonder why they didn't just call them dancers.

The world is dark and terrifying.
All your promises were lies.
The ones who talked of beauty,
Were the first to avert their eyes.

I get it now, a little, why they included them. Jake has turned away, and he's standing at the edge of the screen, and the women have sort of bunched around him, like they've all turned their backs on me.

The face you said was gorgeous,
You now cringe and turn away.

This wasn't part of the blocking, but I turn to face the camera with my left side, my burned side.

The world has made it ugly,
Your gorgeous monstrosity.

I can barely see past the bright lights, but even with that limiting my vision, I can see the cringey looks on a few faces —the closest cameraman, for one. I channel my feelings about that, about all the people who cringe when they see me, about the people who are supposed to love me the most, but turned their faces away in disgust. That always makes it easy to keep from crying and instead hit my cue.

Anger trumps vulnerability every time.

You told me I was gorgeous.
You told me I was beloved.
You said you would be faithful.
No matter what the world did.
All the joy inside me,
My hope for a brighter day,

The monster consumed it all,
And I became beast and also prey.

This wasn't in the blocking, but Jake turns back my way. He walks away from the women in grey beside him, and he holds his hand out toward me. When I come in again, he joins me.

The world is dark and terrifying.
That much, at least, was true.
But those who spoke of beauty
Were the villains, not me and you.
It's not my face at fault here
It's those who glare and jeer
The real beast lives inside of them,
They get back what they give.

I'm not sure why he did it. Maybe it was their plan all along. Maybe he meant to surprise me by providing support before the song called for it. Either way, it works. Tears well up in my eyes and spill over, streaming down my face. I choke them back though, and when the final rise comes, I'm ready for it.

Again, Jake sings a harmonizing line, just below mine. And as we first start, singing the lines, *Stop looking to slay monsters,*

And start working on yourself, he slides his hand over mine, lacing our fingers together.

My voice hitches a little, but I keep singing.
The gorgeous monstrosity you should fear
Is the one you see in the mirror.
Work on the creature only you can tame,
And when you see the ugliness,
Call it by name, oh, call it out by name.
Total silence follows the close of the music.

"I didn't really understand," I hear the camera guy saying.

"I didn't, but now I do."

If we reach anyone else, anyone at all, maybe this was all worth it.

"What didn't you understand?" Jake asks.

The camera guy coughs. "No, I just meant that with her voice, I mean, I've never heard anything like it. It just doesn't match. . ." He cringes.

A muscle in Jake's jaw pops, and he opens his mouth.

Before he can say anything, I drop a hand on his forearm. "It's fine. Please let it go."

Jake's head whips toward mine.

"It's in the song," I whisper. "They have to realize what they're saying and thinking themselves, or it won't change anything."

"But, I have to say," a small voice off to the left says, "White Knight looks good on you. Are you sure you're not the one who leaked the video?" Bea steps to the side, her smirk front and center on her face.

"Do you really think I'd have done that?" He glances my way. It's the first time I realize that he does get some things— he wouldn't have released a video that let everyone see me being mocked, even if it would have shifted the public image in a way that helped me.

"I guess you're right." She's frowning, though. "It's someone who wanted to help, but didn't really *get* it."

We redo the whole thing another five or six times, but in the end, I'm pretty sure the studio's going to use the first one, where I was crying.

"I think we can call it a day," Eddy finally says, spinning his hand, index finger out, round and round. "That's a wrap."

"That went fast," Jake says. "Right?"

"It helps that the singer you found never misses a single note." Eddy's half-smile is encouraging. "I couldn't believe how in sync the two of you were. It felt like you'd performed together a dozen times."

"Instead of the truth—that they barely know one another." Patrice is leaning against the wall. I hadn't even realized she stayed. I hate the thought of her seeing me performing at all, much less such a vulnerable song. Maybe her mean words bothered me more than I realized. Even after all these years, some barbs still slip through my armor.

"Oh, I don't know. I think I know Octavia pretty well." Jake wraps an arm around my shoulder.

Patrice frowns. "She's your sister's friend, and I heard Bea say they only met a few months ago."

"In addition to being my sister, Bea's my roommate and my best friend," Jake says. "As usual, you're totally wrong about all your assumptions."

"I'm totally wrong about which ones, exactly?" Patrice steps closer. "Because it seems like a mistimed comment on my part is causing all sorts of problems. It might even put the movie's success in jeopardy, and instead of shoring things up for the movie, you're over here. . .whatever it is you're doing." She waves her hand. "You backed the wrong person."

Jake's arm tightens around my shoulders. "I backed Octavia because. . ."

It was the right thing to do.

He's a good guy.

He couldn't support Patrice when she's a jerk.

I'm not sure exactly what he's going to say, but I can almost hear his voice already, defending me in the same way Bea always has. She's fierce, like a tiger. She's strong, like a hurricane. And she's determined, like a donkey.

"It's fine," Patrice says. "This will all blow over and you won't have to do stuff like this with her anymore. By the time the movie comes out, everyone will have forgotten about all the nastiness, and they may even re-record this whole thing. You don't have to worry about your image or being linked to her."

Is that what Jake was worried about? Is that why he hesitated?

Jake slips his fingers in between mine and tightens his hand around mine. "Oh, that's not at all what worries me. Octavia hates being in the limelight, so I've done as she asked until now, but I'm done with it." He steps closer to Patrice, dragging me along.

What's he saying?

"Octavia Rothschild's the most talented singer I've ever met, ever *heard*, and we just started dating. The only reason I've bitten my tongue until now is that she doesn't like to make a scene."

Gasps from *all* over the room confirm that I heard him right.

Dating.

Jake Priest just *lied* and said we're dating.

That's how he's defending me against Patrice being an idiot? By making up some lie about how we're dating? What good will that do? Who would ever believe it?

Right on cue, Patrice starts laughing. "Her? You want people to believe you're dating *her*?" She scoffs. "So I came in for a fake apology, and you go straight to fake dating." She shakes her head.

Jake's hand tightens again, but this time, instead of saying anything, he turns toward me. The look on his face is thunderous. His eyes are flashing, and his hand's holding mine tightly when his mouth moves toward mine, slowly.

His eyes search mine, softening a bit.

"Sorry, Octavia," he whispers.

And then he kisses me.

CHAPTER 6
JAKE

Dear Dad,

You're never going to believe this, but remember how I joined choir just to have something in common with the Fansee family's dumb foster kid, Bea? Well, they left me enrolled in it when I stayed with them, and I didn't really care. I was just killing time, right?

Only, it turns out, I'm, like, really good at singing.

The choir teacher, Mr. Kline, says I could be a singer, like a real singer. The Fansees said they'd pay for me to get voice lessons from this really awesome lady who lives in the City, and I know you always say to take whatever you can get for free, so I know you'll be excited to hear they're paying a ton for them.

I'll keep milking them for plenty, yeah?
Love,
Jake

~

Jake:

Quit choir right now. It's for losers and dream-
ers. We only go after sure things. Stupid dreams are
just that—stupid. Don't waste your time on it for
another second.

And stop worrying about the Fansees. I have
something amazing in mind for them that will cover
everything they've done and then some. Keep your ties
to them minimal. I can tell you're getting soft—it's
because you're so young. You think they really care
about you, but they don't.

Remember our first rule. Never try to protect
anyone else. It's you and me against the world. Taking
pity on losers is how you get dragged down with them.

Whatever you do, never let yourself get entwined
with people weaker than you. It's far, far easier to
get dragged off a chair than it is to pull someone
else up.

Never forget that either.

-Dad

When Bea says, "White Knight looks good on you," I can barely make sense of what she's saying.

White knight?

Is she saying I'm being. . .protective?

Bea's smirk has always irritated me. "Are you sure you're not the one who leaked the video?"

Octavia's eyes widen.

She can't think I'd be that stupid, right? I've been paying attention. I don't go fighting wars for people they don't want me to fight, at least, not in ways they would clearly hate. All I did on social was tell the studio I wouldn't let them push my family around.

"Do you really think I'd have done that?" I look at Octavia to see if she thinks it was me, too.

"I guess you're right." Bea's clearly not convinced. "It's someone who wanted to help, but didn't really *get* it."

That's her reminder to me not to push this too far. All of this back and forth and making a big deal out of things is clearly upsetting the very person it's meant to help. I get that. It can't be nice to have public support only because someone mocked you so horribly about your greatest and most visible sensitivity.

I can't help thinking about it, over and over as we record the scene another half-dozen times. Is Octavia upset or pleased that she's doing the vocals and now the video as well? Or does she wish she'd just been cut out? I can't tell.

She's the same as she's always been.

Which means she's even better at putting up a front than I am. She must be hurting, though. If Patrice's initial insult didn't hurt, seeing it again and reading the callous and offensive comments must sting. The fact that the studio only did the right thing when their hand was forced can't feel nice either.

"I think we can call it a day," Eddy finally says, making the same looping wave he always does. "That's a wrap."

"That went fast." I force a smile. "Right?"

"It helps that the singer you found never misses a single note." Eddy's half-smile is irritating. He may know how excellent she is, but he didn't stand up for her when it mattered. He sees her as too weak to matter. That probably pisses me off more than anything else. "I couldn't believe how in sync the two of you were. It felt like you'd performed together a dozen times."

"Instead of the truth—that they barely know one another." Patty's extended artfully against the wall, her chest forced up and out in a pose I'm sure she's practiced in the mirror a dozen times. Everything about her is so fake it turns my stomach.

An urge to show her that Octavia's strong rolls over me. But how?

She doesn't mess with me—we're on par, really, because I have social media accounts and fans who will defend me. They'd turn on me in a second for a few misplaced comments, but as long as I'm careful, I do have some power. That's why I'm not at risk like Octavia is.

But how could I extend my immunity to Octavia so Patrice would just leave her alone already? An idea hits me, but it's a terrible one. I ignore it.

But the idea persists.

The more I think about it, the more I can't seem to let it go.

"Oh, I don't know," I say, wondering as I do. Would Octavia go along with my stupid idea? Or is she the kind of person who insists on strict truth at all times? I decide to find out—maybe I do like playing the White Knight after all. "I think I know Octavia pretty well." I sling an arm over her shoulders.

Patrice's frown tells me it's working. "She's your *sister*'s friend, and I heard Bea say they only met a few months ago."

"In addition to being my sister, Bea's my roommate and my best friend," I practically spit. "As usual, you're totally wrong about all your assumptions."

"I'm totally wrong about what, exactly?" Patrice steps closer. "Because it seems like a mistimed comment on my part is causing all sorts of problems. It might even put the movie's success in jeopardy, and instead of shoring things up for the movie, you're over here. . .whatever it is you're doing." She waves at Octavia. "You backed the wrong person."

She's clearly sore about my social media post, even though I kept things polite about her. "I backed Octavia because. . ."

This is the moment. But will claiming that we're dating make Octavia's life better? Or am I doing it because of some kind of caveman imperative to protect her? Sure, being tied to me will give her some notoriety, and it'll grab more attention for the movie, too. It'll also make Patrice look *jealous*, which she is. She's jealous of Octavia's talent, but no one will realize that. Any way I look at it, the rumor should help Octavia.

Unless she's like Bea.

If she wants to be left alone, well. . .

She's in the wrong career for that. If she wants to sing songs, if she wants to make music videos, she's going to have to come to grips with people looking at her face and saying mean things. It's the world we live in. While I work through things, my obnoxious co-star can't keep her yap shut for three seconds.

"It's fine," Patrice says. "This will all blow over and you won't have to do stuff like this with her anymore. By the time the movie comes out, everyone will have forgotten about all the nastiness, and they may even re-record this whole thing. You don't have to worry about your image or being linked to her."

Is that really what she thinks? That I can't stand the thought of being linked to Octavia? Have I had that great a poker face, or is she just utterly delusional?

Her total cluelessness decides it for me.

I slip my fingers through Octavia's delicate ones and take advantage of her surprise to tighten my hand around hers. "Oh, that's not at all what worries me. Octavia hates being in the limelight, so I've listened to her, but I'm done with it." I tug Octavia along with me as I round on stupid Patty. "Octavia Rothschild's the most talented singer I've ever met, ever *heard,* and we just started dating. The only reason I've bitten my tongue until now is that she doesn't like to make a scene."

That news hits just about like I expect it to. I've been in a lot of movies now, and so far the studios have loved me, because I've never had a single confirmed girlfriend. Lots of rumors, and lots of interest, but not a single actual scandal.

When I turn toward Octavia's beautiful face to see how she's taking my proclamation, I feel something strange.

Pride.

Unsurprisingly, stupid Patty laughs. "Her?" Her giggle's so annoying and high-pitched that I can't fathom how any man in America could find her attractive. "You want people to believe you're dating *her*?" She snorts. "So I came in for a fake apology, and you go straight to fake dating."

I swear, one of these days, I'm actually going to strangle her. It's like she can't help herself. But this isn't about Patty's idiocy. It's really not. I force myself away from the moron and turn to look at Octavia.

She's not watching Patty. She's looking up at me, and she looks. . .unsure. Her eyes are wide, confused. It guts me, really. I wanted to strengthen her position, not confuse her.

It won't hurt her, I promise myself. "Sorry, Octavia," I start. I want to promise her it will go well. I want to tell her that this will make things easier on her. But I'm worried I might be wrong.

In that moment, she looks so gorgeous, so trusting that I act without thinking. My head drops, my hand slides to cup her cheek, and I drop my mouth over hers.

I've probably had more first kisses than most guys the world over.

It's a common part of an audition—at least, for beginning actors it is. Sometimes once I've been cast, I have to kiss a dozen different women to see whether the directors think we have chemistry.

I doubt many men are technically better at kissing than me.

But it's like anything you do for work. When you've made a hundred copies. . .or filled two thousand coffee cups. . .or mopped a million floors, it gets a little boring. I expect to feel what I always feel during a first kiss when my mouth presses up against Octavia's.

Nothing.

But that's not what happens.

On what might be my four hundredth kiss, for the first time in my life, I feel. . .*everything*.

There's an explosion in my chest.

My arms and legs feel light and full of energy.

I want to dance around and sing a ridiculous Disney song.

Birds should be singing, and fireworks exploding in the

sky. As her mouth moves against mine, as her body softens against me, I realize something *is* making noise. Only then does my brain kick into gear, reminding me what the noise is: the flashes of cameras.

Shoot.

We're still on set.

By the time I release Octavia, Bea's standing right behind me, and her wide, wide eyes tell me better than anything else could what I already should have known.

This changes everything.

CHAPTER 7

OCTAVIA

The hospital has these little charts.

They used to have numbers on them from one to ten. Now they have little smiley faces that are green, and then a bunch of other faces, changing colors as they go all the way down to a bright red angry face. When you present in the ER or your doctor's office for some complaint, they always ask you how you're feeling. You can point at the chart and let them know if you're green or red or something in between. Part of their job these days is supposed to be to manage your pain.

Maybe it's because it happened a long time ago. Maybe it's because our insurance sucked, so I was pretty much always a charity case. But when I was small, during the months I spent in the hospital after my burn, they didn't ask me about my pain level, not even when they were debriding the wound. They just threatened to sedate me if I screamed too loud.

Being *sedated,* the way they said it, felt like a terrible threat.

Now, I realize I should have insisted on it. Because their

little scales that went from one to ten were insufficient. Even now, with the faces? They'd need a drawing of someone writhing in agony to represent how I felt when they scraped the burned flesh off of my face, my neck, and my arm.

If you'd asked me for a number, it was a twenty-seven.

During those weeks, I got really, really good at ignoring pain.

Even so, there was one pain I couldn't ignore. During my first weeks at the hospital, my mom never came. She didn't hold my hand. She didn't lie next to me and tell me stories. She didn't tell me that my hair would grow back where it had melted off, or that everything would be okay.

She wasn't there at all.

Only my dad came.

He's the one who held my hand when they did grafts from other places to get the hair back. He's the one who held my hand. He's the one who told me it was going to be okay. When I begged him to get my mom, he told me that she'd come as soon as *My Fair Lady* was over. She had finally gotten the part she wanted, and she wasn't going to let that chance pass her by, wasted.

I wished I hadn't ever made the dumb deal.

If I hadn't, I wouldn't have worn the wig and gotten burned. And I wouldn't have been sitting in here alone all day while my dad went to work. Unlike me, my mom never seemed to struggle with regret. She took her shot, no matter what. But at the time, it felt like she cared more about that cursed play than she did about her daughter.

That thought hurt.

It hurt more than the pain of debridement.

And it hurt more than the looks of pity I got from the hospital staff while they worked on my face. It even hurt more than the recovery from repeated surgeries, including the one that failed after they tried to expand my existing flesh.

I learned that it hurts to feel like you don't matter.

I knew then and there, I never wanted to feel like that again.

So when Jake kissed me—I'm not sure I've ever felt *more* special than I did in that moment, but that was terrifying.

Jake Priest—when I first met him, I was absolutely starstruck.

The Jake Priest.

Then I became friends with his sister, and I realized he was a real person, like any other. Even so, the more time I spent with him, the more I realized that he *is* a person, but he's also like a walking Adonis kind of person.

He's handsome.

He's hilarious.

He's clever.

He's brave and he defends what he thinks is right.

And he can act.

He sings pretty darn well, too.

When his mouth presses against mine, and it feels like *that* scene in every single romance I've ever read, I realize that I'm not just starstruck.

I *like* Jake Priest.

Like, I really, really *like* him.

And that's bad, bad, bad. The reason it hurt me so much when my mom didn't come to the hospital is that I cared, deeply, about what she thought. I cared whether she loved me. I cared whether she was willing to sacrifice for me.

So when she wasn't...

When Jake Priest releases me, my entire body's trembling. My hopes are soaring, and my heart is hammering, and my whole body cries out for just one more touch. Which is the most terrifying thing I've experienced in more than a decade.

There are some things in this world that just *are*.

Gravity keeps us all grounded.

The earth rotates around the sun.

And Jake Priest will wind up with some kind of goddess.

I don't hate myself. I'm an exceptionally talented vocalist. I'm smart, too. But a goddess, I will never be. No surgery, no magical mask, and no amount of makeup will ever make me someone who can walk alongside Jake Priest without causing the entire world to laugh.

Plus, he just lied to protect me.

We haven't been dating.

He threw me a bone—a charity bone to a pathetic stray. That's what this kiss was, and I need a nice bucket of ice water, pronto, so I remember that. "I have to go," I whisper. "I'm sorry."

Jake's brow furrows and his mouth dangles open, but Bea catches my eye and nods, and then she practically drags me out like I'm Princess Diana. We're crashing past crew, actors, and onlookers alike, and then we're out the door and she's waving at the driver who brought us.

"Octavia's sick. We need to go straight back."

It's not strictly a lie. I do feel pretty lousy. When we hop in the van, I notice people trailing us—with their phones out.

Bea swears under her breath. "Step on it." She drops a hand over mine, but she doesn't say another word.

I'm not sure how she always knows the right thing to do. Maybe it's a gift from those amazing foster parents she's always going on about. When we get to our hotel, Bea goes right to the room, points at the bathroom, and says, "Pajamas."

"It's barely noon."

She shrugs.

Once I have the makeup washed off and I'm in pajamas as ordered, Bea's ready for me. She's got six pints of ice cream on a tray and her laptop's perched on the end of the bed.

"We're watching a movie and having a contest."

"Contest?"

She quirks her brow. "A taste test?"

I can't help smiling. "That sounds better than a contest. What flavors did you get?"

"Rocky road, mint chocolate chip, cookies and cream, peaches and cream, strawberry, and fudge ripple."

"Shoot, you already missed the boat."

She frowns.

I cross to the freezer in the corner of the room and pull out my secret stash item. "If you've never tried gooey butter cake, you've never lived."

Bea straightens so fast she nearly knocks the tray over. "Butter cake?"

"It's a Southern flavor my dad showed me—Blue Bell ice cream makes it, and it's hard to find here, but Walgreens will get it if you request it. It's the best southern ice cream company, and it's about to change your life."

"A little like that kiss just did?" She smirks.

My hands wobble, but I don't drop the ice cream.

She pats the bed. "We don't have to talk about it." She scootches over as I get on. But then she whispers, "But I swear, I've never seen a kiss on the screen that looked that hot." She bites her lip and her eyes dance.

"Hot?" I hate that now my voice is wobbling.

Bea's nose scrunches. "*Hot.*"

"Well, I'm sure that's just Jake's version of charitable outreach, but even so, it wasn't bad." I cough. "Not bad at all."

"Then why are we binging ice cream?" Bea's lip curls.

"Should we be *celebrating* instead?" Her eyes light up. "Because I've known Jake for a very long time, and I've never seen him do anything charitable." She leans forward. "Never ever."

I laugh. "I'm sure that's not true."

"No." Bea shakes her head. "It is true. Jake's many things, but charitable isn't among them. And he also only kisses someone he doesn't want to kiss if they're paying him a *lot* of money." Now her smirk is one hundred percent back in place.

So she's saying that if he kissed me, and no one was paying him. . .he wanted to do it? Now my hands are wobbling again as I set the ice cream next to the others on the tray. "It's different for me," I say. "Because I'm your friend. He wanted to help me because of you."

"Maybe." Bea stares at me for a second, and then she spins on her toe and grabs the laptop to pull up Netflix.

"*The Kissing Booth*?" I can't help my snort. "Really?"

"It has a great kiss scene," she says. "And I want to see whether it's better than what I just saw. . ."

We're both laughing as we try the different ice creams. The show's worse than I remember it being, but strangely compelling, too. We both have a good time making fun of it. And I can't help noticing that the couple in the show gets their start with a kiss that isn't quite the normal 'post-date-lip-mash' that most things start with.

Just like the kiss I just had.

My fingers brush against my lips.

And my phone rings.

It's an unknown number.

"Who is it?" Bea peers over the tray of melting ice cream. "Is it. . ." Her eyes widen and she whistles. "First he kissed you, and now he's calling you?"

"Wait." I wave the phone at her, because it's displaying a number I don't have saved. "Is this Jake?"

Bea rolls her eyes. "Of course it is."

My heart accelerates. Do I answer it? Do I ignore it? Right before it can go to voicemail, I swipe to answer. "Hello?"

"Hey, there," a man with a pronounced Southern accent says. "My name's Roy, and boy do I have a great offer for you."

My heart sinks.

"Today only, I can offer you fifty percent off on an auto-warranty extension."

"Um, that's okay," I say. "My warranty's fine."

The accent disappears. "I'm kidding," Jake says. "It's me."

I choke a little, but I hope he can't hear it through the phone. "I knew that."

"You did?"

"I mean, I—well."

"Bea gave me your number. I hope that's okay."

I glare at her and mouth, "A little heads up next time." Next time she gives a movie star my number at his request? *Breathe, Octavia, breathe.* "Well, since we're dating now, I guess it's fine." I snort.

"About that."

There's a knock at the door of our room. "Shoot," I say. "There's someone here. I have to go. Should I call you back so we can work out some kind of story to get out of this?"

"Sure," he says. "Call me back."

I hang up the phone and point at the door. "You get it," I hiss.

Bea shakes her head. "Not a chance. I'm in pajamas here."

"So am I!" I protest. "But you look lovely in yours."

"Lovely?" Bea squeaks, and then she disappears into the bathroom. Her voice is muffled when she shouts, "You look adorable. You can do it!"

"Coward," I shout.

It's probably just housekeeping running late or something. It's only three in the afternoon. I check my pajamas to make sure they're not too appalling. I'm wearing a pink t-shirt and blue plaid pants. Other than an ice-cream blob on my left boob, I'm fine. And really, is anyone from housekeeping going to care? Let's hope not.

I yank the door open. "We don't really need any—" My mouth dangles open.

Jake's holding a box and smiling at me. "Surprise."

I am going to *kill* Bea. She had to know.

"I know you didn't *say* I could come over, but I thought after the shock I gave you earlier, you might want some sugar, and. . ." His eyes cut past me and widen as he notices the multitude of empty ice cream cartons.

"Your sister had the same idea." I smile. "But that was very nice."

"I'm sorry." Jake's hands droop, the box with the words 'Cake Monkey' emblazoned on the top tilting a little.

"You're sorry?" I can't keep my lip from twitching a little. "For what, exactly?"

"All of it," he says. "Kissing you without warning. Telling people we were dating. I shouldn't have just done that, but Patty was being *so* annoying, and I just thought—"

"You didn't think at all." Bea storms out of the bathroom. "You're such an idiot."

Jake's gorgeous face flushes. "Like you think things through before you do stuff."

"This isn't about me, though." Bea drops her hands on her hips. "And what you did was *rude*. Octavia can defend herself."

"Only, she doesn't," Jake says. "I watched you just say 'okay' when they were shafting you, and Patrice should have known what she was doing was wrong, but she didn't. So I thought that if Octavia could get a little boost on social from—"

"A boost from you *kissing* her?" Bea's really on a roll now. Her eyes are flashing, and she tosses her hair, which is tantamount to pressing the big red button for her. "As if you're God's gift."

"You gave me her number," Jake says, his hands waving in response. "You said I should come over and try to make things right." The box is now totally sideways.

I know it's strange, but I've become almost fixated on the dessert box. What did he get? Nothing from a bakery is ever better for being turned sideways. If it's cookies, maybe they'll survive, but a cake?

It's a goner.

The two of them have totally forgotten about the small, peace-offering cake, and I feel a little like it must.

Superfluous.

"What is that?" Bea follows my eyes to the box, finally noticing it.

"Oh." Jake's eyes widen and he rights it. "Cake Monkey makes the *best* cakes in LA, I swear. I had a gluten free one once, which is usually code for 'tastes nasty,' but I had no idea it was even gluten free. Like your singing, they're the very best at what they do, so, anyway." He holds it out to me again.

"Uh, thanks," I say. "But for the record, I'm not upset. You don't need to apologize. I get it—you were just trying to lend a hand."

"Or a *mouth*, you dirty slut," Bea mutters.

"Sure," I say. "A mouth, and I appreciated the sentiment."

"You did?" Jake's grinning now.

I take the box. "I like cake, too. Even if I can't eat it right now, having recently consumed half a gallon of ice cream."

"And does taking my peace offering indicate that you're not mad at me?" Jake arches one eyebrow.

"Sure," I say. "I'm not angry. I think I understand why you did it, and—"

"Actually, that's why I came by, really." Jake steps closer.

Bea inhales sharply.

"To tell me you were defending me." I nod. "I get it, believe me. And I appreciate what you were trying to do, but you don't have to do it anymore. We can say whatever you want—break it off officially whenever is best for you."

Jake shakes his head. "I did get mad at Precious Patty *and* the studio, and I did want to protect you, and when I said we were dating, I thought maybe. . ." He sighs.

"See?" I say. "It's fine."

Jake steps closer still, his broad chest awfully close to my face. "It's not that, though. Because when I kissed you. . ." His eyes trail up, up, up until he's looking right at me. "I liked it, a lot. More than I thought I. . ." He swallows. "It was surprising."

I have no idea what to say.

"And when I thought about how I wasn't really dating you. . ." He shakes his head. "I wanted it to be true. So I came over to see if maybe you would want to go on a date."

"Right now?" Bea's voice sounds a little choked.

"Not now, idiot," Jake says. "I have to go in to film a scene in an hour." He clears his throat. "But tomorrow night, I'm off." He lifts both eyebrows. "We could maybe go somewhere and talk *without* my sister's commentary." The side of his mouth curls up.

My stomach lurches, and I can't believe it when I say, "Sure. I'd like that."

As if the idea of me dating Jake Priest *for real* isn't the most ludicrous thing in the world. As if the kiss we shared really meant something. As if it's not really just an extension of a publicity stunt.

Probably to protect me.

If we do go on a few fun dates, it's definitely going to hurt more when reality really sets in. There's no way someone like Jake really likes someone like me. And there's no way America will ever accept it. And and and.

But he *is* standing right in front of me, and that was the singular best kiss of my entire life. It was better than I ever imagined a kiss might be. So. . . Instead of being smart and telling him it's a bad idea, instead of calling off the insanity, instead of making the smart move, I just smile as he leaves, and I keep right on smiling as Bea squeals. And then, after I go to sleep, I dream of kissing him again. And again. And again.

CHAPTER 8
JAKE

Dear Jake:

You probably don't remember the time we went to Vegas to meet with a friend of mine. You were only four years old. But when we were there, you saw a sign. You could read just well enough to see that it said the slot machines paid out 99% of money paid in. The actual numbers are closer to 85-95%. How they can lie like that in print is a mystery to me. The bigger the company, the more they get away with their lies.

But Jake, what you must have forgotten was the lesson I taught you that day. Only suckers play those odds. If you're going to put your money in a slot machine, over time you will lose. Wanting a career as a singer or an actor is worse than playing slots.

So don't ever write me a letter telling me that you're a talented singer or even worse, that you have promise as an actor again. Not ever, you hear? The

Priests aren't chumps, and we aren't suckers. Don't waste your time or the Fansee's money on something that stupid. Skip the lessons and pocket the cash. We'll need it when I get out to run the big con on those idiots. I'm lining things up—don't worry. It won't be much longer now.

We'll get our revenge and then some.

-Dad

Moments after I leave the set, still floating when I think about my date with Octavia, I get a call. It's a strange call. My agent almost never calls me unless we're negotiating a new contract, and I like it that way. He's a horrible person, as nearly all agents are, but he and I see eye to eye in a way few people really can.

"Priest," he says. It amuses him to call me by my ironic last name. He knows I'm the opposite of Godly.

"Bradley." His name is Brad Hawthorne, not Bradley, but I like to make him sound even nerdier than he is, and he's mildly irritated by it, so I persist.

"I want to start out by saying that I do remember our deal."

When I signed with him, I told him my one stipulation is that he must *never* try to manipulate me. If he tries managing or manipulating me, even once, I'll walk. Our contract has a clause. I can terminate at any time for any reason. "Good." Then this should be a short conversation. They always are.

"You're making a mistake, dating the burned girl."

"Don't call her that," I say. "Octavia has a name, and it's a beautiful one. Just like her face."

He clears his throat. "So it's not just for publicity?"

I want to hang up.

And then fire him.

"Okay, well, I still think it's a mistake. There are way too many ways it could go wrong, but it sounds like you're set on this."

"I am."

"Then I guess I'll do my best to manage whatever happens. But Jake?"

"What?"

"When you dump her, and you will dump her, be prepared. It's going to be ugly for you."

I do hang up then, but I don't blame him for being worried. I can see why he'd assume that it was a mistake for me to date someone if the public might not approve. I haven't dated anyone in. . .well, ever. Not really and truly dating, anyway. One night stands, the occasional passionate week-end. Sure.

And I've 'officially' *dated* plenty of movie stars. The tabloids are always claiming I'm secretly involved with my co-star, and usually the orders from the top brass are to foster those rumors right up until the movie hits the box office. Sometimes they even orchestrate big public break-ups when buzz starts to wane. People like it when their favorite leads are dating "in real life," and they seem to like it even more when we crash and burn.

Not that any part of my supposed life is "real."

What I eat, what I like, and what I do for my hobbies has all been carefully crafted by PR teams to make me look both tough and approachable. Handsome and yet vulnerable. It's all a big steaming pile of garbage. Of course I don't love Red Bull. It tastes like gym-sock-soaked-cola. I don't enjoy cycling, but Peloton pays me a *lot* to pretend to love it. And I definitely don't think tofurkey tastes anything like the actual roasted flesh of the bird, but here we are.

Imagine my surprise when, in my attempt to help Octavia, I discovered that I actually do like her. And then, when I came over to try and figure out what to do about it. . .she seemed to like *me* back. She's not vacuous, selfish, or greedy, so I'm confused about what motivations she might have for liking me.

Could Octavia really be as shallow as all the girls who show up on set holding signs? Is she only interested in me because of my dimples? There's no way she likes me for my brain. It's mediocre at best. My singing voice—same. But for some reason she said she wanted to go on a date, and I'm embarrassingly excited about it. The problem is, I'm not really sure what to *do* on our date. I've just typed in "best first date ideas" on my laptop browser when there's a knock at my door.

I groan.

It's probably someone who wants to clean my windows. Or a salesman trying to convince me to change my laundry service. I think about ignoring it, but they bang again. "It's me." Eddy.

"And I'm here, too." Shoot. That's Adam Forrest, our producer.

"Coming." I jog to the door and whip it open. "What brings you guys over?" I try to sound casual, but it has to be something about Octavia. The producer and the sound director—who's also coordinating the album launch—is not a coincidence.

"We need to talk." Adam looks ticked.

"About?" I lean against the doorway. "Is this about Octavia?"

"Can we come in?" Eddy has both eyebrows raised.

I sigh and shift, and they both walk through.

"This is a pretty nice place," Adam says.

I can't help my frown. "You should know. Your people found it for me."

Adam walks toward the bay window overlooking the ocean.

The Pacific is pretty far from here, so the waves are teensy, but you *can* see it. I don't really care, but apparently ocean-view places cost way more. It's like everything else in Hollywood—inflated and misguided.

"You know," Adam finally says, "every actor's career makes some sort of parabolic curve. You gain in popularity, demanding more and more money, gaining more and more fans." Adam drags one hand downward, downward, downward. "Until you don't." He brushes his hands together. "Your popularity, your fans, and the amount of money you command goes up. . . until it doesn't."

He's straight-up pissing me off now.

"We all want you to be the next Tom Hanks." Adam smiles. "And I think you have it in you to do it. You're smart, you're handsome, and gosh darn it, people like you."

I roll my eyes.

"But Tom Hanks didn't get derailed by making poor relationship decisions," Eddy says.

"Really?" I'm the one lifting both eyebrows now. "Do you care to tell me why it's a poor decision to date Octavia?"

Eddy and Adam share some kind of look.

"Because her face is burned?" I swear, I *am* going to punch someone really soon. "That can't be the reason." I start to pace. "She pays her taxes. She works hard. She's smart. She's kind. She never attacks people on set or off. She's got an amazing voice, and—"

"It's her face," Adam says. "And I can't say that anywhere but here, in this private apartment, and if you ever say I said it, I'll lie, but Jake, the optics are bad, okay?

And what I wish the world was and what it is aren't the same."

I can't believe I'm hearing this.

"You shouldn't be dating anyone really," Eddy says. "It's not just her. Lots of guys are good looking, but you're well-spoken, you're clever, and you're single. You've always been single. Rumors, but nothing more, and along with your clean-cut image, it really plays right now."

"It plays all the time." Adam shrugs. "You even have a pretty decent fan group that's hoping you're gay and the few women are a cover-up."

"But dating someone, especially someone about whom everyone will have an opinion?" Eddy sighs. "It's complicated, and complicated is always bad."

"Tom Hanks was married—twice," I say. "And it really seems like his second wife broke up his first marriage—a marriage with kids, I might add. So don't tell me—"

"That was a different time," Adam says. "It was before social media. Now all anyone remembers is that he's been with Rita for a million years, and that he sure made cute movies with Meg Ryan."

I roll my eyes. "Look, I appreciate that you guys want what's best for me, and that you're trying to help, but I'll remind you that what I do when the camera isn't rolling isn't really your concern. That's my *life,* and it's the one place where *I* get to call the shots."

"Alright." Adam drops onto the corner of my sofa.

I take some small satisfaction knowing that it's about as comfortable as a nearby park bench.

"Let's play this out." Adam drops his head on his hand and leans over the armrest. He's hoping it'll be more comfortable, but he's wrong. Their firm's interior decorator sucks. "Let's say you get good press for dating Olivia."

"Octavia," I say.

"Right." Adam nods. "Let's say women *like* that you don't care about her looks."

"I do care," I say. "I happen to think Octavia's face is beautiful."

Adam frowns. "Fine. Then, that. And let's say women believe you, but think about this. If people love her, then how are they going to react when you break up?"

"Why would we break up?" The whole idea pisses me off. "What if we got married?"

Adam splutters.

Eddy coughs.

"You're the one who started this." I start pacing again, my hands jammed in my pockets. "So let's play it out. Let's say Octavia and I get married. Actors get married. It happens."

"Okay." Adam frowns. "And now you're suddenly stuck playing action roles, because your new wife with the. . ." He clears his throat. "Beautiful face is all anxious about you kissing someone else."

"Please." I snort. "Stop saying dumb stuff."

Eddy chucks a pillow at me. "Jake, the point is that people either love her, and they get mad when you break up, making you the villain, or they hate her, and the longer you're together, the more your career nosedives. We brought her in because you insisted, but so far she's been the biggest liability of this entire movie. She almost destroyed our lead's image yesterday."

"You're blaming Octavia for Patty being horrible? That doesn't seem a little unfair to you?"

Adam stands. "It's cute you think that 'fairness' matters."

I walk toward the front door. "My contract has no stipulations on whom I can date. Your angelic lead Patty caused her own problems by being a raging villain, and I have no intention of *not* dating Octavia because you two disapprove. So if there's nothing else. . ." I open the door. "I'll see you on set tomorrow."

"You used to be easy." Adam glares. "But now, you're not great to work with, Priest."

"I could say the same for you." If he thinks I'm scared of him because he came all the way to my apartment to try and bully me into dumping a perfectly sweet woman, he's wrong. I'm not scared. There are other producers in LA, and there are other roles. I'm the good guy here, and I won't be pushed around for it.

I'm not Octavia.

"We came to make you an offer," Eddy says. "Before we go, I'll at least share it with you." He walks to the door, and then he turns around. "We'll agree to double the promotion budget for the album, and we'll even feature Octavia in all the videos and materials. It'll be great for her future and the album's earnings."

"Why?" I can't help my scowl. "Because if you convince her not to date me by dangling this in front of her, you're just going to piss me off more."

"We've said our piece on that. The rest is your call—as you pointed out, our contract doesn't give us the right to stop you." He narrows his eyes. "Our offer for additional promotion has another stipulation." Adam pulls an envelope from the inside pocket of his suit. "All Octavia has to do is promise not to post any more videos on social media between now and when the movie releases." He leans closer and shoves the paper at me. "Not so much as a Happy Birthday song for a friend. Nothing that isn't approved by our office."

"Wait, you think *she's* been posting videos from the set?" I can hardly believe it.

"Another one went live from the music video filming, and

it wasn't pretty. Who else could be releasing these?" Adam asks. "They've all been hugely positive for her."

I shake my head. "It's not Octavia. Trust me, it's not."

"Then she won't have any problems with signing this," Eddy says. "Get her to do it."

But after he leaves, I can't help wondering, if it's not Octavia, and I'm sure that it's not. . .who *is* posting them?

And why?

CHAPTER 9

OCTAVIA

My sixteenth birthday was *perfect* in every way.

My mom forgot about all her stuff and actually planned a real party for me. She was doing a play at the time—*Cyrano de Bergerac*—but she skipped a rehearsal or two so she could finalize the details of a perfect night for me. I had never felt quite so important and loved. I didn't have a lot of friends, so it wasn't a big party, but Mom made it a masquerade, and I got to cover my face entirely for all the photos. For once, I was happy to be in them with my friends.

Mom had bought me a beautiful black mask made of filigreed black lace and spruced up with a big, startlingly red flower on my burned side. A spray of vivid red feathers effectively covered nearly every burned part of my face.

My mom spent almost thirty minutes curling and arranging my hair.

And my parents finally gave me the gift I'd always wanted: eight horseback lessons at a local barn. By the time the party started, I felt like an actual storybook princess.

Of course, after it ended...

"I hope you had a lovely time," Mom said, after my last friend, Rebecca, was picked up.

"Oh, I did." I sighed as I sank into my favorite spot in the worn sofa of our living room. The plaid fabric was threadbare, but it was *so* comfortable. I could take my mask off now, but I didn't. I just sat there, marinating in the joy of the moment.

"Actually, though, sweetheart, your mom and I have some news we wanted to share." Dad perched on the hard leather chair opposite the sofa, cracking his knuckles and biting his lip.

I straightened immediately. When Dad cracked his knuckles, something was wrong.

"Don't worry, though." Mom sat on the other leather chair, separated from Dad by a large wooden end table. "It's going to be good news, I swear."

It sure didn't seem like it. "Okay. What is it? Are we moving?"

Dad forced the most awkward smile I'd ever seen. "Well, you *can* move if you'd like."

I frowned. "What does that mean?" They've never left anything up to me. There's no way they were asking me if I wanted them to find a new house. With just two years of school left, why would I want to move?

"Your father and I have decided to get a divorce," Mom said, her smile as forced as Dad's. "We're still friends, and we just think we're going to be better apart than together."

I blinked. "You—better. . ." I didn't understand *at all.* "What? Why?"

"As I said," Mom said. "Your Dad thinks—"

"Oh, ho, ho, you can't just pin this all on me. We talked about that."

Mom scowled. "You said I could say that 'we' decided."

"You've always said and done whatever you wanted, no matter what I said."

It got worse and worse from there. I didn't have to say a single word, though. They spun out all on their own. It made me wonder how they'd held things together around me before that, because clearly they detested one another. But within a few moments, Dad said something that made it pretty clear why they were breaking up.

"Isn't that just like you? Of course you're keeping the house. You're keeping the furniture. You're keeping all of it." Dad was pacing, and each time he said 'you're,' he jabbed his finger at Mom's head.

Mom's eyes were flashing, however. "I'm not the one demanding we get a divorce."

"I'm only demanding because you were having an affair with Paul!"

Mom closed her eyes and pinched the bridge of her nose. "You know that's not true."

"It is now," Dad said.

"But that only started after you told me you were filing for divorce," Mom said.

"Which I did after I saw you two kissing behind the building!"

I froze then, waiting for Mom to explain. Hoping it wasn't true. Hoping there was some way back.

But there wasn't.

Mom looked as guilty as he said she was.

She'd been kissing Paul—Christian was his real name— on set, and Dad was leaving her for it. I resolved then and there that I would *never* kiss someone in a play or movie, and that I would never date or marry someone else who was part of that world.

I'd never broken that promise to myself.

Until now.

But as I think about going on a date with Jake later, I can't regret it. It's not the same as my parents at all. He didn't start acting when his marriage got rough, and he didn't sacrifice anything and everything to live a dream into his forties.

He's a young, hot movie star, and he kisses people for his *job,* not as some kind of sick hobby he can't quit. He picked *me* to ask out, in spite of being able to have any woman he wanted, really.

So it's not the same.

I'm not being stupid. I'm not setting myself up for the same misery my dad endured. I'm sure I'm not. I keep telling myself that as I touch up my makeup, grab my shoes, and sling my purse over my shoulder. "You ready?"

Bea's grimacing while she stares at her phone. These days, that's never good.

"What now?"

She drops her phone and it clatters against the table. "Nothing." She stands and snatches it off the table, checking to make sure the screen isn't cracked.

But I'm not a moron. "Just tell me. I'll see it eventually."

"It really is nothing," she says. "The same kind of posts you've been seeing—nothing new."

I hold out my hand.

"We need to go or we'll be late." She turns for the door.

I don't move. "Just show me what you were glaring over."

When she finally surrenders her phone with a sigh, it's obvious. The post's still open. It's a movie-critic-turned-social-media-starlet, opining on the pros and cons of me and Patrice. There's a massive, full frontal image of my burn, juxtaposed with the flawless face of one of the most beautiful movie stars of all time.

I do not look wonderful.

But what had Bea scowling, I'm sure, were the comments. One small scroll shows that public opinion has not been on my side. Besides the usual "optics don't lie," and "not the fugly one," comments, some people are being truly awful.

Like, "Wonder what they're paying him to date *that*."

And, "Hope he's getting hazard pay."

Most of them are from men, which doesn't make me feel better. Usually the women are the catty ones, but in this case, the men are probably more likely to be honest.

"It's fine." I hand the phone back to Bea and head for the door. "It's nothing I haven't heard most of my life." I force a smile, not that she can see it. It's good practice either way.

Bea trots to catch up to me. "He asked you out—he loves your face, just like I do."

It would be nice if every single conversation didn't revolve around it and people's opinion of my worth didn't always come down to it, but we don't get to pick the world we live in. We just have to do our best in the one we have.

"Your hair looks amazing, by the way," Bea says. "I always love your pin curls, but they look really *perfect* today."

If only the 1940s look was actually in right now. . . It's the hairstyle that covers the most surface area of my burn, so I've worn my hair like this for years. It doesn't take long for us to reach the recording studio, and we manage to record two and a half songs before we run out of time.

"We're nearly done," Bea says. "A song and a half, pickups, and we'll be finished."

It'll be nice to go home again, but it's sort of lousy that Jake will surely have weeks left of filming after I go.

What's wrong with me? Thinking about where he'll be, like *this* might turn into something. I can be a real idiot. I decided last night that I'm just going to appreciate hanging out with Jake like I did the date to prom lined up by my dad.

He found a really handsome, really smart guy—a kid of one of his friends—who took me. I knew the guy didn't really like me. I knew he wasn't my new boyfriend or anything. I enjoyed the evening for what it was.

Like I appreciate lilies—short-lived, and all the more special for it.

In ten years, when I look back, I'm sure that I'll think about this the same way. My date with Jake Priest. Or if it goes well, maybe even my *dates* with Jake Priest. As long as I don't expect more, I can't be disappointed.

"Let's go grab a drink," Q says. He throws his long hair back over his shoulder. His head's shaved on the left side, but the other side's longer than mine. It makes us almost opposites. I cover my left side, and his is exposed.

"Not today," Bea says. "Octavia has plans." She wiggles her eyebrows.

Everyone starts to crow. "You have to tell us how it goes," Morgan says. "Because Jake Priest." She whistles. "He's most girls' dream."

"Not mine." Bea groans. "Gross."

"Hey," Morgan says. "We didn't all grow up with him, alright?"

"We didn't," I say. "Thank goodness for that. I imagine he wasn't quite the polished ladies' man at ten years old that he is now."

"Actually." Bea chuckles. "Jake has always been the same as he is now. He's always been charming, and he's always had those dimples."

"He didn't suffer through an awkward stage?" I shake my head. "That's just unfair."

"Some people have all the luck," Everett says.

We all turn to stare for just a moment—our bass player almost *never* talks, and when he does, it's always about music. Those six words may be the first ones I've ever heard him utter that weren't about a song.

As if he can tell he shocked us, Everett kicks a can, which skitters down the hall.

And slams into Jake's black boot.

"Hey, O." He smiles, dimples in full force. "I heard you were done, and I thought you might be ready to go a little early."

Morgan's mouth drops open and then turns into a smile as she shifts toward me and away from Jake. She tightens her hands into fists and shakes them at me. "Go O," she mouths. "Have so much fun!"

"She's ready," Bea says. "You two have fun."

"Or not," Everett mutters.

Words seven and eight, all in the same thirty seconds. It's a tiny miracle.

"I'll see you guys tomorrow." I wave as I awkwardly walk away from my friends and toward Jake Priest.

At some point I should try to think of him as just Jake, probably, but I can't. Not yet. He's still Jake Priest to me.

"Where are we going?" I gesture at my dark jeans and hot pink silk blouse. "Am I dressed alright?"

Jake slaps his forehead. "Idiot. Bea told me that when I liked a girl, I needed to tell her how to dress before we went to do something. I'm sorry if that stressed you out. Yes, though, you look fine." He smiles. "Better than fine."

I can feel the heat rising in my face, and I duck my head.

Blushes do *not* look good with my burn.

And I really want to look good tonight, in the spirit of the lily. Or at least, as good as I possibly can look. It's a sliding scale over here, especially standing next to Mr. Perfect.

Jake shoves his hands into his pockets. He's wearing dark jeans too, like we coordinated or something, and his royal blue shirt makes his eyes really stand out. He bites his lip and waits for a few seconds before finally speaking. He's really got the Hollywood actor timing down. "If you think this sounds lame, I can come up with something else. I just try not to go to movies—I get mobbed usually—and you can't really talk during them either."

"You think going to the movies is a bad date?" I can't help raising my eyebrows. "Alert the media!" Now I'm smiling broadly. "Jake Priest, not a fan of movies, ladies and gentlemen."

He grabs my wrist, spins around, and starts walking, forcing me to jog alongside him. And then he slides his hand against mine, entwining our fingers.

It's like a scene in a movie.

He's that smooth.

I can't do a cartwheel, but in that moment, my heart does a back flip.

For the first time, I realize I might be in trouble. The easy-breezy-Octavia who's looking at this like a lily to enjoy and discard does not exist. I've been on my date with Jake for exactly nineteen seconds, and I'm all in.

How pathetic am I?

I do manage to trip along down the hall and follow him into the parking lot. He slides on sunglasses, hands me a pair, and holds up his hand as we round the corner, already blocking the reporters who are waiting in a tiny mob at the edge of the lot.

"No questions, guys. First dates should be fun and exciting, shouldn't they?"

As if his smile has blinded them, the reporters just stare at us blankly for a few seconds before hammering us with questions.

"Where are you going?"

"Have you slept together yet?"

"When did you meet?"

"It's your first date?" one very short lady in spiky heels asks. "How can that be? Didn't Mr. Priest say you were dating already?"

Jake doesn't miss a beat. "First *official* date, yes." He shakes his finger. "But you little vixens, I said no questions. Please have a little respect and shoo." He waves at them with his free hand.

To my utter shock, they actually wander off, muttering, but leaving voluntarily.

"I give the media a lot of access," he says. "They owe me a little space when I ask for it."

I can't help smiling again. He basically just told me that even the media isn't able to withstand his legendary dimples. "So what are we doing?"

"You'll just have to wait and see," he says. "Since I didn't give you enough warning to work on your outfit, you may as well be surprised." He releases my hand, slides his hand up my arm to my shoulder, and steers me sharply to the right. Then he lets go of me entirely and opens the door on a beat-up old Nissan.

"Umm, I hate to be the one to point this out, but that's not your car. You have a Mercedes SUV, or you did when we went to karaoke."

"I traded cars with one of the set guys for the day." He winks. "Flying under the radar."

"Why would you do that?" I glance around the lot, which is clear full of Teslas, Porsches, and Ferraris. "Isn't this Nissan a bigger anomaly here?"

"Wait." He frowns. "Did you only agree to this date for the media attention?" He pauses. "To gain more followers on social?"

I roll my eyes. "Right."

He smiles. "I'm kidding. But it's not the radar on the movie set I'm hoping to avoid. It's when we leave and go out into the real world, or at least, as real-world as it gets in LA."

"You don't want to be seen?" I don't add the, 'with me,' but I can't help wondering.

"Trust me—it's annoying to be noticed. When I'm with you, I'd rather not have people mobbing me and asking me for a signature or a photo."

"Does that happen a lot?" I try to imagine what it would be like to be noticed for something good, for people who want to see me instead of people who glare or stare awkwardly.

"Enough that it's annoying. But even when I'm not on a date, I try to blend in." Jake shrugs. "Hence the plain white SUV. As you noticed, most everyone has something flashy, so driving something like this Nissan almost makes you disappear."

"Your car back in New York isn't boring."

Jake smiles. "Ah, but in New York, I have family and friends to impress. Everyone here's a total loser." He winks. "Present company excluded, of course."

He bends over and clears all the trash off the passenger seat before reaching across and opening the door from the inside. "I'm going to kill Owen, I swear. He failed to warn me that his car smells like moldy Cheetos and is full of trash."

I'm laughing as I slide in. "This is probably more my speed, honestly. I'm not really a very neat person."

"Somehow, I doubt that." Jake's smirking. "I imagine your Honda Accord is perfectly detailed at all times."

"Bea told you what I drive?" I arch one eyebrow. "What else did she say?"

"You actually drive a Honda?" Jake slaps the steering wheel. He shakes his head. "I knew it, though."

"You guessed?"

Jake shrugs. "Reading people's kind of my thing. Don't feel bad about it." He smiles again. "We don't need any more bad energy, thanks to this disaster of a ride." He starts the car up, and it does thankfully turn over, and then we're off, shooting past confused reporters and photographers and heading for the freeway.

"You're really not telling me where we're going?"

Jake weaves in and out of traffic like he thinks we're in a Ferrari, but in between shifting lanes, he whips out his wallet and flips it open. "Tonight's date will require a small influx of capital."

"What?"

He peels a twenty-dollar bill out of the stack of money in his wallet and hands it to me. "Here's yours."

"What on earth—"

"And here's mine." He pulls another twenty out and drops it in the cupholder. "We're almost there, and then I'll explain the rest."

For the life of me, I have no idea what we're doing when he pulls into a Target parking lot and cuts the engine. There's got to be something magical about his dimples, because I don't even care.

CHAPTER 10

JAKE

Dear Dad,

I know you said never to write you about voice lessons or singing or acting, but something pretty cool happened. I stole a song from another foster kid and I got famous with it instead. And I did such a good job stealing it that she thinks she wanted me to have her song.

I swear, these people really are so stupid.

The label just sent me a check for two hundred grand for the song I stole—and to cut a few others with them. I'm not sharing any of it with the Fansees or the girl who wrote it. I think this is the beginning of our greatest con yet. You need to get out soon and help me pull one over on all the stupid Americans who like this kind of crappy, sentimental music.

Your son,
Jake

Once I cut the engine, I turn to face Octavia, and I swear, the look of confusion on her face is almost enough for me to call it. After scouring the internet for unique dating ideas, this one seemed like a winner.

But now it seems really dumb.

"Alright, what are you paying me for?" Octavia narrows her eyes.

"No, no," I say. "I'm not paying you. I'm paying for myself." I nod. "You have to buy some stuff, and I'll do the same, and then we take the stuff back to my apartment, and we each have to make something for the other person's dinner with what we bought."

Octavia blinks. "Your apartment?"

I groan. "No, not like that. It's not creepy. I just can't go to a normal place, because—"

As if on cue, someone raps on the window. "Hey, are you Jake Priest?" A mother and her teenage daughter are leaning closer and closer.

"No way, Mom. I told you—he wouldn't be caught dead in this old junker."

I shake my head. "Nope, sorry. Not famous, but I get that a lot."

But then the mother sees Octavia, and her mouth drops. "It *is* him. I knew it." She points. "Look!"

"See?" I jab my thumb at the mother. "Let's go quick, before they start shouting and other people notice."

Octavia starts to buckle.

"No, not *go*, go. Go inside." I shake my head. "They have

bags of stuff. They're headed out, so they can't really follow us in if any of it's refrigerated." I smile. "Let's go inside." I jam a hat down over my head and toss the sunglasses to Octavia again.

She bites her lip for a moment, and I wonder whether she's going to beg off on the whole thing, but then she nods, and shoves the sunglasses over her face. "Let's go."

Moments later, we're both racing toward the entrance like we're running from the police, and Octavia's giggling like it's all a big game. "Did you see her face?" She's heaving a little. "That mother looked appalled, like we were the jerks." She shakes her head. "She came and banged on your window like it was her right, but running from her was rude?" She rolls her eyes. "People, man."

"People, man, indeed," I say. "They are the worst."

Octavia frowns then, like she's thinking about all the ways people suck. I can't have her all bummed out on our date, so I slap my forehead. "A timer. We need some kind of timer." I set a twenty-minute timer on my phone, show it to her, and snatch a small black plastic shopping basket from a stack. "And don't try to follow me, either."

She frowns. "We're on a date and you're ditching me? Really?"

I blink. "No. That wouldn't make sense, would it?" I shift my basket to the left side of my body. "But no sneaking a peek at what I grab." I arch one eyebrow. "I can't have you copying my epic ideas."

"Are you a chef?" she asks. "Did you pick this to show off your hidden talent?"

I lean closer, close enough to realize she smells like honeysuckle. "You'll just have to wait and see."

She narrows her eyes at me, and then she snags a basket of her own, shoving her borrowed sunglasses up onto her head at the same time. That movement shifts her hair back, away from her face, and I can't help my smile. She looks nice with her hair pulled back. I'm guessing she never does it because of the burns, but I like seeing more of her.

Her skin's smooth and rippled at the same time. So smooth I think I could run my finger across it and barely feel a thing, but rippled in smooth, almost consistent waves that look like the surface of a lake on a windy day.

"Allergies?" She arches one eyebrow. "I'd rather not blow you up like a balloon on our first date."

First date.

The words are like a caress to me for some reason. My first date with Octavia Rothschild. Maybe it's her voice, which is so smooth and silky it could be like a caress. But I think it's more the idea that I'm with someone I chose, someone much better than me.

Someone I like.

She makes me happy. I'm not sure why, but she does. I can count on one hand the number of people I've met who make me happy.

Bea.

Probably my foster parents.

And now, Octavia, too.

She starts walking, and I have to jog to catch up. "I have no allergies," I say. "You?"

She shakes her head. "Not unless you count wasps."

"Whoa," I say. "That's a big one, but I doubt it'll change my dinner plans."

"I carry an epi-pen," she says. "And a fistful of pills. No need to worry."

"But shellfish and peanut butter are A-OK," I say. "Noted."

"Wait, are you going to make shellfish?" She blinks. "And what about peanut butter? Would that be with the shellfish?"

"I can't really say what's on the menu," I say. "But you know, anything but wasp venom is a possibility."

She rolls her eyes. "But with twenty bucks, our options are pretty limited."

"What do you mean?"

She leans over the refrigerated bin. "This steak, for instance, is twenty-four dollars." She shakes her head. "I'm four dollars short, and that's before sides or seasonings are considered."

"Well, shoot." I pull my wallet out. "Maybe I should change the budget a little—"

She shakes her head. "No, no, this is a game, right? We see who can make the best meal with twenty bucks."

Before I can ask her what she's planning to get, she ducks around the corner—into the international aisle, maybe?—and she hollers. "Meet you in produce in two minutes."

She's clearly had an idea, and I still have *nothing*. You'd think that while I was searching for this date plan I'd have found, you know, an idea of what I should buy.

Okay, think, Jake. What do I know how to make?

Nothing.

I'm totally useless. Why didn't I rule this idea out as soon as I remembered that I never cook? I order all my food. That's my one move. Bea doesn't really cook much either. I blame Seren for cooking so well that none of us needed to learn, but I have no ideas and I'm desperate, so I text Bea anyway.

> Mayday! What meal can I cook for under $20?

> Why do you need to cook? You know what? Forget the answer. You're doomed.

She's rude. I forget sometimes how rude she is.

Is this for your date? Ermagosh, I had no idea
you were such an idiot. Don't try to make her
anything, not if you ever want to see her
again. Call in takeout immediately.

She sends me options for places I could order takeout from, and the options keep coming. She doesn't stop until she's sent at least half a dozen options.

With a beleaguered sigh, I call for Korean takeout. "No, not very spicy on the tteokbokki," I say. "I have no idea whether she like spicy food, because it's our first date." At least the guy taking my order can't see my idiotic smile.

"Who are you talking to?" Octavia arches one eyebrow as she rounds the corner.

"Gotta go." I hang up, and then I smile. "Sorry. Work calls me a lot." That's not technically a lie. They do, even if that wasn't work calling.

She purses her lips, but doesn't argue. "Are you ready? You didn't meet me in produce."

"I mean, 'ready' can mean a lot of things," I say. "I need a bit more time."

"You didn't say we couldn't search for ideas online, but I feel like you're supposed to be coming up with it yourself." She stares pointedly at my phone.

"Right," I say. "Yes, no more of that." But since I can't google for ideas on my phone—why wasn't I doing that instead of texting Bea?—I decide to walk a little aimlessly up and down the aisles, hoping that inspiration will strike.

I mean, I know that help from my stupid idea is on the way, but I can't let *her* know or it won't be a surprise. So I walk up the aisle slowly, pondering the items on the shelf until I see something I know.

Pasta Roni.

"They still make this?" I don't even have to fake my

delight. "This was my favorite summer lunch when I was. . .when Dave and Seren were working and Bea was busy." I toss one in my basket.

"You don't call them Mom or Dad?" Octavia looks genuinely curious.

"It's complicated," I say.

"Why?"

"I have a dad," I say. "I mean, presumably I have a mother too, but Dad never really said anything about her. When I asked, he changed the subject. Either way, Bea's mom's a total mess, but my dad. . ." I'm not sure how to defend him when he's in prison for actually trying to steal from people. "I just know he was a pretty good dad to me when he had the chance to be."

"Bea said he's locked up?" She grimaces. "I know that sounds bad, but that's what she said."

I shrug. "Some people make a living by lying to people on their televisions like I do. Others make a living by lying to their faces."

She winces. "Well, I'm sure it was hard for you when he went to prison."

I'm not sure how to answer. "It was actually easy—too easy. My life was hard with Dad in a lot of ways, and when he got locked up." I snort. "I mean, we were actually trying to con Dave and Seren, and then after they testified against him, they took me in. At first, I thought they were looking for a way to punish me. I spent a miserable few weeks, waiting for them to. . ." I sigh. "I'm not sure. Beat me?"

I see a bag of tortilla chips and toss it in my basket.

"They never did anything but make me special treats, buy me clothes, and get me lessons for things I wanted to learn." I can't help my half-smile when I think about the paranoid little kid I was when they found me. "In some ways, I almost feel bad saying this, but in some ways it was the best thing that ever happened to me." I've never said that aloud. Not once.

I feel terrible about it.

I have a father, and one thing I've always prided myself on being is loyal. Saying that it was good for me that he was caught is hard, but it's also true.

"Your dad going to prison was the best thing?" Octavia looks surprised.

I nod slowly. "Dad—what he taught me and what the Fansees taught—they were complete opposites. When I lived with Dad, I believed everything he said, but as I got older, I started to wonder. The Fansees seemed right, too."

"Couldn't they both be right?" Octavia's looking straight ahead, at the floor, talking as if to herself. "I used to think the world had to be black and white, but I think sometimes the truth is somewhere in between."

"Shades of grey," I say. "I like that. My two sets of parents are both extremes. The Fansees are optimistic and idealistic, and my dad's jaded and cynical. Maybe that's the closest anyone has ever come to describing me—something in between."

She nods. "What you need to do is take the best from both. You can see things like Dave and Seren, but you're also smart enough to spot duplicity in situations and people in a way your foster parents probably can't."

It's like I've been waltzing through my life for decades and no one has ever seen me before. Then along comes Octavia, and suddenly, someone *gets it*. The real me. Unvarnished. Grey. Dingy.

But she doesn't seem put off by it.

I throw a bag of gummy bears and a pint of ice cream in my bag and head for the front. Octavia's trying to peek into my basket, probably trying to figure out what I might make with ice cream and Pasta Roni, but I'm going to keep her guessing.

"Just the twenty." I point at the register four down from mine that's lit up. "You go down there."

She tries to steal one more look in my basket and then finally trots away. I don't take the register in front of me—I swing farther right and check myself out. I always do better at self-checkout because no one's staring me in the face, so I'm less likely to be recognized. When I go to pay, I actually have three dollars and eleven cents left, so I throw in a pack of gum and a pair of nail clippers to add volume.

We're spotted on the way to the car, and we run again. When I grab her hand, she startles a little, but then she smiles.

People smile at me all day long. Sometimes they're paid to. Sometimes they're smiling with the adoring grin of a fangirl. So why does *her* smile make something inside my chest spin round and round? Is it because her eyes sparkle? Is it because her voice is so melodic I could listen to it forever? Or is it something else?

On the way back to my place, she tells me about the years of voice lessons it took to polish her abilities. I don't bother telling her I spent just as long for a far less impressive product. While she's talking about one of her voice coaches and his obsession with her keeping her shoulders squared up and back, she's waving her arms and ranting. It's one of the cutest, most dynamic things I've ever seen.

I'm really looking forward to her reaction when the Korean food shows up. I can hear her now, squawking about how unfair it is that I didn't even bother making her something.

"Why aren't you talking?" She frowns. "Did I say something stupid?"

My eyes widen. "Not at all. I'm enjoying listening to you."

Uh-oh. Her frown grows. "I'm not a circus act, you know."

I laugh. "You'd be a good one. You remind me of Seren—she's the most dynamic speaker I've ever met."

"I remind you of your mother?" She grimaces. "Dear Diary. First date went badly. I reminded him of his *mother*."

I reach over and take her hand. "I don't know. I think it's going pretty well."

She clams up like I stuck duct tape over her mouth, but she doesn't pull away. I'm taking that as a win.

"Tell me about your family," she finally says. "I really only know Bea."

Shoot. My family's a tricky topic. "Well, you know I have a dad," I say. "He's locked up, so that's complicated. He was almost eligible for parole when some administrator discovered that he'd helped the prison warden siphon about eight million dollars during the past year, and then he refused to divulge where it was hidden, and he got more time added to his sentence."

"Oh, no," she says. "That's terrible."

"He's only been caught twice in his life," I say. "But I agree it was pretty bad timing for the second one to happen then."

"Wait." Her hand stiffens in mine. "Are you saying it's terrible that he was caught or terrible that he stole that money?"

"Both?" I ask. "I mean, he raised me for the first ten years of my life, and if you'd asked me right after he went to prison and I was being honest, I'd have said the only bad part was that he got caught. But now?" I shrug. "I guess Dave and Seren have rubbed off on me."

"I should hope so," she says. But she doesn't pull her hand out of mine. That's something.

"I do think things are more complicated than a lot of people make them out to be. They're more complicated than my dad led me to believe, too. My dad didn't have an easy life, and people took advantage of him a lot. It was a natural next step for him to do the same to others. But now that I've met Dave and Seren, now that I know there are good people out there. . ." I shrug. "I guess I learned there's another way."

"A better way," Octavia says.

She's like them—the Fansees. She lives squarely in the white. Maybe that's why I like being around her. For the same reason, things could get a little uncomfortable if she spends more time with me. Most of the Fansee family—foster or biological—doesn't really get shades of grey. Bea does, thanks to her mom. I think that's why she and I work and Emerson has never really liked me much.

I've killed the conversation with talk of my dad, I suppose. Luckily, my apartment's close. That's why I chose that Super Target. I pull into my normal space, and I wonder whether this car's going to get ticketed. Exactly no one will believe it's mine.

Right as I kill the engine, Octavia says, "I'm sorry."

"Sorry?" I turn toward her. "For what?"

"I shouldn't say it's a better way when I don't know all the details, but I would usually say—"

I release her hand and then I cover it with mine and squeeze. "It's fine. You're right, of course. Stealing money from other people, no matter who they are or how unscrupulous they've been, isn't as good as working hard to earn it yourself."

"He's still your dad though, so it's complicated," she says. "I get it."

"You do?" I raise my eyebrows. "Do you have a dad who's not always a hero?"

She shrugs. "My dad's pretty great. But my mom. . ." Her smile's a little pained, which means she's being honest. "That's my 'complication.'"

I laugh. "Maybe you do get it." Reluctantly, I pull my hand away from hers and get out. When I reach for my bag, she tries to grab it first. "Ah, ah, ah, Miss 'Better Way.' No peeking."

"Tortilla chips," she moans. "What could you be making that requires tortilla chips and Pasta Roni?"

"You will just have to wait and see what my culinary skills produce."

She follows me to the elevator bay, and once the doors open, I swipe my card and hit the button for the penthouse. "Oh, fancy. I'm assuming that 'P' means the penthouse?" She arches one eyebrow.

"I didn't even pick it," I say. "It's part of my agreement with my management company. They provide me an apartment as long as I film more than two feature films a year."

"Oh, you know." Octavia's using a British accent. "As long as I remain famous and posh, they provide me with a penthouse." She breathes on her nails and rubs them on her shirt. "No big deal."

The elevator doors ding and open.

I roll my eyes. "Get off."

She shimmies past me and into the hallway outside my apartment. "Wait." She looks around. "There are *two* penthouses? I thought the whole point was that you're the top of the building."

"Inflation?" I snort. "Not sure what to tell you. José lives there." I point. "He's a great guy."

"Is he famous?" She arches an eyebrow. "What about hotter than you? Maybe I need to meet this José."

She's ridiculous. "His parents own a huge shipping company, and as far as I can tell, all he does is party all night and sleep all day."

"Sounds like he's just my speed." She shrugs. "I may wait outside in the hall for a bit." She leans against the wall.

I grab her wrist and yank her inside, closing the door behind us.

She pivots and snags my bag, ripping it away and opening it. "Tortilla chips, Pasta Roni, and *nail clippers*?" She scowls. "I'm not eating whatever you're planning to make with this."

"Relax." I laugh. "You'll love it, I swear."

"Nail clippers?" Her voice has turned almost shrill. "Please tell me those don't factor into your dinner plans."

"They do not," I say. "They were an impulse buy when I had money left over and a mostly-empty bag."

"You just buy things without thinking about them?" She shakes her head. "That's a problem, you know."

"What are *you* planning to make?" I tug my bag back and then reach for hers.

"Ah, ah, ah," she says. "If you're making tortilla chip pasta with ice cream for dessert, I'll be making myself dinner from what's in my bag, thanks."

I laugh. "I just want to know what you'll be making yourself."

"Fine." She sighs. "I'll show you so you can be jealous while you eat your gross toe-nail-clipping pasta."

"Eww." I pull a face. "That was way too graphic. Now I'm not even hungry."

She laughs, sets her bag on the counter, and pulls out a package of ramen—not the Maruchan kind I grew up eating. She chose something with real Asian characters on it.

"What's Momofuku?"

"I'm a bit of a ramen nut," she says. "And it's, hands down, the best instant ramen you can buy."

"Well, it's good to know you're not scrimping on this, at least." I can't help my smile. "A friend of mine told me that in Asia, inviting someone up for ramen's like inviting someone up to 'Netflix and Chill.'" I arch one eyebrow. "So I find it interesting you chose *that* to make for me."

Octavia's blush is immediate, but what gets me is how shrill her always melodious voice becomes. "No, that's not—I mean." Her eyes widen. "Listen, if you've never had ramen with kimchi before, this will change your entire life."

"Kimchi?" I pull a face. "The cabbage stuff that tastes like carbonated onions?"

Now she looks horrified. "How could you say that?" She frowns. "Though, now that you say it, that might be right. But I like it even though it tastes like carbonated onions. You have to try it with the ramen to see what I mean. And I might have bought enough for two of us, if you play your cards right."

I chuckle. "Fine, fine. I admire your passion for it. Go right ahead and make it, and—"

"You're lucky I'm kind." She squares her shoulders. "Otherwise, you might have starved, and then they'd fire you." She arches one eyebrow. "And then what would happen to this gorgeous apartment? Would José buy it and make it into a real penthouse?" She spins around, looking at all of it, frowning. "Did you decorate this?"

I shake my head. "The agency got it for me, and it came furnished."

"So this place can tell me nothing about you?" She clucks. "That's disappointing."

"Well," I say. "I brought my clothes, my pillow, and one

decor item." I spread my hands out. "Want to guess what it was?"

Her brow furrows and she walks around the family room, her eyes studying the black sofa, the grey armchairs, and the odd greige ottoman. She runs her finger along the top of the black-painted wooden TV table, the end table, and the strange modular lamp. "Not any of this." She tilts her head and keeps moving, stopping in front of a black-painted book-case. "Not this." She leans closer. "But maybe something on it."

She's getting closer, but I don't say a word. I want to see if she can figure it out.

Her eyes study the headphones resting on a stand. "These aren't functional. It could be this." She touches some weathered books slowly. "But I don't think you'd cart around old works of literature. It's too obviously preten-tious." Her hand trails downward. Her fingers are delicate and long. It makes sense—she's tall, but elegantly willowy. She ignores the fake plants, the strange metallic-painted-wooden horse statue, and then she stops at my raku bowl. She runs her fingers over the strange finish, and then she picks it up.

She frowns as she studies it, and I wonder whether she hates it. "Do you think it's that?"

Her eyes narrow.

"No?"

She spins around and stumbles, losing control of the bowl.

I dive over to catch it, and then I realize it was a trap. She was never going to drop it. Her smile widens, though, and her eyebrows rise. "Gotcha. Tell me about this little bowl, and tell me why it matches the style of that vase over there on the end table." She arches one imperious eyebrow. "Because you said *one* thing, but this is one of two, and I think they're connected to what I heard you telling Patrice the other day."

I laugh. "You're very literal."

"I don't like losing."

"Noted." I take the bowl and place it back where it goes. "I don't make many things. As mentioned, I don't cook, and I have no time for hobbies, but once I was doing a promotion in Japan. Don't ask about it, because that's a long, boring story. Or I guess you can ask, but do it when you're having trouble sleeping. Anyway, while I was there, I saw some raku pottery —that's what that is—on set, and I fell in love. I got stuck there for three days thanks to more boring stuff that you won't care about. I decided to take some pottery classes, and then when I got back home, I found someone here who makes it, too."

"What do you like about it?"

"Other than the wide range of shapes and colors, including a lot of vibrant colors in the Western raku that you don't usually see, I love the erratic nature of it. Raku literally means 'happiness in the accident.'" I shrug. "A lot of my life has felt like an accident, so I guess the whole element of luck thanks to quick-firing the raku, which encourages cracking, spoke to me."

She pokes my chest with one officious finger. "I like that about you."

And I like the feeling of her finger on my body. "Tell me that same thing again, but leave off the words 'that' and 'about.'" I bite my lip.

"That just leaves. . .I like. . .you." Her eyes fly up to meet mine, and her mouth opens just a hair, and I swear, even if I hadn't filmed a dozen scenes that taught me what was happening here, I'd still get it. A complete moron would know what was happening.

I feel drawn to Octavia like a beetle to a light at night.

Hopefully my attempts won't be met with zapping. I lean down, my head angling over hers, our lips drawing closer and closer until—

Bang bang bang.

The door? Really?

Octavia straightens.

It feels like I really *am* filming a movie, but not a good one. A very bad one. "You're supposed to wait until *after* I kiss the girl." I shake my head. "That guy just cut his tip in half."

"Guy?" Octavia's expression went from shock to bemusement, so I suppose I should be happy. All signs point to her being just as excited as I was for us to kiss again.

"I clearly wasn't planning to feed you. . ." I gesture at the melting ice cream and Pasta Roni. "That."

She giggles. "Thank goodness."

"I called in for Korean delivery."

She drops a hand on her hip. "So you *do* like kimchi."

I shrug. "Not especially, but I love tteokbokki."

"Nice." She tosses her head. "Go get it, then."

I jog across the room, realizing with a grin that there will be plenty of time for kissing to come, and yank the door open.

Only, it's not the Korean.

It's a very huffy looking man in a suit. "Mr. Adam Forrest," I say. "I wish I could tell you how nice it was to see you, but honestly? It's not."

"And me." Stu Murray—publicity and marketing—pokes his head around Adam's shoulder. "We need to talk."

Frigging fantastic.

CHAPTER 11
OCTAVIA

"Talk to me tomorrow—at work." Jake slams the door in the men's faces. I can tell by the look on his face he doesn't expect that to work. It's definitely more of a protest than anything else.

Oh, to be a movie star in demand that can get away with that kind of nonsense.

"Open the door," I say. "They wouldn't be here if it wasn't important, I'm sure."

"You would think that, but you would be wrong," Jake says. "What *they think* is important is often really *none of their business*." Jake's yelling by the end, clearly trying to make sure they can hear him.

"We have the code," Adam shouts. "We knocked as a courtesy."

"I'm going to fire my management company," Jake says. "You're not supposed to have that."

"We own that company," Adam says. "Open. The. Door."

Jake yanks it open, but he's not happy. "What's so important?"

"We don't actually need to see you," Stu says. "We're here to see *her*, and your sister said she was here."

Jake tries to close the door again, but they're already walking through. "You can't just barge in at night and demand to see her. She's part of a band you signed, but they don't have social media clauses." He folds his arms. "This is inappropriate."

"Posting our internal video feeds was inappropriate," Stu says, "and thanks to the blueprint on the new version of the video she posted today, we found her." He tosses his head at me. "I'm assuming that now that we have evidence of her guilt, she won't try to deny it any more."

"Deny it?" I shrug. "I haven't seen this new video, and I've had nothing to do with posting any videos at all."

Jake's pulled it up, and he spins his phone around.

I take a step closer so I can see. It's another video taken from the side—looks like a security camera, maybe. And, of course, it's Patrice. "Someone really hates her," I mutter.

"Someone?" Adam rolls his eyes.

Before I can defend myself, Patrice starts talking. Her voice is low, but it's been isolated. "—course it's fake, for ratings, right? I just wish the studio wasn't making me the bad guy every time."

"So he's not really dating Octavia? It's all a publicity stunt by the studio?" I can't see who she's talking to, but I can hear the other woman's voice. I don't recognize her, but I bet someone will. Her voice is ridiculously nasal.

"Of course it is. You think he'd really date that crispy critter?" Patrice snorts in a very un-ladylike way. "He's vainer than I am—which is why we're perfect for each other. Once all this nonsense is past, I'm sure we'll get back together."

"*Back* together?" Jake's fingers are twitching on the edges of his phone. "I swear, she's such a liar. I'm going to kill her."

"You can imagine that this hasn't been great for our ratings." Adam looks quite unhappy. "Who could possibly believe that the studio *wants* these videos out?" He shakes his head. "We've filmed twenty percent of the scenes, and this film's already dead in the water."

"It's only Patrice they hate, though." Jake's scrolling. "And as you can see, it's not fake between me and Octavia."

"I think you meant Crispy Critter," I say, unable to resist.

Jake slams his phone down on the counter. "I won't work with her. I know we've filmed twenty percent of the scenes, but I just can't pretend with her anymore. Not after that."

Adam wheels around and points at me. "*You* did that. Are you trying to get her part? Is that what this is about?"

"You can have it," Stu says. "If you'll sign a cease and desist and stop posting internal videos as weapons to force our hand, we'll give you the role."

"I would rather *die* than take that role, or *any* role in a movie." I blink. "I'm telling you, this wasn't me. I had nothing to do with any of it. There's no way any evidence points to me. I don't know what you think you have, but maybe they spoofed something?" I don't even know what that means, but I've heard it used about computers before.

"Spoofed?" Stu actually looks amused.

"Maybe someone's setting you up." Jake's brow furrows.

Stu says, "But we found the leak—AJ."

"You found what?" I sit on one of Jake's stools. "What's an AJ?"

"It's a person, a tech guy," Adam says. "Are you insisting you don't know him? Because I'm sure, once we bring you in, he'll confirm that it's *you* he was sexting with on the company server—you even joked he *had* to send you the files or you wouldn't. . ." He clears his throat. "You know, you said that you would refuse his advances later."

"He *what*?" I splutter. "You must be kidding right now. You think *I'm* using my feminine wiles to lure tech guys into doing my bidding?" I point at Jake's phone. "Did you hear what she said? That's what *most* people think when they look at me. I'm not a vixen, luring men into temptation with my body."

"We have all the messages," Adam says. "It's only a matter of time before we can tie it all together."

"Great," I say. "Once you've done that and you have the right person, let me know."

"I'm assuming you're willing to share your phone, then, if you're sure it has no trace of what you're saying," Stu says.

I whip it out of my purse and walk toward him.

Jake intercepts me. "Of course she's not handing over her phone when she did nothing wrong. It's *your* job to prove she knows someone named AJ—which she clearly doesn't. You don't get to snoop through her private stuff, and she's not guilty until proven innocent. This isn't Russia." Jake snorts. "Or worse, TikTok."

"Funny you should mention that. Previously those videos were only posted on YouTube and Instagram, but now the user, gorgeousmonstrosity3, has created an account on TikTok and the videos are trending there as well." Stu holds out his hand. "Give us the phone, because we're sure that—"

"Gorgeous monstrosity *three*?" I ask. "That's a weird name to choose. The song was written by Bea, and sung by *me*, so I could see taking the name gorgeous monstrosity, or even that I might claim *two*, but why would I pick three unless. . ." I scratch my chin. "Unless I was the third person to join the group."

"Or the other two were already taken," Stu says. "The video's been up before of you singing it. You competed in that contest."

"You looked like you had a thought," Adam says. "Who did you think could be the third person?"

I actually really hope it's not her, because I like Morgan a lot. I have no reason to think it *was* her, but she was there the first day, and. . . "Have you looked into Morgan Hadley at all?" I wince. "I know it didn't really affect her either way. She was still going to be on the album either way, but. . . She's a great guitarist, and she's a smart lady, and I can't imagine she'd do that, but she did make some changes to the guitar line, so she might feel some ownership of the song."

"You think she might be 'gorgeous monstrosity three,' since she joined you two later on." Adam sighs. "We should have thought of that."

"Could you call her for us?" Stu asks. "Because as things stand, we're running numbers to decide whether to shut this project down or try and find a replacement for Patrice. If we still don't know where the leak's coming from, we may be safer to just pull the plug."

Bea would be devastated if that happened. It's a huge break for her and for me, honestly. "What would happen to Morgan if it *is* her?"

Stu sighs. "The accounts have generated a lot of. . .interest. We can't make her shut them down, but we'd make her an offer, like we have with you, to try and encourage her. . ." He clears his throat. "Er, we'd like to have some *oversight* in the future."

"But will she be fired?" I arch one eyebrow. "Because she was probably just trying to defend me, if it was her. You heard the things Patrice was saying. I understand why she wanted to do it."

"No, we won't fire her," Stu says, "but she needs to know that some people in Hollywood are hard to work with, and that's just how it works."

"So we should let people like that get paid tons of money in spite of being horrible human beings?" Jake asks.

"I try not to judge others," Adam says.

"As long as they're padding your pocketbook," Jake mutters.

"Call her." Stu points at my phone. "Call her, and ask her if she's dating someone named AJ, and ask her if she posted the videos. No matter what she says, you'll be off the hook for now."

"She's already off the hook." Jake frowns. "Innocent until proven—"

"This isn't a court of law," Adam says. "Call her."

I think about it for a moment, but in the end, we do need to know who's been posting all these videos. I'd hate for the movie to be cancelled. I dial Morgan.

"Hey Octavia," she says. "Is it a bad sign you're calling me so early on date night? Did Jake get called in for some reason? Acting emergency?"

"Sort of," I say. "Actually, some work people came by and they were asking weird stuff."

"Oh?" Morgan snorts. "Like what?"

Stu's gesturing for me to put her on speakerphone.

I glare. "They wanted to know whether I was dating someone named AJ, and whether I had posted the videos about Patrice." I cringe, and then I hit the speakerphone button. "I thought maybe you might have some insight."

"Insight?" She swears under her breath. "So you know it's me. That's what you're saying?"

"Why would you do it?" I ask.

"My brother—you never met him, but he's got a cleft palate, and my family couldn't afford fancy surgery for him. No plastic surgeon for us, so his scar's noticeable. In fact, it's bad enough that no one would sign him as a singer, even though he sounds great.”

“Oh.” I did *not* expect her to say that.

“I’ve been watching him deal with small-minded bullies like Patrice my whole life.” The way she says her name, it sounds like she’s swearing. “I guess when I told my boyfriend how upset I was, and he mentioned that he’d seen it too, I freaked out.”

“Your boyfriend, AJ?”

She grunts. “Who’s there asking?”

I look up at Stu, and he nods.

“Listen, you’re going to be hearing from some people. I’m not quite sure who.” I grimace, not that she can see me.

“I figured,” she says. “I’m sorry if I put you in hot water, O, I really am.”

“It’s fine,” I say. “I appreciate what you were trying to do.”

“I knew you would,” she says. “But I know it got you some unwanted attention, and I’m sorry for that, too.”

I take her off speaker and drop my voice to a whisper. “They swore they wouldn’t fire you. If you threaten to post more stuff on your site, you can use it as leverage.” Then I hang up.

“Really?” Adam tilts his head. “Leverage?”

Turns out they have pretty decent hearing. “She’s my friend.”

“And you have your culprit,” Jake says. “Which means you can—”

The knock on the door seems to indicate the Korean’s finally here. I cross to answer. “Hello?”

“Order for Jacob Bishop?”

I quirk one eyebrow.

“Easier name to use,” Jake says with a grin.

"No way." The delivery man whips out his phone. "You're Jake Priest."

"No photos," Adam says. "Or we'll sue."

The boy hands me the bags—how much food did Jake order?—and jets, muttering under his breath. Thankfully *my* hearing isn't cat-like, so I don't hear whatever unkind thing he says.

Jake has them packed out of the apartment within minutes. "We'll be in touch tomorrow about our options to replace Patrice," Adam's saying.

Although he's nodding, Jake doesn't stop moving them toward the exit, and once they're through, he shuts the door.

"You aren't worried about offending them?"

"Oh, I was," he says. "Believe me, at first, I was. But the thing is, they push and push and push and eventually, if you let them have their way, there'll be no Jake left. All that will remain is a shell if you let them carve you out. You learn to push back."

"Plus, the food's getting cold." I point at the bags on his kitchen table.

"We don't want that. Cold tteokbokki's gross," he says. "Trust me."

He knows how to order Korean. Everything's amazing. The tteokbokki's a little spicy and a little chewy, but it's an amazing flavor, kind of like marinara and teriyaki had a baby they dressed in chili peppers. "What do they call these kind of noodles?"

"Rice cakes," Jake says. "Funny, right? Better than the crunchy cardboard we called rice cakes back when I was a kid."

"They still sell that now," I say.

He cringes.

"Right? You know, I've seen this in K-dramas," I say,

"which is where I got the idea for the kimchi with ramen, but I've never had it myself."

"Stick with me," he says. "I'll show you lots of things you've never seen before." He leans toward me then, and I almost forget to breathe. His hand reaches for my face, and his big, strong thumb wipes something off the side of my mouth.

I force myself to blink so he doesn't think I'm a cyborg masquerading as a human, and then I lick my lips.

"Well, I tried to be respectful and keep my distance," he mutters. "But if you're licking your lips, that's too much for me." He leans farther, farther, and then he grabs the back of my head and pulls me the last few inches. When our lips connect, it's like I've just flown straight down on a roller-coaster. My body seems to step away from my brain for a brief moment and then everything slams back online.

My heart hammers.

My lips swell.

My hands tighten on the edge of the table, and I groan.

His free hand cups my cheek, and he deepens the kiss, and I really lose track of where I am and who I am and. . .then I realize he's touching my burn.

That thought's more startling than a bucket of cold water. When I pull back, Jake looks a little confused. "I should go," I say. "I had a great time, and I'd love to do it again soon." I grab my purse.

Jake's nodding as he stands. "Right. We should—putting on the brakes is good. I'll take you home."

I shake my head. "I'll just call an uber. Call me tomorrow?" Before he can argue, I duck out, already clicking yes to the uber. I wave my phone at him. "It's two minutes away." The doors ding, and I hop on the elevator before he can object.

The whole way down, I stroke the side of my face to see exactly what it would have felt like to him.

Alien.

Strange.

Like cooled wax.

I know just how foreign it feels, and that's what worries me.

Because at some point, he's going to realize that he doesn't want someone who's damaged, and the idea of the inevitable end of all this is starting to really hurt.

CHAPTER 12
JAKE

Dear Jake:

I'm beginning to worry that you've forgotten who I am. I'm hearing from you less and less, and you keep telling me to "forget" about the Fansees and move on. You've punished them, you've told me, over and over.

Only, it really sounds like you're forgetting who you are.

Everyone on earth's either a mark or they're a grifter. You don't get to opt out, because there's nothing in between. I left you to be fostered by the Fansees because they proved themselves to be some-what canny for do-gooders.

It never occurred to me you might drink the lemonade.

Snap out of it, boy. Right this moment. Remember who you are. Remember that there's only one true north in this world, and it's not your stupid, sappy, holier-than-thou foster family.

I'm your true north.

I'm the only person who really knows you.

And I'm the only person you can trust to have your back when things get bad. Don't ever forget that. I may be locked away, but I still have your back, even from here. If you go check behind the flowering bush that's a little overgrown right behind the signage for their stupid hotel, you'll find a little reminder of that.

-Dad

When I was fifteen years old, I stopped writing my dad letters. I should've tapered them off, maybe, or written perfunctory ones, telling him I was busy.

I was a teenager.

It would've been believable.

But the truth was, I was embarrassed that he was my dad.

He was in prison.

He had taught me to make my way as a liar and a thief. For the first time in my life, I didn't want to be a cowbird. I didn't want to bump anyone out of their nest and take their food. I wanted to be the kind of bird the other birds could rely on.

I wanted to be a part of the nest, with parent birds who loved me.

So I stopped writing my real dad.

He saw right through my reasons immediately, of course, and he delivered to my door the very thing I imagine he plans to use to destroy the Fansee family at his leisure. When he finally does get out, whenever that day comes, I'm sure I'll see exactly how he uses the information he managed to dig up on my seemingly perfect foster parents while he was in prison.

But whenever I have a weak moment, whenever I think that maybe, just maybe, good people exist. When I think that maybe the world isn't all swindlers and suckers, I look at the photos Dad left in that manila envelope.

I've told myself all kinds of things about them.

Maybe they were doctored.

Maybe they aren't real at all.

Maybe it was a one-time mistake and Dave didn't tell Seren about it because he didn't want to hurt her.

I've hoped all those things might be true.

But at the end of the day, I know people. I know people in a way most people never do. I've peeked underneath the curtain of humanity and seen that we're all pretty lousy underneath our shiny and bright veneers. We all have our most base desires, and we all have our essential flaws, and no matter how hard we try, we all let down the people we love at some point. Usually we let them down regularly. Right now, I really want to be a good person—I want to be what I thought the Fansees were.

I feel like Octavia deserves someone shiny and bright and good.

She's the shiniest, brightest, most beautiful woman I've ever met.

But I'm not the right person for her, even if I can fool her for a little while. After all, my dad's in prison for theft and my foster father's the kind of person who gets caught in bed with a woman who's most decidedly not his wife Seren.

In the photos, Dave's smiling like it's Christmas morning, and every time I see them, I want to punch him until his face caves in.

Which is why I'm flipping through the screenshots I took

of the photos on my phone. I'm trying to prepare for the worst. In the next few days, something's going to happen. I can feel it. Either Octavia's going to realize that I suck and dump me, or I'm going to find out something about her that breaks my heart. It's important that I prepare myself.

No matter how great someone seems, they're either being lied to, like Seren, or they're doing the lying, like Dave. When you know that in advance, it doesn't hurt as hard when the disappointment slaps you in the face.

At first, Dad's pictures hurt me.

It felt like he was attacking me and the family I'd come to see as my own. But with a little time, I realized that he was actually trying to help me. The Fansees weren't the paragons I thought. They were just like the rest of us, making mistakes, hurting people, and covering up their lies. I was better off not idolizing anyone and trusting my dad, because then I'd be able to take whatever I could so no one else took anything from me.

Even from prison, Dad was trying to protect me.

That's why, when Octavia said the Fansees' way was the better way. . .I wished I could believe it. I want to believe in a world like the one she sees. Even with all the people saying ugly things about one of the most beautiful souls I've seen, she believes in that world.

But I know it doesn't exist.

I have Dad to thank for that, and Dave too, I guess.

When I first found out, I hated him, but I came to understand that he's just a normal guy. Every normal guy in the world falls short. They all let their families down. They all ruin things. The key's not appreciating only perfect people. It's assuming that everyone's imperfect and seeing their good things so the bad won't wreck you when you uncover it.

Sometimes I momentarily forget that everyone's flawed.

I always remind myself the same way. After looking at the bad photos of Dave, I swipe through more recent ones, marveling at the disconnect between the man in these bright and cheery photos with his arm around Seren and the cheating philanderer I know him to be.

I only have time to work on these reminders because the scene that was supposed to be filmed this morning was canceled. Since coming to terms with Morgan, they're now working furiously to find a replacement for Precious Patty that America won't hate.

I wouldn't like to be Patty's agent right now.

But I kind of love that Morgan lady. What kind of person is able to, with the posting of just a few videos, effect the total and complete annihilation of someone else's career? I mean, Morgan burned it to the ground as effectively as if she'd lit a funeral pyre, and no one I've met deserved it more.

A lot of people may be awful about Octavia's face, but none of them are supposed to be America's little darling. America's darling shouldn't be the jealous, rude, petty person Patty has proven herself to be.

Good riddance.

I do sort of wish that Octavia had jumped at the chance to be my costar, but she clearly hated the idea. I'd never try to push her into something she didn't want. Or at least, not unless it was really good for her in some way she didn't understand.

When my phone bings, I swipe and see the text's from Jane.

Get here in an hour. We have women for you to screen test.

I hate screen tests. It's like doing a bunch of speed dates, but worse because everyone I'm force-dating's a megalomaniac. I wish I could refuse any involvement and just make them pick someone—it's not like there's going to be a good choice—but it's in my contract. Begrudgingly, I shower, brush my teeth, and then I finally go in.

So what if some of the people reading for the part have to wait?

Hopefully they'll find someone who's a little better than Patrice. I'm about to walk into the conference room when I get another text. It's from Octavia.

> Good luck today. I hear they're re-casting. I hope it goes well.

> You sure you don't want to read for the role? I'd push for them to pick you.

> Ha.

> I'm serious. You'd be amazing.

> They'd have to rewrite the entire thing to address my face. Pass.

> Think of the good that could come of it—how many people you could reach.

> No after-school specials for me, thanks.

> Fine, but for the record, I vote Octavia.

> Checked the ballots. You were the only one.

I'm smiling when I walk into the room, and I hope on the other side of the phone, she is too. As predicted, the next few hours are pretty brutal. I read with a half dozen women I've met before, and two new faces.

They're all terrible.

Some of them are decent actors, and that's what matters.

It is, at the end of the day, a job. That's why they pay us. I grit my teeth, and I tell each of them in turn how lovely it would be to work with them. I nod in agreement when they say how horrible it was to discover what a bad person Patrice Jouveau was, as if it was a surprise to any of us.

But then, the last screen test walks in.

It's May Markson.

She's literally the girl-next-door in my favorite sitcom. I'm honestly bummed to see her here. I like to at least pretend, with the few shows I watch, that the person in them is decent. Kind. Funny. Smart.

I know it's unlikely, but I can hope.

And all my hopes are about to be dashed.

"Hey," she says. "I'm May, and you can call me May." She shrugs, and with a half-grin says, "Plus, it's my actual name, and May's better than April, right?"

It's a little corny, but there's not enough of innocent humor in Hollywood. After we read our lines, the producer, director, and their finance team disappear to talk, leaving me with May.

"I really enjoy *Just Three Neighbors*," I say. "It's refreshingly honest and still upbeat."

"Oh, thanks." She beams. "I hardly have to say that I would be honored to work with you. Stepping up to movies— I've wanted to do that for a while."

Is it possible I've just met the only non-arrogant actress in LA? "Well, they don't really let me vote, but I'd vote for you for sure."

"Honestly, I'd vote for Octavia Rothschild," she says. "After seeing those videos, it seems like a movie role is the least of what she should get after dealing with Patrice." Her lip curls. "Who knew she was such a jerk?"

"Everyone," I say. "But as it happens, I agree with you."

"So you're really dating her, then?" May's eyes widen. "She's really pretty, and her voice." She whistles. "I've been listening to the soundtrack raw cuts on repeat since they called me about the role. I can't get enough of it."

"Those raw cuts aren't—"

"Supposed to be on the internet?" She shrugs. "I know, but they leave them to build hype, and I think it's working. They weren't even hard to find. I think YouTube's pushing them, to be honest."

Probably. People always do whatever they can if it's in their interest. Dad got that right. "Well, it's nice to hear that you appreciate her, and yes, we're dating."

May closes her eyes and exhales. "You didn't hear this from me, but my boyfriend will be all kinds of relieved."

"You have a boyfriend?" I lean closer. "I haven't seen a whiff of that on social."

"Posting about your normal-guy boyfriend is really more of an 'established actress' kind of move," she says. "My agent says I can't let anyone know I'm serious with someone until I've gotten a few movie deals. So far... none." She shrugs. "I think all the secrecy makes Stuart nervous, so he'll be so happy to hear you're dating Octavia."

I imagine Octavia will like that May's not pursuing me, either. A moment later, I stand up. "Restroom." I point.

That was a lie. I sneak around the back and barge in on the meeting. "It's May, hands down," I say. "You have to pick her. She's as great as Patrice was lousy."

"Oh, good," Stu says. "Someone smart." He points at me. "Listen to him."

"But she brings no star power," Adam says. "And when you're replacing someone high profile, you don't bring in a nobody—"

"Unless you're doing it to clear out the stench that high

profile person left. Then you *do* bring in a breath of fresh air," I say. "That's what May is. What little notoriety she has, and it's growing, is all good. And out there, did you actually listen to her? She's as nice as she is wholesome. She's perfect. She fits the description of the role to a tee."

"She's a blond," Adam says.

"Then dye her hair," I say. "And stop being an idiot."

"I agree with him," Stu says. "Except not the idiot part, of course."

Jane covers her mouth, but it's clear she's laughing. "I vote for May, too."

"So do all of you want her?" Adam looks around.

Everyone's nodding.

"Oh, good." He beams. "Then it's unanimous. I was just playing devil's advocate to see how much you'd fight me."

We've just shared the news with May, who's giddy enough to be jumping up and down, when Bradley calls. "Two calls from my agent in two days?" I ask. "What is it now?"

"I thought you deserved a warning," he says. "I just got a call from someone with the state of New York, and they said—"

In that moment, I *know* what the call was about without Bradley saying the words. I hang up the phone and stand up to prepare. Like most of the biggest moments in my life, I'm not sure whether to shout or cry.

When the door to our tiny meeting room opens, my hunch is confirmed.

"Excuse me," Adam says, "but this is a closed set. You can't just barge in here—"

My father's smile spreads slowly. "But I'm Jake Priest's new manager." He bobs his head at Adam. "I assume you're Adam Forrest."

"His manager?" Adam frowns. "Last I heard, he didn't want a manager assigned."

"That's because Jake was holding the position for me," Dad says. "I'm his father." He holds out his hand. "And it's so nice to finally meet you."

CHAPTER 13

OCTAVIA

I've always wondered whether my mother liked acting so much because she never felt happy with who she was. Not that the same principle applies to everyone. Perhaps I hated it because it made my mom angry when I took attention from her. Or maybe I just wanted to be happy with who I was—I didn't ever want to pretend I was someone else entirely.

That's why Morgan's proclamation isn't very exciting to me.

"I got them to agree to exactly what I wanted." It's eight-thirty in the morning, and she's shrieking, waving a paper in my face.

"You—what?" I glance at Bea, hoping she has some idea what's going on.

"They're eliminating *Patrice*, for one." Morgan makes a retching sound. "But for another, they've officially offered you her position. I told them you have past acting experience, and they agreed that the video of Jake kissing you—"

"Absolutely not," I say. "I won't take it."

"Why not?" She steps closer. "Look at the contract.

They're keeping your pay the same as it was for Patrice, and—"

I shove both the paper and Morgan back a full body length. "I appreciate you caring enough to do this for me, but it's still a hearty 'no thank you' from me. I want nothing to do with any of this."

"They tried to offer her that part when they first accused her," Bea says. "She turned them down then, too."

Morgan's shoulders slump. "But if you don't want it, then—"

"They'll find someone else," Bea says. "You can't throw a rock in this town without hitting a wannabe actress."

"None of them would be as good as Octavia," Morgan mutters.

"What else are you going to ask for then?" Q asks. "If you had to negotiate for this and she doesn't want it, then what?"

"I'm not sure." Morgan frowns. "But something. They want to control my content, which is ridiculous. I post the truth."

"A truth that was stolen from their security feeds through use of an undeclared relationship," I say. "Aren't you worried they'll fire your boyfriend?"

She snorts. "My boyfriend? As if. Have you met AJ? He's a total dork."

"But you said—"

"I could tell you were calling with an agenda," she says. "Geez."

I don't want to think about what that means. It might lower my opinion of Morgan, and right now I like thinking she's a warrior. "Let's get to work," I say. "We have songs to finish."

Good songs, thanks to Bea.

"This movie soundtrack's going to be amazing," Everett says when we finish.

All of us exchange a glance.

He frowns. "I do talk, when I have something to say."

"I guess you just haven't had anything to say for weeks," Q says.

"Never had much space to talk in this room." Everett shrugs. "Then it kind of became my thing, so I leaned in."

I think about that while they get machinery and instruments put away. How often do our perceptions of other people shape people's future action? How often do our preconceptions become reality because we made assumptions and they get boxed in?

We all go to lunch to celebrate, and then we help Morgan read through the agreement the studio wants her to sign.

"It's basically just a right of refusal for your posts," I say. "And for that, they're doubling your royalty share for the songs." I shrug. "I think it's fair."

"I'd be making the same thing as you and Bea. Doesn't that upset you? I'm just hired talent." Morgan's frowning.

"It's not coming out of our cut, though," I say. "And you kind of saved our involvement in the project. Patrice was demanding that she take over the vocals. We'd have been out, except for behind the scenes."

"Ooh." Morgan beams. "Maybe I should insist that all of us get to make a cameo on one of the music videos."

"All of them," Q says.

"Count me out." Everett grimaces. "I don't do video."

"Video killed the radio star," I sing. "But you have a nice face, Everett."

He smiles, his white teeth bright against his dark brown skin. "That's the problem. I have too many ladies after me as it is."

We're all laughing when Bea gets a call. "Hey, Mom," she says. "We just finished recording."

There's a pause.

Everyone quiets down, like we're all listening. I can't tell whether we're being quiet in a rude way, to try and eavesdrop, or a polite one, to keep from distracting her.

"Yeah, I guess we'll probably be coming home pretty soon. We may be in a music video, though." She winks at me. "And we have some promotional footage to record and some photos for the album to take, but probably in a few more days or a week."

Another pause.

"I'm not sure about Jake—I think they have to start over on all the filming, which is a huge drag."

When she pauses again, I poke Morgan. "What did they say about the music video?" She was texting Eddy right as Seren called.

Morgan shakes her head, presses her finger over her lips, and points at Bea. So it's clearly snooping. I'm just not sure why they care what Seren thinks about Bea or Jake.

"But Mom, I think Octavia may *want* to stick around, to see more of Jake." Her whispering's pointless. We can still hear her.

Morgan actually leans closer—she's that obvious.

"No, I mean, I know birthdays are a big deal, but. . ." She sighs. "Fine. I'll talk to Jake and see if he can come back for a weekend. I'm sure they have some breaks in the filming schedule. They just aren't very long ones." After a very short pause, she almost shouts, "No, don't book tickets to come here. I'm sure he won't want you walking all over the set."

I'm laughing when she finally hangs up. "Whose birthday is it?"

"Jake refused to tell us his birthday at first—he had so

many falsified papers, no one was quite sure when it really was—so we celebrated the day he joined our family every year. That date is this weekend—Saturday. Dave and Seren take birthdays seriously."

"But more importantly, it seems like the two of you *are* still dating." Morgan rounds on me so fast it makes my head spin.

"I thought we were spying on Bea's conversation," I say.

Q rolls his eyes. "Only because of the off-chance she might let something spill about the two of you." He crosses his arms. "You've told us *nothing* about your date."

After I finally give them enough information that they're satisfied, Bea and I go shopping for a new outfit for the album cover. I've never cared much about my clothes, opting for classy and boring business casual stuff mostly, but now that I'm supposed to be on an album cover. . .

"What look are we going for?" Bea asks.

"I'd have said opera for my first album," I say. "But your stuff is more pop meets soul."

She laughs. "Which means Doc Martens, argyle socks, and mini skirts?"

I groan. "I hope not. That was bad enough in the nineties."

"I hear it's come back."

I hope she's kidding.

We look all afternoon, checking out store after store, but don't find anything that feels quite right. Or at least, nothing that costs less than five grand and feels quite right.

"Man, everything here's so expensive," I say.

"Yeah, and not like, 'Whole Foods' expensive. It's like 'sell a kidney' expensive," Bea says.

I chuckle. "I doubt my kidneys are worth as much as some of those purses."

"Right?" She holds one hand out. "Here, sir, how much for a slightly used and possibly not very pretty kidney? Half of the price of that tiny pink coin purse?" She ponders for a moment and then nods her head. "Deal."

"Who buys this crap?" I ask.

"People with more money than sense."

"I wish that was me," I say. "But I think you lose a little bit of your soul when you have that kind of money. Like, how do you justify buying a ten thousand dollar handbag when people, hardworking people, can't pay their rent?"

"Or when some kids don't have dinner?" Bea asks. "Did I tell you that Easton's putting me in charge of charitable giving, or he said he will, once his new startup goes public?"

"Wait, he has a new startup already?" I blink. "I thought he *just* got out of the other thing?"

"It's early stages," Bea says. "But he knows what he's doing now, so he thinks he'll get there faster." Bea stops walking. "Ooh, what do you want to eat for dinner? I'm thinking sushi."

For some reason, that bums me out, and I can't help glancing at my phone. Not that I'm expecting anything. There've been no messages all day. Not even my mother's calling.

"What's up?" Bea peers closer to my face.

"Nothing." I slide my phone into my pocket.

"My stupid brother hasn't texted you all day, has he?"

I shrug. "He's busy. I'm sure they're trying to find a replacement for the great disappointment."

She snorts. "I sure hope so, but how long does a text take?" She grabs my hand. "It's not the nineteen fifties. *You* should message *him*."

Duh.

I whip out my phone.

> Find anyone to replace P yet?

What does P stand for?

Poopy?

Pathetic?

Pimple Popper?

I chuckle.

"Oh, good. He's doing something right at least," Bea mutters. "I told him if he makes you cry, I'm going to castrate him."

That makes me stumble. "You're sure violent—it feels strange from someone so small."

"You have to be very clear with Jake. Vague threats do nothing, and I always go a level or two higher than I really mean, to make sure he knows I'm serious."

"You go nuclear," I say.

Bea kicks a rock, and it skitters a dozen sidewalk squares down. "Look, there's a lot of angry shoved into this tiny package. You can thank my parents for that one." Her head whips up. "Not Dave and Seren. My bio parents."

"I figured," I say.

Jake texts again, even though I hadn't replied yet.

Putrefic? Presumptuous?

> Patrice is already the worst name that starts with P. Speaking of, did you find a new actress to take over for her yet? Or are you still looking?

Morgan said you refused the offer they made to you. I thought you might reconsider. You're sure?

Yeah, that's not for me.

I get it. We did just find someone, though. May Markson. Have you seen Just Three Neighbors? It's a great show. I really like her in it. I think you will, too.

Bea and I are thinking of grabbing dinner. You busy?

I'm glad you have Bea—I'm busy. Something just came up. I'll text you later with my filming schedule tomorrow once they confirm May can start right away.

"Whoa." Bea's reading over my shoulder. "So they hired the cutest actress I've ever seen, someone he likes too, and *now* he's busy?"

I hate that she's seeing the same thing I am.

"He didn't say he's busy with her," I say. "Maybe it's something else that's come up, and—"

"Jake's really simple," Bea says. "Think of him like a river. It flows downward. If he said they chose her and then he said he's busy, it's with her." She looks ready to rip something—or someone—in half. "I swear, I should have warned you off from the start. I'm going to have to kill him, and. . ." She turns toward me and meets my eyes. "I'm going to miss that jerk after he's dead."

She's such a crazy person. "You aren't killing Jake, even if he moves on. I always knew we were unlikely to be a long-lasting love connection."

Bea grabs my hands. "But you were excited. I could tell. You liked him, and you're a hundred times better than he deserves, and just. . .ahhh!" Bea's shouting on the sidewalk, and people are starting to stare.

"Let's order some delivery and change into pajamas and watch another romantic comedy."

"Yes!" Bea's nodding with some real energy. "Any movie you want."

"Great," I say. "Let's do *How to Lose a Guy in Ten Days.*"

"I love Kate Hudson," Bea says. "Let's do it."

"You love Kate Hudson?" I snort. "I like Matthew McConaughey."

"I mean, yeah, but saying that now that I'm engaged sounds weird."

"You don't have to say, 'I like staring at his pecs,'" I say. "You can just think he's funny, cute, and a little strange."

"He actually is a pretty odd guy." Bea's eyes widen. "Or so Jake says."

"But he's a movie star. Aren't they all a little strange?"

Bea laughs. "I guess so."

On the way home, she tells me stories about Jake as a kid, most of them involving some strange behaviors for a kid his age. Or, anyone, really.

"He ironed his underwear?" I can barely believe that.

"I know he seems like he'd be messy," Bea says. "And he does take up way too much space, but he's actually really fastidious with clothing and stuff. He only did that for a year, but he likes things to be crisp and clean."

"Better than him being a disgusting slob, I guess," I say.

"Like you?" She's grinning, though, so I know she's kidding.

By the time we get back to the hotel, and our takeout arrives, and we've got the movie queued up, I can't keep myself. My finger's hovering over the keyboard of the laptop, but instead of hitting play, I ask, "Do you think Jake likes May? He said her show was great."

"Oh." She drops her chopsticks and meets my gaze. "Well,

he watches it sometimes," Bea says. "He does like it, and her too, I think. But I don't think he likes her like *that*."

It's easy for Bea to say that.

Her boyfriend isn't out right now with his new costar, who happens to be cute, kind, and accessible, while still having flawless skin, shiny white teeth, and a proportioned figure that would make Angelina Jolie jealous.

I have a really hard time focusing on the movie, even though I really like it. I just keep thinking that as cute as Kate Hudson is, May Markson's even cuter. And as pouty and flirty as Kate is, May's even more enticing.

Ugh.

I always felt like Dad had some culpability in my parents' break up. Yes, Mom shouldn't have gotten carried away with her role in the play or whatever, but Dad blew it out of proportion, too. He could have done more to make her feel seen and special. He could have tried harder to make her happy.

I resolve not to do what my dad did. I won't assume the worst about Jake. I mean, we've been on *one* date so it's not like he owes me anything, but I'll assume he likes me until I see that's wrong. I won't ruin this with my own insecurity.

That night, it gets harder and harder to stick to my guns as I toss and turn. I dream, when I finally do sleep, of Jake kissing May, over and over.

Ugh.

What a horrible night.

The sound of Bea's phone alarm going off over and over wakes me up the next day. I rub my eyes and force myself upright, then I notice the time. It's five-eleven in the morning.

"Bea," I croak. "Bea, your phone."

She mumbles something.

I realize it's a phone call, not an alarm, just as it goes to voicemail. Oh well. I flop back down on the bed. But when it starts ringing again, I drag myself over and pick it up. It says "Mom," on the phone. I'm assuming it's Seren, but I'm not totally sure as I swipe to answer.

"Hello?"

"Bea?" It's definitely Seren. "Bea, is that you?"

"It's Octavia," I say. "Sorry, it's really early here."

"No, I know, and I'm so sorry to be calling this early, but it's really urgent. Can you put Bea on the phone?"

My whole body freezes up. A lot of horrible possibilities run through me, like Easton dying or Dave having a heart attack. When I shake Bea awake and hand her the phone, I do it with the knowledge that I have the phone volume turned up to max.

I'm dying to hear what's going on, and I'm praying it's not as bad as I've already imagined.

"Bea?"

"Mhhmph." Bea's rubbing her eyes. "Wha?"

"Wake up, Bea," Seren says. "You're my boots on the ground."

She straightens. "What's going on?"

"Jake's dad got out of prison."

Bea's eyes fly open. She swears loudly under her breath. "No way."

"They sent us a letter—or rather, the letter for Jake came here to our place. But I guess it got put in the stack of bills, and you know I only pay those twice a month, but when the water line—"

"Mom, focus."

"We didn't see it until this morning, so here we are."

"When did he get out?" Bea asks, yawning. "Today?"

"Three days ago," Seren says. "Have you seen him yet?"

"I'm sure he's on parole," Bea says. "He won't be allowed to travel, right? Won't he be stuck in New York?"

"Yes," Seren says. "Because he strikes me as someone who follows all the rules." I barely know her and I can hear her eye-roll through the tinny speaker of Bea's phone.

"Okay, so he'll show up here, and then. . .what do I do? What do we expect?"

"His dad's not a good person," Seren says. "First and foremost, he'll be demanding money from Jake, I'm sure. And then beyond that. . .I was hoping you could tell *me* what happens. We'll have to kind of make decisions as things happen."

They talk about options for a few more minutes, but eventually, they hang up. I expect Bea to collapse back into a gently snoring heap, but instead, she rounds on me. "What did he say last night? Did he say he was with May?"

I shake my head. "He said. . ." I whip out my phone so I can read the text. "He said, 'I'm busy. Something just came up. I'll text you later with my filming schedule, once they confirm May can start right away.'"

Bea sighs. "So maybe he went out with her, and maybe his dad showed up. He didn't give us any clues at all. I can see why you were a mess."

My shoulders square. "Hey, I wasn't a mess."

Bea rolls her eyes. "Well, it's too early to do anything but plan. Today, we have the videos they want us to film for social, and then tomorrow we have the endorsement meetings."

"Okay," I say. "But what does that—"

Bea holds up one hand, like she's a mob boss, or an officious mean girl. It makes me smile. When I peer over her shoulder, she's typing out a text to Jake.

> Seren just told me your dad's out of prison? Have you seen him? Heard from him? Text me back when you get this, or I'll come over to your apartment and refuse to leave.

Of course there's no response. It's barely five-thirty in the morning.

"Hey, this is good." Bea looks up at me. "He told me two days ago that he's filming this morning starting at eight a.m. Let's get ready, and we can stop by on our way to our filming or whatever."

I have no idea what we might possibly do if his dad *is* here, but I suppose Bea's just desperate to know. She seems utterly convinced that his dad will hunt him down now that he's out, but I'm not so sure. On the way to the set, I ask, "Is it possible his dad might ignore him? I got the impression they haven't been talking much."

Bea's brow furrows. "That would be nice, but I doubt very much if he'd really be able to leave Jake alone."

"He was an embezzler, right? That's what he did?"

Bea's frown deepens. "What did Jake tell you?"

"Not much," I admit. "But he said that when his dad was supposed to get out, he got caught stealing money and got stuck in there even longer."

She sighs. "That's true." She glances at our driver and drops her voice. "But the reason he went in the first time is that he tried to pull a con on the principal at our school the same time Jake was pulling one on Mom and Dad, and the principal was talking to Mom about something, and Mom put two and two together, and they managed to convict Jake's dad—with my mom's testimony."

Shoot.

He didn't tell me that part. "Wait, and then Jake was

fostered by your parents? Isn't that weird, since they sent his dad to prison?"

Bea shrugs. "His dad apparently encouraged it, but I always felt like it was a 'know your enemies' kind of thing. I don't think Jake's dad is a good person, and I doubt he's gotten much better. I'm worried what he may do now that he's out. Or more specifically, I'm worried what he might convince Jake to do."

Now I am, too.

It can't be easy for Jake. I'd have thought living with Dave and Seren would've been hard on him, too. "Could they not find him another placement?"

Bea leans her face against the window, so her voice is a little muffled. "I mean, they could have, but. . ." She sighs, her breath fogging up the glass. "Everyone loved Jake, even then, but once the truth came out, he didn't really have any friends."

"Except for you."

She nods. "I think, or I've always thought, that he stayed with Dave and Seren because of me, but I know he grew to care about them, too."

Jake was right. It's complicated. "Alright, so we'll be at the studio soon, and if his dad has reached out, what do we say?"

Bea shrugs. "I guess I'll do what I always do. Ask him what he's going to do and then tell him that he's being an idiot." She turns back to face me. "Prepare yourself for that, if you do like him. He usually makes the wrong decision before he makes the right one."

I do try.

But nothing can really prepare me for Jake's dad.

CHAPTER 14

JAKE

My dad's a bad person.

I've known that for quite some time.

Ironically, it wasn't seeing my dad lie shamelessly in his testimony in front of a judge that convinced me. It wasn't watching other people call him a criminal. It wasn't even the judge reprimanding him, saying he was what was wrong with America, and it certainly wasn't watching them sentence him to the maximum penalty for his crime.

No, what convinced me that my dad was a bad person was living with two truly *good* people.

You can't really understand dark until you've seen light. You can't comprehend salty without tasting bland. Most concepts are really defined by the existence of their opposite, so it wasn't until I saw how good people handled the same situations I'd already encountered that I really came to understand that my dad was the opposite of that.

Also, his letters provided evidence of his thoughts I could go back and study. Even after dozens of letters from me, extolling the many things the Fansees had done for me, he never relented in his hatred of them. At first, I thought that I could convince him to let it go.

I think that idea was inspired by Julian. We adopted him, a small, wiry-haired dog, a few months after I went to live with the Fansees. He wasn't much to look at, and he limped. Even after we bathed him, he smelled pretty bad. But the longer he lived with us, the better he looked. Most of the awful things he did—like pooping on Seren's favorite rug over and over—gradually improved.

One thing he never stopped doing was chewing on shoes.

We learned to hide our nice shoes, or they would quickly become *not* nice. We should've kicked that crappy dog to the shelter. He was a real mess. Seren was far too soft for that, and she felt like him finding the hotel was some kind of sign that he should be part of our family. But if he managed to get one of your shoes, and you caught him before he did any real damage, the only way to save your shoe was to distract him with something he wanted more and trade them out. He was a terrorist, really.

After watching that, I had an idea.

I could entice my father with other ideas—other people or companies—he could defraud when he got out instead of the people I cared about. Sadly, my clumsy efforts only made my dad more doggedly determined to punish the Fansees for turning me against him.

And now that he's out, I'm worried.

I was able to put him off last night, at least a little, by telling him how tired I was. My dad knows movie stars need to get enough rest, so after I bought him an expensive steak dinner, he largely let me go to sleep.

Not that I could fall asleep until quite late indeed.

But now that I'm awake, I can't really put him off any

more. The second he hears movement in my room, he taps on the door. "Coffee?" He pokes his head in.

I hold out my hand. "You want to be my manager?" I take a sip, and then spit it right back out. "Black, Dad? Really?"

"Real men take their coffee black."

"I've seen you add a bucket of cream," I say. "And sugar."

"That was before." He sips on his own mug. "Now I take it black."

"You said one day I should take it any way our mark was taking it, so we could bond." I arch one eyebrow. "What happened to that?"

"Black's a way they could take it," he says. "You should be ready for that."

"Not with you." I shake my head. "You're true north, right?"

He snorts. "You don't think that, not anymore." He sets his coffee down. "Yes, to answer your question. I think the least you can do is pay me a generous salary for being your manager."

"I don't have a manager."

"Now you do," he says. "And I'll only take a paltry twenty percent. And for that, I'll make sure no one else is fleecing you the way that I am."

I roll my eyes. "Gee, thanks."

"Speaking of, I spent a few hours reviewing your contracts last night—"

"Wait, you did what?"

He plows ahead. "Several of them have clauses that concerned me. What kind of agent lets you sign a non-com—"

"Dad, I don't want you digging through my stuff." Not that I'm surprised. I knew he'd have pawed through everything. He probably placed bugs, too. "But if you need a job that badly, maybe I'll let you be my manager *from New York*, where your job couldn't send you back to prison."

"Please." He rolls his eyes. "I'll tell them I had to come here because of work." He beams. "It's a high profile, honest position. My salary will impress them, and it'll drag their ex-convict averages way up. Trust me, they'll grant me a waiver."

I can't help staring.

"Relax," he says. "It's all going to be fine now that I'm out."

He still hasn't brought up the Fansees at all.

Maybe he won't.

"I have to film early today," I say. "We're way behind, thanks to—"

"I've been following along," he says. "I know all about Patrice Jouveau." He shakes his head. "What kind of a moron is that blatant anywhere someone else could see her?"

"Clearly her father was less rigorous with her education."

"You're mocking me, but I'm serious." He leans closer. "I taught you well, at least. You've never been naive or clueless."

He's right about that.

When I go in to work half an hour later, he insists on following me. He *tries* to drive, but there's no way I'm allowing that.

"A manager's supposed to drive."

"They drive if it's a van," I say. "Or maybe a charter of some kind. Even a limo, but not this." I shake my hands over the steering wheel of my Mercedes. "Only I drive this."

Once I get out of the car, my phone bings, and I realize I have quite a few messages, including one from Bea asking about my dad. I can't really text her about it now. She'd just come rushing over. I'm stuck hoping she's bluffing about confronting me in person.

I've just come out of costume and makeup when my dad

almost runs into me with another black coffee. "Dad, be careful," I snap. "You almost dumped that all over me."

He leans closer. "That was the point. Then you can get a better shirt."

I roll my eyes. "I like this shirt. I picked it."

"Oh." He eyes me sideways. "Interesting."

I might dump the coffee over his head in about thirty more seconds. "What do you want?"

"Can we chat for just a moment? They said you had five."

Of course he was listening, but he didn't really get it. They told me to take five minutes so I could go pee, not to argue with him about my shirt. Even so, I just nod. "Sure."

We duck into the janitorial closet since my trailer's a hundred and fifty yards in the wrong direction. The door won't close all the way, but that's fine. I don't really want to encourage a long heart-to-heart anyway.

"What did you want?" I arch one eyebrow. Maybe if I'm rude enough, he'll give up and go back to New York without me. I can deal with him later, once I've made up a plan for how to keep Dave and Seren safe.

"While you were getting ready, I was able to walk around mostly unnoticed." He nods slowly. "It's helpful to have someone around whom no one knows. We'll have to remember that, once everyone knows who I am."

I blink.

"What I heard might surprise you."

"What did you hear, Dad?" In spite of my efforts not to insult or offend him, my tone's flat. Too flat. "Just tell me."

He purses his lips like he's not sure I really want to know.

"I just have five minutes, remember?"

"Here's the thing. I'm sure you've seen some of the positive chatter, and you definitely didn't want to wind up on the wrong side of things there. That Patrice woman. . ." He shakes his head. "That was a total disaster, and you wisely steered way clear. But I will just say that your acting has improved dramatically." He slow claps.

I'm still not quite sure what he's saying. "Dad, can you get to the point?"

"No one likes the idea of you dating that burned woman."

I ball my hand into a fist and grit my teeth. Neither action helps me calm down. "Octavia," I hiss. "Her name's Octavia Rothschild, not the 'burned woman.'"

"Well, I know you didn't want to be the one attacking her, but can I just say how impressed I am that you've been able to convince everyone you're actually dating that Crispy Critter?" He chuckles. "The funniest thing Patrice said, hands down." He leans closer. "And give the man an Emmy. I didn't think your acting was very good until I saw the video with you and her. I mean, you really look like you like her in the clips I've seen."

I don't think about it or clench my jaw or grab the sides of my jeans.

I just punch him.

With the position of the door, and the fact that it's not entirely closed, the impact of my blow sends him sprawling. He spins, grabs for the handle, partially slows his fall, and slams face-up, back-down on the ground. Someone almost trips over him.

When I look up, I realize that someone's Octavia.

She looks as pale as, well, as pale as a ghost. Which means she probably just heard everything my stupid Dad said. Now I wish I'd punched him a whole lot harder.

CHAPTER 15

JAKE

My favorite food as a kid—hands down, no contest—was Pop-tarts. I could eat an entire box, and my dad was fine with it. He called people who 'hated' on sugar 'Mary Andrews,' not that I knew what it meant. I found out in high school that the phrase was supposed to be Merry Andrew, meaning someone who makes a lot of jokes.

But to my dad, it was an officious idiot.

When I got to Dave and Seren's, they didn't agree with his breakfast policy. They thought Pop-tarts were empty calories that added nothing to my nutrition and would lead to an unhealthy diet that might stunt the growth of a growing boy.

Their refusal to buy me Pop-tarts downright pissed me off back then.

Of course, they didn't slow my consumption much. There was a never-ending parade of chumps at school who were happy to bring me Pop-tarts over the years. But somewhere around high school, I kind of stopped eating them. That was about the time my desire to be cool overpowered my nostalgia about my favorite childhood food.

On the very first movie I ever made, they had Pop-tarts in the break area one morning. Not having had one for years, I snatched a silvery package right up. Imagine my surprise when my beloved Pop-tart was dry, over-sugared, and downright crumbly around the edges. After a few bites, I tossed what was left in the trash.

I'm realizing now that I've grown in more areas than my palate.

I've put up with a lot from my dad over the years, though much less than I would have endured had he never been locked up, I'm sure. But even knowing that he wasn't quite perfect, I've held on to a lot of gratitude for what he did teach me. I love Dave and Seren, but they're starry-eyed optimists most of the time, and the world's a lot darker than they wish it was. I always credited my dad with preparing me for the reality of life.

I didn't realize he was so toxic.

Hearing him echo Patty's rude ignorance about Octavia. . .hearing him say that I must be acting and that I couldn't genuinely like her filled me with an unspeakable rage. Not just because the world is so ugly, and people care about all the wrong things, but because my own dad's part of the problem. I knew he was a con man. I knew his whole life has been based on stealing from others.

But I always told myself he stole from people who probably deserved it. People who hadn't worked hard for what they had. People too stupid to hang onto what they'd been given. His comment about Octavia was mean, predatory, and low. It was indefensible.

I feel terrible to be related to him.

And to make everything worse, Octavia clearly heard what he said. After laying Dad out cold, I stomped off. I probably only have a minute of my five-minute break left, which means they can start dinging my pay at any point for breach, but I don't care. I can't go film, not right now.

"You didn't need to punch him," Octavia says. "He doesn't know me."

"Or me." I stop and pivot, finally facing Octavia, who's been trailing after me. "He doesn't know me at all. I'm not like him." I'm shaking my head, and I'm pacing, and I'm still so mad that I can't seem to stop.

"Jake." When Octavia tilts her head, her eyes are soft. Kind. They're so *her*.

"I'm so sorry," I say. "Sorry you heard that, sorry he said it, and sorry that's my dad."

She hugs me then, her arms snaking underneath mine and wrapping around my body. A wave of her scent—honeysuckle and something else. Citrus?—washes over me and the twitching stops. The anger recedes a little. "I know you don't agree with any of what he said."

"I'm really sorry you had to hear it."

"You didn't have to knock him out cold, though. The poor man's only been out of prison for what? A few days?" When she lifts her face upward toward mine, her lip's twitching.

"I wish he were still stuck in there," I mutter.

"You don't." Her hand brushes my cheek. "I know it's hard, but people can only change for the better when they're around people who can help them."

I realize, as she says it, that she might be talking about me. I changed, thanks to Dave and Seren, and they may not be perfect, but they're trying. She might also be talking about my dad, though, and I've never met someone less interested in changing. "He's not the kind of person who—he won't change. He doesn't even want to."

"No one really wants to change." She shrugs. "And he may

not substantially improve, but at least in small ways, you could be a good influence on him.”

That makes me laugh.

“What’s funny?” She frowns.

“I’m not sure anyone has ever called me a good influence,” I say. “But aside from that irony, my dad’s the last person in the world who would ever be influenced by me. He teaches me, end of story.”

“I’m sure that’s not true,” she says. “First of all, he’s your dad, so he must care what you think, at least a little. But secondly, try to imagine how proud of you he must be, and how potentially embarrassed that might make him.” She smiles. “His son, a handsome and well-known movie star, making loads of money. . .the right way?” She shrugs. “Let comments like the one he made go, or just gently tell him that it’s too much, and then try to show him how much better he could have handled the situation with what you do.”

She does not know my dad at all.

“Try to remember that he hasn’t seen you for as long as you haven’t seen him. Maybe he won’t be what you remember.”

“I guess.” I’m honestly worried he might be worse.

“Aren’t you supposed to be filming right now?” She glances behind her. “I thought I saw May, all dressed and make-upped and—”

“Shoot.” I sigh. “Yeah, I’m probably holding them all up.”

“Let’s head back,” she says. “The last thing you want to do when there’s a new co-star you want to impress is make her wait.” She ducks her head as she starts back toward the set, and I’m not sure how I can tell, but something’s still off.

“Hey.” I grab her hand. “Wait.”

She stops and turns, but her eyes are shuttered. “What?”

“Come here.”

She swallows, and then she looks around. "Come *where*?"

I tug on her, and then I step toward her myself. "Closer." I lean over and press a soft kiss to her mouth before she can stop me. "I've missed you. Our date got cut off, and then I spent yesterday helping find a replacement for the 'rank one,' and then my dad showed up uninvited, telling everyone he's my new manager." I shake my head. "It was a terrible, long day. I needed to see and touch and hear you." I smile, and then I press another kiss to her cheek. "I'm sorry I didn't call last night. I was too tired, and my dad was hovering and snooping, and I just couldn't."

She ducks her head. "I thought you were with May."

"With May Markson?" I release her. "Why would I have been with—"

Then it hits me.

She was *jealous.*

And now I'm grinning from ear to ear. "You thought I was with another woman, and you were upset about it."

She's shaking her head, and she's walking back toward the set. "No, I mean, I wasn't upset."

I jog ahead of her and trot along backward so I can see her expression. "You were."

She finally stops walking and drops her hands on her hips. "Bea said you love her, and now you're working with her, and she's really cute, and—"

I grab her arms, and I yank her right up close, and I really *kiss* her this time. I kiss her until I can't think. I kiss her until I can't *breathe,* and then I kiss her until I can tell she's gone weak in the knees, and only then do I let her go.

"When I kiss May, it'll be because someone's paying me. The only person I *want* to kiss is *you,* Miss Rothschild. Besides, May knows we're together, and she said she has a boyfriend who feels the same way. She seems to be just as nice in person as she acts on her show, and that's why I was happy they chose her." I lower my head until we're eye-to-eye. "Capiche?"

She's smiling. "Yes. Aye, aye, sir."

I turn back around, slide my hand down her willowy arm, and then lace my fingers through hers, tugging her along with me all the way back to the filming location. "I have to go *work* now, but I hope you'll come back for a late lunch. After that we have a sunset scene, so I should have loads of time before I have to report back." I lift my eyebrows. "Yes?"

She shrugs and nods.

"Good. Because I'll miss you this morning."

There are people watching, and I'm glad. Maybe it'll keep them from saying anything stupid. I lean closer. "And if anyone ever implies that I'm a good actor because I look happy when I'm with you, I'll lay them out cold, even if it's the President himself."

"Maybe especially if it's the president," she says. "He can be a little annoying."

"It's actually *because* everyone knows I'm not a good actor at all." I wink. "That's why they can see just how I feel when I'm with you and know it's true."

I watch sideways as Bea circles around, grabs Octavia, and they leave. Then it's time to focus on getting through these scenes quickly—not that it's too hard. I'm great at memorizing lines, and we're filming scenes I've already done with Patrice. Even so, the first few scenes with a new actor are always the most critical. You have to find your stride.

It's easy with May, *so* easy.

She knows her lines. She has a natural cadence, and she's genuinely funny. This isn't a comedy, but I almost wish it was. She makes things that aren't even supposed to be jokes mildly comical.

Before I know it, we're filming the very last scene. Our third cut felt great, but now we have to wait to see if they want us to run it again, or if we're done until four.

"Heard you have lunch plans," May says.

I nod. "I should, yeah. She has some filming for something today, or that's what my sister said."

"So you're dating your sister's best friend?" May's eyebrows rise. "Is that complicated?"

"I guess I am." I hadn't thought about it like that, but Octavia has basically transformed Bea since meeting her. "You know, they haven't even been friends too long, but Bea has grown so much with Octavia to push her."

"The best friends are like that. It's easy, it's just *right*, and they make us better."

"That's exactly it," I say. "I'd known Bea for a really long time, maybe too long. I didn't realize she needed a push. I had let her become complacent, but Octavia saw the problem right away." I can't help smiling. "I hated her at first—she personally ruined Bea's chance of winning this jingle competition. My sister was *so* upset."

"I bet." May's smile is just like it is when the camera's rolling.

"Anyway, now they're almost inseparable. I think Bea said they should be done around one or so."

"I can see why you like her," May says. "She's really, really pretty."

"You haven't even heard her sing in person yet."

"Still," she says. "Even in recordings, it's really something, her voice."

"It fits her," I say. "All of it."

Jane waves our direction. "We're done."

"Nice," I say. "That was way faster than with Patrice the first time."

"When it's right, it's right," May says. "See you later." She's already on her phone, probably with her boyfriend.

When I call Octavia, she says, "Hey! Are you done already?"

"Yep, so much easier with May. Wrapped up early."

"Awesome. We have a few things left—wanna text me a place? We can meet you there?"

"Hand the phone to Bea, would you?"

"Oh, uh, sure. Hang on."

"Hey, stranger," Bea says.

"Why are you crashing my date?"

"Do you not remember how obnoxious you were when I was dating Easton?"

"The difference is I was doing it because I didn't want to lose you," I say. "And you're doing it because Seren wants to make sure I'm fine."

"I can't believe you would—"

"Can it, Hornet. We both know it's true."

"Fine." She huffs. "So I'll tell her you're fine?"

"Maybe don't tell her I punched him."

She laughs. "Too late. She sent me the '100' emoji, so I think that's old person code for 'no problem. More punching, good.'"

"I figured she'd worry more about the prospect of me joining his cabal."

"Exactly," Bea says. "Have fun at lunch. . .without me." She sniffs.

"Hand the phone back to Octavia."

"Oh, fine." She doesn't even sound like she's really annoyed.

"Hey."

"I don't actually have anything else to say," I admit. "But I didn't want to hang up without hearing your voice one more time."

"It's my best feature."

I can't argue with her, because her voice is amazing, but that feels like a trap. "Your voice is obvious, but I'd actually say it's your eyes." As I say that, I realize I do think that. Everyone can hear her voice, but only I get to study the flecks in her eyes up close.

"Aww, well, thanks." Someone's calling to her in the background.

"Alright, go. I'll find a good spot and text you."

"See you soon!"

I search for a new, hot place for a minute, but I'm not great at this stuff. I decide to just go with what I know and text her the address of the Clark Street Diner.

> I'm happy to come pick you up if that's easier. Send me an address. I'll even bring the nice car this time. :P

She doesn't text back for more than forty-five minutes, but then she's pretty curt.

> They'll drop me off—I can be there in twenty.

Since I'm a solid twenty-five minutes away, maybe more, I race to my car and take off. Thanks to LA traffic, I can't even speed to pare down the time. When I finally find a valet parking attendant, I fling my keys at him. Even so, Octavia's standing in the corner, waiting, when I arrive.

"Sorry," I say.

"They don't have any tables," she says. "Did you see my text?"

"Jake!" The manager, Philippe, rushes over. "Corner?"

I nod.

"Oh, right." Octavia rolls her eyes.

"It's my favorite place for a patty melt," I say.

Octavia frowns as we follow Philippe. "That's not on the menu. I'm pretty sure—"

"No, it's not." Philippe gestures to a table with a smile. "But it was, and we've always got one ready for Jake." He turns to Octavia. "He's been so good about choosing us for ordering in on movie sets. We try to give him anything he wants."

"Plus, Philippe's daughter's a little obsessed with me, and I've come to *two* birthday parties," I say.

"She'll want a photo," Philippe says.

"With or without Octavia?" I ask.

"I think with." Philippe smiles. "My little Georgina isn't delusional. She knows she's not going to marry Jake. She just likes knowing the handsomest guy on the movie screen."

"Yeah, yeah," I say, slinging an arm around Octavia and dragging her over. "Snap away." I can't help noticing that Octavia still turns what she thinks is her good side forward. I guess I can't blame her, but it bugs me to see it.

"Can I get a California club?" Octavia asks.

And then we're finally alone. I reach across the table and grab both her hands. "So good to see you."

She smiles. "You don't look so bad either, 'handsomest man on the big screen.'"

I roll my eyes. "She's thirteen. She also loves Timothée Chalamet and Tom Holland."

"At least you're in good company."

"Well, I am right now too," I say.

She rolls her eyes so hard I'm worried they might pop out of her head. "No corny lines, please."

"Look, I don't have someone here to write them, so you

get what you get. Beauty and smarts like yours don't often coincide. Sometimes you have to settle for just beauty."

She's still chuckling when our food comes out, and her eyes widen until they're enormous. "We placed our order like two minutes ago!"

"Maybe I picked this place for that reason—they really do love me."

"Wow," she says, as the waiter walks off, "you may have to hide in grocery stores, but being famous has some perks."

"Unless you *like* spending food prep time chatting with someone," I say. "Then I guess it's a little annoying."

She blushes again, and I realize that I really like making her do that. She looks almost like an errant child. It gives me an idea of how young Octavia must have been. She was every bit as adorable as she is now. "Well, after a morning like you had, I'm sure it's nice to have some things go right."

"You can say that again."

"Did your dad come back to yell at you?"

"I'm assuming he's at my apartment," I say. "He has the code, and he disappeared after he stood up, or so the crew told me. Maybe he's slashing my pillows and scrawling lewd words across my walls at this very moment."

Octavia can't tell whether I'm serious.

"Don't worry about my boring walls. That's not really his style. He's more likely to steal all the money from my accounts and leave me with a pile of debt."

"Shoot," she says. "Would he really do that?"

"I'm his son," I say. "I don't leave any papers that would let him do something like that lying around, and my passwords would be hard for the Pentagon to crack."

"At least there are some advantages to having a dad like him—you learn a lot."

"You can say that again," I say. "But it has plenty of disadvantages, too."

"Like?"

I could tell her about the times I risked criminal incarceration as a child. I could talk about the times we were thrown out of apartments and hotels. Or I could share the feeling a kid gets when he walks away from his friends after stealing from them, knowing they'll soon hate him, but instead, I shock myself by saying, "He stole the one thing that mattered to me when I was in high school."

"What?" Her brow furrows. "Wasn't he locked up? What do you mean he stole from you in high school?"

And now I'm stuck. I've never said a word to anyone about the photos Dad sent, but for some reason, I suddenly *want* to. Maybe it's because I want someone to tell me that Dave's not a bad guy, someone whose opinion I might believe. Even if a miracle's unlikely, I want my dad to have been wrong. I want my faith back, in Dave, in life, and in the existence of goodness in the world.

Not that Octavia's a miracle worker, but she's a good person. I'm hoping that somehow, Dave might be, too.

"Well, it's a little complicated." I take a bite so I can use chewing my food as an excuse to think about how to tell her this.

She sets her sandwich down on the plate and stares, waiting.

Chewing time didn't help. There isn't a great way to broach this topic. "So, when I was in high school, my dad got upset. He swore when Seren's testimony sent him away, that he'd get his revenge. At first, I thought that was fine. I was keen to help him. But then, as I spent more time with them, when I saw that the Fansees genuinely liked me and weren't trying to punish me, I wanted to spare them."

"That's good," Octavia says. "You were growing."

"Maybe, but I guess my ham-handed attempts at getting my dad to let go of his anger were a little obvious. Dad sent me a message with. . ." I cough. "Some damaging stuff about Dave. He told me my foster parents weren't perfect, and that I shouldn't even be trying to protect them. He threatened to share what he sent me with my foster mom, so that they'd break up and I'd have nowhere to live."

"And now that he *is* out, you're worried he'll take whatever he sent and use it against them."

Shoot. Why wasn't I worried about that? "Well, Dad's usually more of a blackmail kind of person than an outright aggressor," I say. "I guess I'm more worried, well. Two things. First, I'm worried about whether what my dad said and sent is true, and what it means about my foster parents. And second, I'm worried he'll finally take his revenge—maybe even in a way that's totally different than spreading the information he's shared with me."

"Tell me what he knows about Dave that's so bad," Octavia says. "I don't really know him, so I won't be as emotional about it."

I grimace. "I mean, it's not great."

"So, what? He bribed someone? He stole something? Or did he, like, have an affair?"

I'm not sure what she sees. I usually have a pretty good poker face, but I definitely give something away, because she gasps. "No. *Dave?*"

I nod slowly. "Well, at least, I think so."

"Why do you think that? He just said he had an affair?"

I sigh, and I pull out my phone. "Not exactly." I have to tap on a few things, but then I swivel it around.

At first she leans closer, and then she gasps louder, and

then her eyes widen like saucers. "And that's for sure him?" She bites her lip. "Could it have been photoshopped?"

"One of my friends from before is pretty good at photo analysis. I mean, I can't trust him one hundred percent, because I knew him through my dad, right? But he said this had no hallmarks of being fake. He thinks it's totally real."

Octavia nods slowly, and then she drops a hand over mine. "You just found out people you thought were really good weren't."

I swallow.

"I'm sorry," she says. "That must have been really hard for you."

I shrug. "Look, I'm a big boy, but the thing is. . ."

"You can't trust your dad either," she says. "It might be fake. You just want to know whether it's true." She leans a little closer. "And maybe, even if it is true, Dave could have some explanation."

"Like what?" I ask. "They were 'on a break?'"

She frowns.

"I don't know, but it doesn't look good."

"What if," Octavia says, "this was from before they met? It's not like he was a nun before they got married."

I blink. I feel like a complete moron for not thinking about that before.

"I mean—how would they be able to prove that?" I ask.

She tilts her head. "He could just *say* if it was, right?"

Duh. Because when people are honest, when they trust each other, they believe what the other person says.

"You should ask him about it," Octavia says. "You don't have to tell Seren. If it's really something as awful as you've thought for all this time, maybe this will be the impetus he needs to come clean to her. But it's possible there's an explanation that won't hurt anyone."

"I guess."

"My parents got divorced when I was young, because of infidelity," she says. "I think it was actually better for them and me than it would have been if they'd just lied to each other."

"I can't think of anything I could do that would be worse than breaking them up," I say.

"I can," she says softly. "How about not trusting that they're who you think they are? Not giving them a chance to explain and do the right thing?"

Maybe she's right.

"Because, Jake? Even good people make mistakes sometimes. You know, it's possible your dad was right *and* Dave's already confessed and been forgiven. People are complicated, but not knowing is hurting you, and it's within your control to put a stop to that."

I can't believe she thinks that, just like that, I could *ask* him.

"It would probably have to be an in-person conversation." I frown. I won't be back home for weeks yet.

"I may have overheard a conversation with Bea where Seren was saying something about a birthday or anniversary or. . ." She lifts both eyebrows.

Not this again. "Look, we never celebrated birthdays growing up. Dad said they were a manipulation by society that forced us to celebrate mediocrity at an arbitrary time. So when this new do-gooder family wanted to celebrate the day I joined them, which also happened to be the day my dad went to prison?" I'm not sure what to say. "It felt contrived. I wasn't really their kid. They didn't really care when I was born. They didn't even know I existed when I was born. I didn't have a 'real' family, so I tried to stop them from throwing me a party."

"Then you don't want to go back to celebrate your birthday-slash-anniversary of joining the Fansee family?"

I wish I didn't sound so angsty. "I would actually like to go back. I tolerated it for years, but it has grown on me. It's just that if I tried to leave now, especially after the re-casting, I doubt it would go over well. Catching up again means working long days, even on weekends."

Octavia drops a hand over mine again, and a nice, warm feeling suffuses my whole body. "Jake, I support whatever you really want, but I disagree with one thing." She pauses.

I like her holding my hand, so I don't rush her.

Finally, she says, "Everyone, born into a family or not, feels like they don't quite fit in at some point. No family is perfectly homogenous. Talking to people when you don't want to, squeezing in when you don't quite fit, and asking them the questions that are hard and being open to their answers. . ." She taps her pointer finger on the top of my hand. "That's what family *is*." She scrunches her nose. "That's their job. They do it because they love you, and you have to meet them halfway, or in this case, find a day to fly home."

"Then do you like birthday parties?"

"Not even a little bit," she admits. "But I'm an introvert—not as bad as Bea, but I prefer to spend my nights in—and my family isn't harmonious. When I was a kid, I liked them." She squeezes my hand. "But that's because I felt safe, then. Maybe you could like them now."

The real reason I should go home is to ask Dave whether the pictures have some explanation. The risk is that my questions might blow things up.

"Some risks are worth taking," Octavia says.

When she answers a question I didn't even ask, it makes

me genuinely wonder whether she can read minds. "You might be right."

"About this?" The corner of her mouth turns up. "I am."

After we finish our food, we talk a little while longer. I ask her about her birthday parties as a kid. She asks what my real birthday is, and I evade. But then, I give her a ride back to her hotel and prepare to head back to the set.

"Don't go yet." Bea races out. "I got you a ticket home."

"Oh, come on," I say. "I'm not five. I can get my own plane tickets."

"But you wouldn't do it," she says. "And with all the drama, you need to go home." She hugs me. "So do I," she whispers in my ear.

"Are you coming?" I glance over Bea's shoulder at Octavia. "I know you guys have some stuff left next week, but I hope you can."

"I figure the flight and this hotel cost about the same," Octavia says. "I may as well come for the day."

"But the label's paying for our hotel," Bea says.

Octavia rolls her eyes. "Not the point."

"You're flying in Friday night," Bea says. "You can fly back Sunday morning. They can spare you for *one day*, and trust me. The filming crew will thank you for forcing a short break."

Thanks to Octavia, for the first time, maybe I'll get some answers. It's partially because of what she said—I need to trust him enough to ask—but partially because. . .if I do blow things up, at least I'd still have her. For the first time in my life, I have something other than just the Fansees. Risking that relationship doesn't feel quite as terrifying.

But when I start to walk away, Octavia standing in the doorway and waving, I'm suddenly struck with a moment of panic. "You should know that I'm going back to the set, but

there are no kiss scenes today, and I'll be wishing I was here."
I can't help smiling when I see her looking sheepish.

"Yeah, yeah," she says.

I walk back her direction, and I grab her waist, and I kiss her right on the mouth. Her little sigh, the way she leans into me, and her delicious smell all lighten my heart. "I'm sad to be leaving you."

"Mhm," she says.

"It's hard to leave your girlfriend, I guess," I whisper.

The corners of her mouth both rise exactly the same, the burned side and the smooth. Her eyes light up, and she goes up on her tiptoes. I think she's going to kiss me back, but her head turns and she whispers in my ear instead. "I guess now I *have* to go back home that weekend. My *boyfriend* needs some support if he's finally going to talk to Dave."

For the first time, that prospect doesn't seem quite so daunting.

When I do force myself to walk away, glancing back at Octavia two more times, I'm not quite as scared. Everything's better with Octavia.

She had to define family for me, but I think I can define girlfriend for her now. It's the person you're happier and safer and more light-hearted with. It's the person you want around all the time.

And I've finally found mine.

CHAPTER 16
OCTAVIA

My mom loves me.

I really believe that.

She was never a *bad* mother, she just didn't like doing it very much.

That's why, in spite of my begging and pleas, and in spite of my dad's longing for more children, I remained an only child. Sometimes I overhead her telling people that she wished she hadn't had a kid. It hurt back then, but as an adult, I've come to understand a little more.

Some women shouldn't have kids.

Society tells us that we all should. It says without having children, we aren't complete. There's something wrong with us. We'll be sad when we're older. For a lot of women, having kids helps them step back from selfishness and learn to care about other people more than they do themselves.

But some people, some people don't want kids. They don't want to let go of their own desires. They can be good people, but they just don't *want* what they were stuck with. For them, kids are like an anchor dragging them down and drowning them.

My mom's like that.

Knowing you're an anchor isn't really very fun.

When my mother calls, I groan a little, but it's early enough that we haven't even reached the store to shop yet—we still need an outfit for the album cover, because so far Bea has hated everything I like—so I answer. "Hey, Mom. What's up?"

"When are you coming back?" she asks.

I haven't talked to her in weeks, but there's no lead-in, no niceties. That's just how she is. "Good to hear from you," I say with a half-smile. "Yes, I'm loving being in LA, especially as New York's probably getting colder and colder."

"Well *of course* it's nice in LA," she says. "That would be like saying it's cold in the North Pole, or it's sunny in Iraq."

"I have two more weeks here," I say, even though it's technically just one day more than a week. When I get back, it'll be nice to have a few days that she's not sure I'm home yet. My mom tends to ask for a lot of favors when I'm around. "We've recorded the songs, but we have some promotional stuff to do, we'll have some edits to make, and we've got album cover photos to take."

"Can't they just do a little icon or something?" She coos. "A gremlin would be great. That fits your beautiful disaster theme."

"That's another song, Mom. Ours is gorgeous monstrosity."

"I also forget you copied them." She sighs. "Fine, no gremlin. What do I know? I'm just a washed-out community theater actress."

She means washed-up, but I'm smart enough now to never point out inconsistencies in her sayings or vocabulary. "I'm not saying that, Mom. They don't let me make the decisions on really anything, though."

"Yes, yes, I'm sure it's all very hard to be stuck dealing with the whims of a big studio and a huge album deal." She snorts. "My condolences."

"I'm not saying that, either. All I'm saying is—"

"Two weeks," she says. "Then you'll be back home."

"Right." Why bother arguing? It's pointless.

"Your father's driving me nuts, you know. He doesn't want to bother you, but he's desperate for information, and for some delusional reason he thinks I might have it. As if my now-famous daughter cares a bit what her mother knows."

"I'm hardly famous," I say. "And I've texted to tell you all the relevant information as it happened."

"You haven't said a word about any handsome movie stars, so I'm guessing that's all just a publicity stunt? Were the little clips staged, too?" She doesn't wait for me to even say anything. "How is Jake Priest in real life? Is he just horrible? I bet he's rude, and brags, and he's demanding. They always are."

I think about correcting her, but it doesn't seem to be worth the energy. "Mom, I have to go."

"Great, yes, you go and do all your big, important things. I'll just hang around here, ignoring messages from your father since you never text or call him."

"Okay, Mom. You do that." I hang up.

"What about this?" Bea's standing in front of a shop, her gaze locked on the work of art in the window.

It's a massive, full-skirted ball gown that's entirely and completely impractical. The skirt's touching the ground for at least a foot all the way around, and it's made up of dip-dyed, bold, autumn-jewel toned swaths of crepe fabric that fall down from the bodice in a stunning cascade. The bodice itself is made of what look like carefully shaped and possibly embroidered sections of chiffon feathers and leaves.

It may be the most beautiful dress I've ever seen.

"That thing must cost an absolute fortune." Like, the same price as a car.

"The shop's called Helen Spinelli." Bea frowns. "I've never heard of it. Maybe things that are new are cheap."

"Well, let's go inside and you can try it on, but I'm telling you, there's no way our budget will cover that. We'd need the movie's costume budget." I shake my head. "But you do have exquisite taste, and I'd be happy to kick in my entire share for that—I can wear anything."

"Wait." Bea drops her hands on her hips.

"What?" I point. "We won't know how bad it is until we ask. Places like this don't exactly post a price card in the window."

"We may be operating under a misunderstanding. Are you thinking I want this dress *for myself?*" She snorts. "Because that would be ridiculous. I'm five feet tall and the most introverted person you know. I would never wear this dress, not in a million years."

"It's perfect for you. Your face's basically a work of art," I say.

"No." Bea shakes her head. "That dress screams Octavia."

"That?" I can't help pointing at it to emphasize my incredulity. "You think that gorgeous ball gown with a million brilliant colors that swirls and poofs and highlights my shoulders—one of which I never expose—and puts all the focus on my face, neck, and hair. . .you think *that* dress screams *Octavia?*" I can't help laughing. "Have you met me?"

Bea tosses her head. "Just go in there. I'm getting a call— I'll meet you inside in two minutes. At least ask what it costs and try it on. If you hate it, I'll never bring it up again, and I'll agree to whatever other outfits you pick."

Trying this dress on is a ridiculous suggestion.

There's no way that I would ever wear that dress for anything, much less to be the focal point of an album cover that's going to be pushed hard. But once I do it and say no, she'll let me pick something less *in your face*, and we can finally be done with all the never-ending searching. I've always hated shopping, but finding the perfect outfit for an album cover is the worst shopping task I've ever been set.

"Fine, but no photos once we're in there." I point.

She nods, presses her phone to her ear and waves.

I go inside—reluctantly—and then I see the price of the gown. It's seventeen thousand dollars. I almost laugh my way out of the store, but there's no way that even Bea could justify spending that. That means that once I try it on, she'll have to concede to me. As I'm standing here, I can't help wondering whether shops like this even let people like me try on gowns like this one.

"Can I help you?" The woman walking toward me is exquisite. She's the kind of person who should be wearing this. She's tall, thin, and just perfection all around. There's not a blemish, not a wrinkle, and not a single discoloration marring the beauty of her face.

I feel really stupid even asking about trying it on. "I'm looking for something to wear on the cover of an album we're about to release." Why did I say that? "This is probably out of our budget." I swallow. "But my partner really thought it might be the perfect thing."

"Are you wanting to borrow it?" The woman frowns. "Because we don't really do that."

I shake my head. "No, of course you don't."

Bea blows through the door like a tiny hurricane. "She's going to try this on." She folds her arms.

The woman blinks. "We don't really do—"

"You don't allow people who are looking for clothing to come shop in your store? Or you don't let people who are going to be spending. . ." She glances down, and her eyes widen infinitesimally, but she doesn't react beyond that. ". . .seventeen thousand dollars on one of your works of wearable art try them on?" Her eyebrows shoot up. "I find that hard to believe."

The woman frowns, and even then, she looks like a print model. "Your partner here says it's out of your budget."

"Did she?" Bea laughs. "Good thing she's not in charge of the money part." She waves. "I imagine it's a one-of-a-kind, for that price?"

The woman's frown deepens, impossibly. "It is."

"Perfect." Bea's beaming, the counterpoint to Grumpy Bear. "My friend is, too, as you can see. They don't make beauty like hers more than once."

I expect Grumpy Bear to laugh, but she glances my way again and her eyes widen. "You're Jake Priest's girlfriend."

I swallow.

"Here, let me get it off the dress form." She keeps her eyes down the whole time, never meeting my eye. I can't tell whether she's embarrassed or just finds my face hard to look at. I suppose it doesn't really matter.

It takes her longer than I expect to get the whole thing off the mannequin, but once she does, it takes all three of us to bundle it back and into the dressing room. I actually feel a little bad, making her go through all that, even though she was a little snotty. Bea must know we can't afford this now that she's seen the price tag.

"We should not be doing this," I hiss, once I'm in one of their two massive dressing rooms with Bea helping me into the rainbow cupcake.

"Hush, you." Bea slaps my arm. "Bra off, loser. There's no way you'll like this with straps showing all over the place."

I turn around just to glare at her. "There's no way we're getting this, so why does it matter?"

"Just do it." Bea's glaring so fiercely that I almost laugh.

It's not often someone like me gets to dress up like they're the Princess of Monaco. This might be my one time, ever. And if I stand with my right side toward the mirror, I might not even hate it. I might even have Bea snap a photo after all.

I tug my bra off, and then Bea helps me zip the back up. I'm surprised to find that they have supportive bra cups built into the sleeveless sheath form, so I don't even look like I'm sagging to my knees. Though, for seventeen thousand dollars, it should play the piano, clean my room, *and* lift and shape my bosom.

Now that I'm looking at it up close, I realize how very delicate the carefully shaped and embroidered chiffon actually is. When I gather up my skirt, the tiny bits flutter and shift, and even looking down on it from above as I am, it almost looks worth the steep price tag.

For one tiny moment, I find myself wishing I could buy it.

I'm far too practical, of course. I would never. But I can see why Bea wanted me to try it on. "You know we can't buy it," I whisper. "But I don't regret putting it on, other than feeling a little guilty."

Bea arches one eyebrow. "You have to leave the dressing room to get the full effect."

I turn around and realize for the first time that there aren't mirrors in here. "Why don't they have mirrors in a dressing room?"

Bea grabs the handle on the door. "They have a wall length floor-to-ceiling mirror outside. Didn't you see it?" She tilts her head. "These aren't the kind of clothes you can appreciate without something like that."

When we walk out, I realize I didn't even glance to the left as we walked back. I was too busy shifting the dress inside the room without letting it snag on anything. I couldn't imagine the horror of tearing a seventeen thousand dollar ball gown. I would die.

"How would I even move in this?" I ask.

"There are spots in four places where we can gather the skirt underneath when you need to move in it, but they would be custom tailored based on the purchaser's height." The woman's voice startles me. I had no idea she was waiting outside for us, like a spider. Is that normal?

In places like this, maybe it is.

I swallow, and I move slowly toward the mirrors, but to see how I look, I'm forced to climb up onto the raised dais. It's all such a big production, like I always imagined trying on a wedding gown would be. Though in my wildest dreams, I never considered I'd wear an off -the-shoulder dress for my wedding. Even if this thing wasn't seventeen grand, the bare shoulder would be enough for me to rule it out.

I spin around and face the mirrors, and it's. . .

The gown was gorgeous in the window, but it looks much, much better than I ever thought it could. I shift naturally so that my left side's hidden, and I smile just a little. "It's really stunning."

"Turn straight," Bea says. "You look *amazing*, like the masterpiece I always knew you were."

"Maybe a Picasso," I say.

Bea shakes her head. "Stop and look in that mirror."

I do as she asked, and when I really look. . .I don't look bad. I mean, one side of my face still looks melted. My shoulder, too. I hate it. But it's. . . In this, I almost don't care. The asymmetry of the dress makes the asymmetry of my face less displeasing.

Not that it matters.

Our costume budget's a grand—for the two of us. I'm not about to pay what I'd pay for a car to buy a dress I'd never have anywhere to wear and couldn't even fit in my closet.

Bells jingle up front, indicating that someone opened the door.

The woman clears her throat. "I'll be right back. Take your time." She ducks down the hall, presumably to talk to the customer who's currently staring at the mess we left of the front window display.

"We have to buy it," Bea says.

"We?" I snort. "Absolutely not." She's standing at the very back of the shop, so I turn to look at her while we talk. "I humored you. I put this on, and we took way too much time away from this poor woman, and now I'm going to change and we're going to go pick out something completely fine, like a pair of dark jeans and a chunky sweater from Anthropologie. Heck, I'll even let you pick something weird, like an asymmetrical sweater." I nod slowly. "Yes, that will be fine."

A soft exhalation behind me has me spinning around in panic.

Jake's jaw's almost draped on his chest. "That's—it's—you're." He swallows, finally closing his mouth. "You have to get that. It's *the* cover."

The shopkeeper's literally standing right behind him. I shove the words past the rictus of my fake smile. "Bea, did you call Jake?"

She grunts. "I knew I needed reinforcements."

"I'm glad you like it," formerly Grumpy Bear, now Sunshine Bear, says.

Jake snaps a photo.

"Hey," I say. "Bea promised me no photos."

He shrugs. "I wasn't a party to that short-sighted promise."

I'm going to have to steal his phone and purge any photos later. "Do *not* send that to anyone, or I will straight up murder you."

"You can't do it now," Jake says. "Even if Bea won't testify against you, Cordelia just heard that threat." He tosses his head. "She'd make sure justice was done."

I roll my eyes. "Alright, well, the show's over. I'm going to change."

"Wait." Jake throws up a hand.

"What?" I pause.

He smiles.

"*What?*" I ask.

"I just wanted to see you in that for one more minute."

"While she changes," Cordelia mutters, "I'm just going to go kill myself."

"What?" Bea looks as confused as I feel.

"You two are disgustingly cute," Grumpy-turned-Sunshine-Bear-whose-name-is-really-Cordelia-but-I-will-refuse-to-use-it-in-my-head says. "Meanwhile, I'm still single."

The jealousy from her almost makes me smile. Perfect Cordelia's single. Not for long, I imagine. "Okay." I throw my hands up in the air. "That's enough silliness. I'm going to change." Only, no matter how I turn, I'm going to walk right past Jake with my burned shoulder. While I'm trying to work out how to back up in this dress, he walks toward me.

And he picks up one side of the dress—the left.

I suppress my cringe and force a smile. "Thanks."

"A true pleasure," he says. "You are literally the most beautiful person I have ever seen in my entire life."

Bea makes retching sounds, but she's smiling. "You two really are disgustingly adorable."

"You have to get this," Jake whispers. "It's perfect for the album cover because it looks like it was made for you."

I gather up the right side, and he helps me into the room much more elegantly than Bea did before. The fact that I'm wearing the dress now probably makes the process much simpler, but still.

As he releases the gathered skirt folds, he leans close to me, his face pressed against my left side. "I mean it. This will make the album. It makes me want to refilm our music video."

I roll my eyes. "Did Bea fail to mention that it's seventeen thousand dollars?"

"So what?" Jake asks. "You're worth a hundred million."

"That's so corny."

He sighs. "Well, get changed and I'll try and convince you over lunch."

He and Bea both try, and both fail utterly to make any headway.

"How did you get away for lunch?" I ask. "I thought you were working basically all day and most nights this whole week just to try and get caught up."

"Bea actually called my director and said she hurt her ankle and was in the hospital." He sounds pretty ticked. And then he smiles. "It was brilliant."

I can hardly believe it. "So the entire crew's waiting on you, and they think Bea's injured?"

Jake shrugs. "This was important."

"Hardly," I say. "Because under no circumstance are we buying that dress. Neither of you is going to do it, either. It's too expensive, and it's not practical, and most of all, it makes me uncomfortable."

"Because of her face," Bea mock-whispers. "She thinks she looks bad."

"I don't think I look bad." I don't bother saying that I *know* I do. "But you know when you see people wearing something that's too small? It's just not flattering on them. That doesn't mean they're fat. It just means that outfit isn't their best option."

"But that *was* flattering on you," Bea says. "So stop with all that."

Jake holds out his phone and points. "You looked. . .like some kind of pop legend."

"At least that's better than what Bea said."

Bea frowns. "What did I say?"

"She said I look like a Picasso." I can't help myself. I wiggle my eyebrows.

"Oh, shut it," Bea says. "You got me." She glares Jake's direction. "I one hundred percent did *not* say that. I said she was a masterpiece."

"Picasso was probably the most famous painter of all time," Jake says. "I won't even laugh at that joke."

After lunch, Jake has to rush back—reporting that Bea made a miraculous recovery from her "sprain," but we keep shopping and I practically shove her into Anthropologie for a look around. It's just pricey enough we may have luck, but cheap enough it could come in under budget.

We've barely walked past the front display when I see it— a minidress that would be utterly indecent on its own, but covered with a mermaid-silhouette lace overlay, it'll cover me from wrist to throat to ankle.

They even have it in both black and ivory.

Bea sighs. She turns to face me slowly, but then she nods. "Fine."

It's not a work of art, but we look pretty darn good. We also come in under budget, and no one's going to be bugging me to wear something I have no business wearing. But as I pack for our quick trip back to New York, a tiny part in the deepest corner of my heart laments that I won't ever own that Picasso ballgown.

FILTHY RICH

In another life, it would have been epic on me.

CHAPTER 17
OCTAVIA

Fall in Scarsdale, New York is either *magical* or it's *diabolical.*

Of course when I was younger, I lived for the diabolical days. I remember one day in particular that the weather forecasters were just plain wrong. A front they said was going to swing south came north instead.

It dumped six inches of snow overnight, and when I woke up, it looked more like a winter wonderland than anything I'd ever seen outside of a snow globe. I was absolutely entranced. My mom? Not so much.

When she saw they were still holding the audition, but public transit into the City was closed down, she swore a *lot.* Apparently she had an audition she'd now miss thanks to the storm.

"If we didn't live in the bumpkiss middle of nowhere, I could still go, but thanks to your dad's job, we're stuck out here, away from the epicenter of the acting world."

"I'm sorry, Mom," I said. "Maybe they'll get it cleared up soon, and then—"

"What do you know about snow?" Mom shook her head. "Just go clean up your room."

I'd learned by then that when Mom was in a bad mood, nothing I did helped. Instead of arguing that my room was already clean, I ducked out of the kitchen without finishing my now-soggy cereal. I walked around my room, wondering what I could possibly clean. It took a minute, but it finally hit me—my closet had a box full of old toys from when I was a kid. I could go through them and pull a few things out to keep. I could donate the rest. It was only a few weeks until Christmas, and I'd heard that was the best time to donate toys. Parents who were on a limited income could pick them up at the donation center in time to put them under the tree.

About halfway down in the box, I found my favorite dress for playing dress up, Belle.

The enormous, glittery golden dress had a massive skirt, an off-the-shoulder, drape neckline, and long sleeves with tiny sequins sewn at odd intervals. At the time, I thought it was the most beautiful dress I'd ever seen. Since I didn't go to church very often as a kid, I didn't own many dresses. I knew I should donate it so another little girl could enjoy it, but I couldn't bring myself to do it if it still fit.

Alone, hiding in my room, trying it on seemed like a good idea.

To my utter shock, even though I was almost thirteen, I could zip it up! I remember spinning around in my room, wishing I had a friend here to tell me how it looked. Sadly, I couldn't see for myself.

Mom had covered my full-length mirror, my dresser mirror, and the bathroom mirror after my accident, "so you won't feel bad every time you look at yourself." But it had been more than a year and a half, and I'd had loads of painful surgeries and also recoveries. Mom was homeschooling me, to her great dismay, and I wondered—with a dress this stunning on, how bad could I really look?

I whisked off the sheet covering my mirror, and I stared at myself.

The gown was a little too short, showing my ankles, and the bodice was tight, since I was just starting to have the beginnings of a chest, but with the sparkles and the pin-up floofs decorating it, I didn't even care. I stepped closer, looking at my own face.

It wasn't like everyone else's, but it wasn't grotesque. In fact, it sort of looked interesting and unique.

Where the unmarked side of my face had tiny holes and hairs, the burned side was smooth and rippled. On that side, I looked a little like a statue. I rummaged around in the box until I found the gold shoes that went with the dress. They had tiny, one-inch heels, and I slid my feet into them. Then I posed again, turning my left side, my damaged side, facing the mirror.

I smiled, and I looked really nice.

When I took this off, it was definitely going in the keep pile.

My door burst open, and Mom froze, holding my backpack in her outstretched hand. "You left this in the kitchen." Her lips compressed into a flat line. "What on earth are you doing?"

I blinked. "I—well, you said to clean my room, but it was already clean, so I thought I'd go through my old toys, and I found this—"

"Go through? It looks like you dumped out every toy you ever owned into a massive pile." But when her eyes tracked up to where I was standing, her eyes widened precipitously. "What on earth are you doing right now?"

"It still fits," I said lamely. "Can you believe it?"

"I'm downstairs, depressed that I can't audition for my play, and you're up here frolicking around in the most ridiculous outfit I've ever seen?" Her lip curled. "Why would you uncover the mirror? You're the only person in this house who's not forced to—" Her nostrils flared, and her mouth snapped shut.

Forced to look at me? It had to be what she was going to say. That was the moment I realized how horribly ugly I was. My own mother wished she didn't have to look at me. When she left, I tore that dress off and stuffed it in the trash can. The shoes were heavy enough to keep it tamped down. I stuffed all my toys back into the box and never donated a single one. In fact, I never opened that box again.

So when we land in La Guardia, I check the weather on my phone to see if it's a snow day. They're rare this early, but not unheard of. Thankfully, it's fifty-eight degrees—a *lovely* fall evening in New York. No snow. No delays.

"You excited to sleep in your own bed tonight?" Bea asks.

I shrug.

"I am," Jake says. "If you're indifferent to your place, you could always come back with me." He winks.

My heart races, but not in a good way. It occurred to me last night, as Jake was kissing me good night in front of my hotel room, that if things keep going well, one day he'll want to see me as bare as I was in that dressing room. He'll want to touch my shoulder.

The whole idea makes me sick.

"I'm kidding." Jake's brow furrows. "I'm not in a hurry."

"It's refreshing, really," Bea says. "To meet a girl who's not tripping him with her six-inch platform heels and trying to dump him into bed." She snorts. "Bunch of tramps, in and out of our place like—"

Jake kicks her.

"Make him buy new sheets first," Bea says. "That's all I'm saying."

"Eww," I say. "Just, ew." I grab my bag and hustle out of the plane before the people behind us get any ideas.

Not that there are many. We're in first class, thanks to Jake's face. They upgraded all three of us the second we checked in together. They said it was to keep anyone from bothering him, but I think it was because the flight attendant liked him and he *insisted* we all had to sit together.

The flight attendant in question's snapping photos of her and Jake as I wheel past. There are definitely some obnoxious things about dating a famous person. Jake catches up with me about two minutes later, taking my bag off my shoulder and slinging it over his.

"Why were you in such a rush?"

I shrug.

"I'm driving you home," he says. "I had someone from my agency drop off my car."

"What about me?" Bea asks.

"Please," Jake says. "As if lover boy isn't waiting at the exit with a rose clenched between his teeth."

I can't help my snort. But then, as we turn the corner past baggage claim, Easton's literally standing there with a goofy grin and a bouquet of red roses. None of the flowers are clenched between his teeth, but I swear, Jake was pretty darn close.

"See?" Jake hisses. "Pathetic."

"At least my boyfriend *wants* to sleep over." Bea lobs that one over her shoulder as she jogs toward Easton.

"Ouch," Jake says.

I drop a hand on his shoulder. "It's not you," I say. "Trust me. You are—I definitely—" I cough. "This isn't coming out right."

He slides his free hand through mine. "You don't need to explain. At some point, it'll feel right, and trust me. It *will* be right." His sly smile's adorable.

When we walk outside, I don't expect his ridiculous sports car to literally be waiting outside in the car-pickup line. A man hops out of the driver's side and hands him the keys. "Pickup on Sunday?"

Jake nods. "Thanks." He hands him something, and then he's loading my bag—thank goodness it's small—into the tiny trunk of his electric blue Nissan Z.

"Who was that guy, and what did you give him?" I ask, once he's pulling out into traffic.

"I have no idea who he is," Jake says. "Which is why I tipped him."

"You let someone you don't know drive your car?" I'm surprised. Most guys I know act like their car's their baby, at least if it's nice.

Jake shrugs. "Stuff never matters a lot to me. I mean, I try to take care of my things, but it's not worth stressing about."

"Really?"

He merges so fast, I'm flung back against the seat. "It's only money, O," he says. "If your problem can be solved with money, it's not a real problem." He winks.

I might be in trouble, because he says things like that, and I think he's pretty clever and balanced, too. I really, *really* like him. "So if you don't care about pedestrian things like money, then why did you buy a car that cost. . ." I pause. "Actually I have no idea what this would cost, but I'm guessing it was more than my Honda."

He glances at me sideways. "No one has ever asked me

why I bought this one, not even Bea." He turns back to the road, but his brow is furrowed. "Actually, it's stupid, the reason I picked this monstrosity."

"Wait," I say. "Don't you like your own car?"

"It's fun to drive." He grunts. "But I would have bought a less obnoxious color if this hadn't been my dream for more than a decade."

I'm confused.

"My dad promised me once that if I'd help him with a big job, he'd get me a Nissan Z. It was the car our mark drove. I had to do some dangerous and pretty scary things on that job, but it worked, and at the end, he didn't break his promise." He chuckles. "I failed to clarify that I wanted one that was larger than a pack of gum."

"He gave you a matchstick car?"

"He said that lesson of hammering down details was more valuable than a car would have been. I should've known he wasn't going to buy me a real car. I was nine, but I was pretty sore about it for a while. After staring at that stupid car for ten years. . ."

"I guess when you got your first big paycheck, you knew how to spend it."

"Exactly. This was the first thing I bought," Jake says. "The rest of my money's saved. I'm actually not a very big spender."

That doesn't surprise me. He doesn't wear brand names I haven't seen him paid to market. And if all his dad valued was money, it makes sense he'd be slow to spend his once he got it. "I bet that makes you an anomaly in Hollywood."

"It's why I spend all my free time here," he says. "And why my agency got me an apartment in LA. I refused to buy a ridiculous house, and they got sick of paying hotel bills, which I always insisted they cover in the contracts as a New York resident being asked to travel for work."

"Maybe your dad's lesson was worth something after all." One of my favorite songs starts on the radio before he can respond, and I start to sing along.

Jake goes utterly quiet.

After a moment, I stop. "Why aren't you singing?"

"There are very few things in the world I like as much as hearing you sing."

That makes me blush. "You can't just say stuff like that."

He drops his hand over mine. "I plan to keep speaking the truth so often that you finally accept it. I'm not sure who convinced you that you're less than you are, but I'm going to be the one who undoes that damage."

For some reason, that makes tears well up in my eyes. "No one did that."

"Someone," he says. "Otherwise, you'd know how stunning you are. In appearance, in talent, and in friendship, you're as good as it gets. Other than Bea, there's never been someone I couldn't get enough time with." He glances my way. "Until you."

On the next song, he sings with me, and that's even better.

The drive to my place flies by, and before I know it, we're parked and he's unloading my bag.

"I can take it from here." I hold out my hand.

He steps close—way too close, so that we're almost touching—and then he bites his lip, lowering his head until we're eye-to-eye. "I'm going to kiss you right here, Octavia Rothschild, so that you know exactly how much I like you. I'm going to kiss you so long, and so hard, that you have not a single doubt in your mind about all the many things I want to do to and with you." He smiles, and his dimples. . .*his wicked dimples*. . .and then he kisses me.

It's every single thing he said it would be.

Fireworks, an explosion, barking dogs—none of it would even register if it was happening right beside us. The world ceases to exist beyond Jake's arms, Jake's mouth, and Jake's words still ringing in my ears. And then, slowly, reluctantly, he pulls away.

"And now I'm going to carry your bag upstairs and place it in your entryway, and then I'm going to turn around and come back downstairs and get in my car." He runs one finger down the side of my face, on the left side.

My bad side.

"I'm doing this so you don't have to get as spooky as a horse eyeing a rippling Texas flag. Got it?"

I laugh. "Do horses hate Texas flags?"

"Texas flags specifically?" He shrugs. "No idea, but they hate every other flag I've ever seen near them. I had to ride in—"

"*Memory of Tomorrow*," I say.

"Stupid name, but it was a decent film," he says.

I laugh. "And you rode that white horse."

"Horse people call them greys," he says. "They get downright unreasonable about it, even if the horse isn't grey at all."

"I didn't realize you were funny without a script," I say. "What a relief."

"You." He shakes his head and points at me. "I've known you were funny all along. It's one of the things I like best about you."

Jake grabs my bag, and then he clicks the key to lock his car. He grabs my hand, and we're suddenly headed up.

"How do you know where my apartment is?"

"Did I mention that my agency is your agency? Bradley's

appallingly bad at choosing passwords—it's literally his birthday—so I can get anyone's address that you want." He squeezes my hand. "Ask me how fun it is to toilet paper Tom Cruise's house."

"You didn't."

He shrugs. "How else would I know he shouts and pumps his arm like an old man when he runs out wearing Sponge Bob boxers?"

"Sponge Bob?" I'm laughing harder because I have no idea whether he's serious.

"Sponge Bob and Patrick," he says. "Not even Squidward."

I'm laughing so hard when I open my front door that I'm worried I'll snort.

"Octavia?" My mother's standing in the kitchen in her underwear.

I scream.

Then I cover Jake's eyes. "What on earth are you doing here?" I shout.

Mom hasn't moved a hair, but she is glaring. "You said you'd be gone for two more weeks."

"I didn't say you could move in! Why would you be in my apartment?" I look around at the haphazard piles of crap all over my apartment. "And did you bring Oscar the Grouch with you? What is all this garbage?"

Mom wasn't the tidiest parent around, but we didn't live like this.

Jake pats my hand and whispers, "Can I have my eyes back?"

Mom swears loudly. "Is that Jake Priest?"

I clamp my hand down harder. "Go put on some clothes, Mom, right now."

Mom actually arches her back, thrusting her chest out. "I *am* dressed."

"I swear, I will kill you myself," I hiss.

She rolls her eyes. "Fine. *Fine!*" She saunters across the room and finally ducks into my bedroom.

I release Jake and collapse onto the couch in my family room. "My *mom's* here."

"So—you want me to go, right?" He's glancing back at the door to my bedroom, which is still wide open. I suppose if you're comfortable strolling around in your undies, why would you bother closing the door just to put more clothing on?

Mom comes out a moment later, clearly as curious as Jake. She's pulled an oversized t-shirt over her head, but that's it. I really wish I couldn't see the backside she's always bragging still looks like a teenager's.

It doesn't.

But it looks much better than someone who's almost fifty-four has any right to look. "I'm Miss Phillips." She bats her eyes.

Bats her eyes. Like she's auditioning for *Gone with the Wind.*

"Mom, this is Jake Priest." I can't help it if my tone's a little flat. "Now, can you please do me the favor of explaining why you're here, in my apartment, without my permission or even any notice?"

"I needed a place." She shrugs. "Mr. Phillips was bothering me."

Her husband Roy's a real jerk.

Other than Dad, they all have been. "That's when you get a hotel."

Her eye twitches. "I would, but the thing is, I'm between jobs."

She's always between jobs. Roy's probably canceled her

credit cards again. I don't even blame him. She spends money on the most ridiculous things.

"Can we talk in your room for a moment?" Mom literally shoves her face into her patented pout and glances Jake's way, like she's going to *flirt* him into listening to her.

"Jake was just leaving," I say. "Goodnight, Jake."

He opens his mouth like he wants to argue, but then he snaps it shut and nods. "Yep, I sure was. I'll see you in the morning."

I wish he hadn't added that. Mom will never let it go.

The second Jake shuts the door, Mom practically shouts, "You're actually dating him? How? He's about one million times too hot for you."

"I get it," I say. "Believe me. But he likes me, and I like him, so can we focus on where you'll be moving, and who's helping you get this crap all cleaned up?" That last bit's a joke. We both know it'll be me, but at least she could have the decency to act guilty or grateful or both.

"Are you in town for a while, then?"

"Just a day and a half," I say. "But you need to go back to Roy and apologize, because—"

"I won't." She folds her arms under her chest. "You don't get it, because you've never really even dated anyone, except. . ." She waves her hand. "Whatever this thing with Jake is."

"Mom."

"But if I go back there, and if I apologize, he wins, and he cannot win. I'm way too pretty for him, so he should be doing everything he possibly can to keep me happy. That's how it works." She grabs my wrist. "Which is why you can't possibly date Jake." She closes her eyes and shakes her head slowly. When she opens them again, she says, "Tavie, believe me when I say, you need to find a very rich, very ugly man. He'll be grateful, and he'll treat you so much better."

"Mom." I'm pulling my hand away when my door whips open.

"Mrs. Phillips, with all due respect, you're going to have to leave." Jake's eyes are flashing.

"I beg your pardon?"

"I know you're Octavia's mother, and I want to be polite, but I've been dying to figure out who treated her so badly. I couldn't fathom who would damage such a beautiful soul, but it was clearly you."

Mom blinks, dropping her hands at her side. "Have you been listening at the door?"

"Like a peeping Tom," he says, "yes. I have, absolutely, and that's how I know it was you." He steps closer, his eyes narrowing. "In my twenty-six years of life, I have never once punched a woman, but that's about to change if you aren't out of here by the time I reach the count of ten."

Mom turns toward me with the most disbelieving look on her face.

"One," Jake says.

Mom snorts.

"Two." Jake steps closer.

"You can't punch me," she says, spluttering. "I'm—I would charge you with assault, and that would be bad for your image."

"Three," Jake says. "I have plenty of money, and I bet my lawyers are better than my girlfriend's homeless, unjustifiably proud mother's." His lips flatten.

"Unjustifiably?" My mom would fixate on that.

Jake's mouth over-enunciates the word. "Four."

Mom straightens as if she's just now wondering whether he's serious. "I don't even have pants on."

"You better hurry and grab them," I say.

"Five." Jake smiles. "This is going to be really fun."

Mom practically leaps out of the room. Thankfully, I hear her rummaging around in my bedroom.

"Six," Jake shouts.

Mom whimpers.

"Seven," Jake says, not slowing down.

"Are you really going to hit her?" I ask.

"Do I look like someone who wouldn't follow through?"

I shake my head slowly.

"Good," he whispers. Then he raises his voice. "Eight, and tell your daughter to stop trying to distract me."

Mom shoots out of the room, her eyes wide, but at least she's wearing pants. Praise be. "I can't find my purse." She's looking around frantically.

"Nine."

Mom's hands are shaking, and I should hate this, but for some reason, it makes me want to laugh. He's really made Mom think he'll hit her. "I'm—Tavie, do you see my purse?"

I hand it to her, and I point at the door.

"Ten." Jake lunges at my mother, and she shoots out the door, stumbling over the threshold. She turns slowly, and rights herself. "Now that I'm *outside* of the house, let me tell you what I think about—"

I slam the door in her face.

Jake's smile grows until he's beaming. "You slammed it." He steps toward me. "So you're not mad?"

I shrug. "She'll be back. She's like a cockroach."

He laughs. "I can sense that."

"I'm sorry," I say. "She isn't perfect, but she's really not that bad. Plenty of other mothers were worse."

He presses a finger to my mouth. "Your mother *is* bad. She might be worse than the mothers who don't feed their children. Anyone in the world can feed a child that's hungry. Anyone in the world can wrap them in a blanket." He crouches until he's staring right at me. "But it takes a mother to convince such a gorgeous woman to believe the outrageous lie that she's ugly, and your mother has done that. I don't know why, but she's never doing it again. No one is." He runs one finger down the left side of my face so lightly, so slowly, that I can barely feel it. "You, Octavia Rothschild, are the most stunning woman I have ever seen. I've said it before, and I'll say it again and again until you finally start believing it."

CHAPTER 18
JAKE

One of my dad's favorite plays was to convince some rich guy that I was his kid. He'd ask for some kind of finder's fee, and then, like the little liar I was, after Dad got it, and after I'd convinced the poor man that I was his perfect, shining star, I'd escape out a window and he'd never find me again.

I've always worried that now that I've 'made it,' someone might recognize me and come after me for my part in the duplicity.

Thankfully, our faces change a lot in adolescence.

In fact, sometimes people I knew in junior high come shrieking up to me and I don't recognize them at all. I always try to be as nice as possible, because I'm hoping all the karma I didn't earn as a kid might be replaced by my generosity as an adult.

I'm not sure that donating a large chunk of my paycheck will really make up for the kinds of things Dad and I did, but it can't hurt. I suppose today's the day I find out what kind of life is possible. If the best people I've met are all liars, then maybe goodness is just unattainable. Now that I've reached the inn, Octavia by my side, I'm absurdly nervous.

"What will you do if Seren's here?" Octavia asks.

"That's why we're here at exactly seven-fifteen," I say. "She's always leading the staff meeting right now—the few night shift workers are leaving, very few people are stupid enough to be checking out now, and the day shift people are just showing up to clean. As they change over the front desk tasks, Seren meets with everyone."

I'm just lifting my hand to knock when Octavia asks, "How many employees do the Fansees have?"

I freeze. "Really? That's what you want to know right now?"

She slides her arm through the space between my body and my elbow. "You look like you're marching to the town square to stand in front of a gun-squad." She bumps me with her hip. "You need to relax. So yes, how many employees do your parents have?"

"Dave and Seren had fifteen, last I checked," I say. "But one or two of those only comes on weekends." Before I can knock, Dave whips the door open.

He's smiling his enormous, eye-sparkling smile. "Jake!" He hugs me immediately, dragging my body against his.

"How'd you know I was here?" I barely manage to gasp.

"We got the new Ring doorbell." Dave points. "I can't believe you came early—of your own volition." He turns immediately toward Octavia. "I really, really hope you're here to tell me that you and this stunning beauty are getting married or something."

Poor Octavia's face blanches. "We—we just started dating."

Dave shrugs. "I mean, crazier things have happened.

Love's a leap." He slaps me on the back. "Come on in and tell me why you came while Seren's busy."

I swear under my breath. Sometimes I forget how freaking smart he is, because he's so darn happy and kind. "Um, well."

Octavia's head tilts. "How did you know—"

Dave's laughing. "We have five kids, you know, and they're all as different as they can be. But Jake? His excellent timing is never an accident."

"Oh." Octavia's looking around intently, as if she's going to be quizzed on the contents of the Fansee's small cottage. "It's nice to meet you."

"Same." He grins again. "Even if you're here as a buffer for my son who knew Killian would be sleeping, Seren would be busy, and I'd be right here, going over numbers." He turns to catch my eye, daring me to correct him.

"Can we sit?" I start walking across the family room to the breakfast table.

"Of course." Dave trots ahead of me and closes his laptop, sliding it away from him. He stacks his crazy, tracking notebook in which he scrawls a bunch of numbers every day on top of the laptop and sits, leaning on his elbows.

Octavia waits for me to sit down and takes a chair behind me. She really didn't want to come, but when I told her I needed her with me, she didn't argue. She just agreed. I don't want to evaluate why I wanted her here so badly, but I'm pretty sure it's because I'm scared this is going to go badly.

"So, the thing is, a few years ago, my dad started sending me letters through—"

"His old partner Quintin?" Dave nods. "Go on."

"Wait, you knew that?" I swallow.

Dave chuckles. "You were a kid, Jake. Give us some credit for paying attention to the people you met."

I'm shocked. I was so careful to make sure. . . Dave's an

easy guy to underestimate, but that makes me nervous. Could he have been cheating on Seren all this time, and no one even knew because he looks so trustworthy? "Did you read all the letters he sent me?"

Dave shakes his head. "We wouldn't have read them even if they came through the system. We tried to give you the chance to learn to make your own choices, even ones we disagreed with."

"Well, the thing is, one of the things Dad told me after his letters started coming through. . ." I clear my throat. "He told me that you. . ."

I can't say it.

There's a reason I've never asked him about this. Now that we're down to it, I don't want to know. I'm about to make something up and get out of here.

Octavia drops her hand on my knee under the table. Her voice is soft and even. I've come to expect that from her. Most girls get shrill or demanding or acerbic in times of stress, but not Octavia. "Maybe it's easier if you text him an image of what your dad sent."

Dave's eyes rise. "What did he send you? Is it something about me?" In spite of his curiosity, he doesn't look the slightest bit guilty or nervous. That calms me down some. One thing I'm very good at doing is reading people in the moment. It's probably the thing Dad drilled into me the most. Dave's either a complete sociopath, or he's not worried in the slightest.

"I—I'll text you the image. Octavia's right. That's best." My hands are fumblier than they've ever been, but I do manage to pull up one of the images and text it to him. Then I swallow, inhale slowly, and force myself to look up as he pulls it up on his phone.

His eyes widen. He zooms in, and then his mouth drops open. "How did he get this?"

Not, "What on earth is this fake photo?" Or "That's not me!" Just "How?" My stomach sinks.

"My dad's very, very good at data mining," I say. "He used to train other people how to live like us." I clear my throat. "For a fee, of course."

"Okay, so one of his people somehow dug this up?" Dave sets his phone down and looks at me. "And why did this upset you so much?"

I can hardly believe what he's saying. "I mean, well, I know you and Seren aren't my real parents, but I do think—"

"Are you religious?" Dave's eyebrows rise. "I didn't realize that."

I blink.

"I think what Jake's trying to say is that he was disappointed when his father told him you were unfaithful to your wife. His dad used this as leverage to force Jake into doing things he didn't want to do, I believe. He threatened to send this to your wife if Jake didn't listen to him, and now he's out of prison, so you can see how that's become more dangerous. He could send this or other images like it to Seren at any moment."

The front door opens, and Seren darts through, her eyes wide.

Shoot.

"Oh, hey." I stand up. "We were just—"

"David Fansee, what on earth did I just see?" She waves a paper at him, and I realize with horror that it's the photo I just sent. It's Dave, leaning back against the headboard of a bed, clearly naked, with just a sheet covering things no one should see, smiling. There's a woman's head in the bottom part of the image, and it's clearly not Seren's.

"I am so sorry," I whisper. "I was actually trying to avoid this exact situation."

Dave hops to his feet, but he doesn't look upset. He's smiling. "Jake's dad sent him that."

Seren starts laughing. "I've been telling you to take that hard drive in to recover our honeymoon photos. If you'd done it, I wouldn't have to use this one, *with another woman in it.*" She waves it at him. "Don't worry. I'll crop her out before I tape it to the fridge."

"I told you, it's not that I don't have motivation." He snatches the printed image out of her hand. "It's that you make such *good* treats that they always overwhelm my desire to rediscover my six pack."

She laughs and grabs the paper back, balling it into a wad and tossing it at the trash can. She misses and it bounces across the tile floor, coming to rest by my foot.

Seren's eyes followed its trajectory, and now she's staring at me and Octavia. "Oh, you didn't tell me we had company."

"Are you kidding? Jake's car must be parked outside," Dave says. "It's so obnoxious that it's hard to miss."

I stand up, too freaked out by their bizarre reaction to know what to do. Are they in some kind of open relationship? Why does Seren think it's funny?

"We parked on the street," Octavia says. "There was a truck unloading something. . ."

"Sit back down." Dave points. "We can explain this." But he's smiling like it's all no big deal.

"Do you not care that he cheated on you?" I need to be looking at Seren when I ask. If she's faking, I'll see the signs.

Seren's smile is a knowing one. "Just listen to your dad."

I sit back down with a sigh. Octavia immediately takes my hand. I knew I was right to bring her.

"But how did Seren get the picture?" Octavia asks. "Did you accidentally group text it?" She's looking at me.

I whip my phone out, but no, just Dave.

"There's some kind of weird glitch with our phones," Dave says. "We managed to disconnect them, but anything you send through iMessage to me goes to her laptop, too. She probably got it the second you sent it. They pop up whenever she's using her laptop."

"I did run out of that meeting pretty quickly," Seren says. "But they're probably relieved. They were getting a little annoyed with me talking about the cost savings of installing more energy efficient fixtures."

"I'm confused, too. You thought this was evidence that I was having an affair?" Dave reaches down and grabs the wadded-up paper off the ground and slowly smooths it out. He points at his shoulder. "This happened before I ever met your mom."

I frown. "You look—"

"He's gained some weight," Seren says, "but the Fansees are like Keanu Reeves." She shrugs. "They never age." She slugs his shoulder. "The jerk."

"If you make me lose a lot of weight, I might be all saggy and baggy." He sighs.

"It's not me making you lose weight," she says. "It's your doctor." She turns toward me. "At his last appointment they told him he's prediabetic."

Dave unbuttons his shirt and yanks one shoulder down, showing me a tattoo. "We really should have gone swimming more often. I blame the New York weather. You haven't seen my shoulder?"

I lean closer, squinting. There's some kind of tree tattoo. Or is it a shamrock? "What is that?"

"It's our family symbol," Seren says. "I got one too, on our honeymoon."

Dave points at his shoulder in the image. "See? No tattoo. Pre-Seren Dave did all kinds of stupid things." He shakes his shirt back into place and wraps his arm around Seren. "She knew I wasn't a saint before, though."

"I mean, are you really a saint now?" She leans her head on his shoulder.

"What were the little red blobs?" Octavia asks.

"For our symbol, we chose a tree," Dave says. "To represent that we're growing our own family now, but we gave the tree a four-leaf-clover shape, because we believe that we make our own luck." The look he gives Seren is almost disgusting, it's so sweet. "And the *blobs*, as you phrased it, are small, red, apple-hearts. Each of them has a single letter printed beside them. The first had an E. Then a B. The next was a J, an A, and a K." Dave looks at me.

"Our names?"

Octavia says, "Aw, that's so sweet. I love it."

"Except Seren only has the tree with one heart," Dave mutters.

"Tattoos hurt a lot more than I expected." She taps her fingers on the table. "I went to get the other apple-hearts added two different times, but I had to wait for a while for my turn, and I always chickened out before they were ready for me and left."

"She does love you guys," Dave says. "Just not as much as she hates needles."

"To be fair, if I'd known how much it would hurt before I got the first one, I'd have backed out on the matching tattoos entirely."

"I've never seen yours either," I say.

Dave clears his throat. "It's in a place you'd be unlikely to see."

Ew.

"Which is good," Seren says, "because otherwise, the kids would probably be upset I only have Emerson listed on the heart. He was the only one of you I'd met when we got it done."

"But how did you have those photos to begin with?" Octavia asks all the great questions.

"Did you want to tell the story, or should I?" Seren's lip's twitching.

Dave scowls. "There isn't a story. My stupid friend Bernie asked me to housesit and didn't tell me he'd installed security cameras."

"Wait," I say. "You didn't *mean* to take these?"

The expression of irritation on Dave's face is hilarious. "Of course not. I'm not a weirdo."

"Hey, I'm not ready to rule that out yet," I say. "You vacuum out the utensil drawer once a month."

"That's just good hygiene," Dave says.

"And I'm not sure photos—if both people want them—*are* weird," Octavia says.

"Really?" I turn toward her. "You don't say."

Seren's got her fingers stuffed in her ears and she's saying, "Lalala."

Dave grabs her arms and tugs them down with a smile. "Anyway, when Bernie was checking the surveillance feed, it told him when there was. . ." He coughs. "Motion at an unexpected time. He saw what I did at his place, and he took issue with it. To make his point, he took some still shots and did more or less what your mom just did, shoving them at me."

"And you never got to housesit again," Seren says.

"That was a real *trial* for me," Dave says. "Bernie's stupid yorkie wouldn't go outside to potty if it was raining. Do you know how much pee I had to clean up that weekend?" He shakes his head. "He deserved what he got, snooping around on what I did while I kept his house clean and his tiny, cricket-of-a-dog alive."

The next half hour is one of my favorite breakfasts of my life. Octavia slides right into the conversation like she's always been a part of the family. She makes jokes, she laughs at theirs, and she even manages to make a reference back to both Bernie's video camera and Seren's fear of needles before we finish eating the eggs, turkey bacon, and cinnamon toast Seren makes.

And when we're done, Octavia insists on loading the dishwasher, which wins her lots of points with Dave since that's usually his job. Even though we're not supposed to get together to celebrate my party until much later, Killian rolls out of bed at the end of breakfast, his nose turned up and sniffing. He rubs his eyes. "Is that bacon?"

Seren laughs. "I saved you some."

He wraps his blanket a little tighter, but I notice that he's not wearing a shirt underneath.

I stand up. "Please tell me you have pants on, at least," I say. "I brought my girlfriend."

"Wait, you brought a dirty little tramp home to meet Mom and Dad?" Killian's eyes widen.

"She's not a tramp." I slug his shoulder.

Which makes him drop his blanket.

Seren starts shouting, because, in fact, he was not wearing pants.

"Ew," Dave says. "Tighty whities? Really?" He groans. "A son of mine."

Before Killian has even finished the breakfast Seren saved for him, and just after Octavia finishes the dishes, Ardath shows up. She looks pretty tired. "You okay?" I ask. She's always been the least talkative of my siblings, but when she's tired, she barely says a word.

"I'm fine." She yawns. "Stuck with an overnight. Couldn't sleep at home—they're doing construction next door." She points at the hall. "Can I?"

Seren waves her back. "You need your beauty rest."

"Sick burn," Killian shouts at Ardath's retreating form. "Mom says you're an ug-oh." Then he freezes and turns slowly toward Octavia. "I'm sorry. Should I not have said burn?"

Octavia's eyes widen, and she half-smiles. "No, I'd say my traumatic reaction to that word has sufficiently healed. You can use it with impunity."

"Does that mean it's fine?" he hisses at me.

I just roll my eyes.

But Ardath laughs. "Educated people need to scale things back a few levels when they're here." She shakes her head in commiseration, clearly talking to Octavia. "You get used to it."

"I guess when you save people as part of your job, you get used to adjusting the vocabulary you use," I say.

Ardath's still smirking as she ducks into my old room to sleep. It was turned into a spare bedroom about eight minutes after I moved out. I guess I should be grateful they didn't take the opportunity of the vacancy to adopt another kid.

Not that any of us were ever formally adopted, but you know.

"Hey, does anyone want to play a game?" Dave asks.

"Dad and his games." Killian scrunches his nose. "No, thanks."

"I love games," Octavia says. When Dave practically

sprints across the room, she smiles, and I realize she might have been serious.

"You don't have to," I hiss. "He'll get over it."

"I really do love games," she says. "I was an only child, so when I was a kid, I'd make my brown bear and my giraffe each pretend to pick a game piece—and we'd play Monopoly."

"That may be the saddest thing I've ever heard," Killian says.

Octavia sticks out her lower lip. "Oh, no. Do you feel sorry enough for me that you'd like to let me beat you?"

Killian frowns. "I know you're baiting me, but I still find myself saying yes."

I slap his back, and this time, no clothing falls to the ground. "Good man."

In the end, we all get roped into playing a bizarre, 3D printed version of Settlers of Catan. When Easton and Bea show up, arms full of wedding samples they want us to evaluate, they get roped into joining us, too.

The party isn't anything special.

Seren makes my favorite pie while we all argue over resources and something called a development card. I don't win, but to my surprise—and Dave's—Octavia does.

"It's because she was so nice," Dave says. "Everyone kept making trades they shouldn't have made."

"And no one was watching her road length," Killian says. "Jake, your girlfriend's a bigger snake than you." But he's smiling, and so is she.

It's funny, but somehow, even with all these people who care about me, I never really felt like I fit. I didn't think that would ever change, but by bringing an outsider, I finally feel like I belong. That makes me think...

Maybe they haven't changed.

Maybe it was me all along.

As everyone jokes and chats around me, Octavia zinging Killian as much as he goes after her, I wonder what might have changed me. Octavia told me to trust Dave and Seren. She made me tell them what's been bothering me—scaring me—for the past few years, and she was right.

It wasn't the horrible threat I worried it was.

My dark view of the world, my experience with so very many dishonest, untrustworthy people had colored my view. My dad must have counted on that when he sent me the photos. For the first time, I know the truth, and now I feel like there's nothing in the world that can ruin this day.

Until I hear Killian going head to head with Bea.

She trots out the same threat she's used for years. "I'll tell them about the funnel." She scowls. "Unless you apologize."

I consider coming clean to everyone. I'm tired of her holding it over our heads. But before I can say anything, Ardath walks into the room. "You will *not* tell them about the funnel, or I'll tell them about *your* thing." Ardath never jokes.

She's the strangest person in our family, hands down.

I'm a little bit terrified of her, honestly. She's a good person, but she's weird. All she does is work, and when she's not working, she's sleeping. When she's not sleeping, she does and says as little as she can, and then she leaves.

If someone told me she was a drone, I'd believe them.

Thankfully, Emerson gets there then, and Elizabeth immediately starts complaining about how she's so hungry she could eat an elephant. It's not as shocking, since she's been married for. . .I do the math.

"So, are you pregnant yet?"

Elizabeth blinks. Then she rounds on Emerson. "I'm going to kill you."

Emerson swears. "I swear, I didn't say a word, and it's Jake. A hundred bucks says he was testing you."

"He wouldn't—" Elizabeth freezes. "You got me, didn't you?"

Seren shrieks then, and some kind of massive family hug-fest follows. Octavia, Ardath, and I retreat slowly.

"You're not about to hug me, are you?" Ardath asks. "I'm not a very touchy-feely person."

"It's one of the few things we have in common," I say.

"Please," Ardath says. "If I told your girlfriend about all the girls you touched and felt, she'd be sick to her stomach."

Octavia laughs, and I realize. . .Ardath just made a joke. Is it the first one she's made? Or have I missed the others?

Once people finally calm down, or at least, as much as they're going to, Seren pulls out a massive chocolate cake.

"I know cheesecake's your favorite, Jake," she says. "But everyone else likes this better."

"Seriously?" Bea asks. "On his birthday, you make what we want?" She shakes her head.

Octavia looks genuinely upset on my behalf.

"She's got a cheesecake in there, too," I whisper. "She'll let them fall on this like locusts, and then she'll pull it out. They all know it, but they play along. She does this for literally every party. At first, I thought it was kinda corny, but it grows on you." Actually, I've always thought it was dumb. But, tonight, explaining it to Octavia, I feel like I'm in on the silliness.

So when everyone has a slice of cake and I ask for one, Seren gets a sly look on her face and says, "Actually. . ." Then she shoves my hand away, stands up, and pulls the cherry cheesecake out of the fridge. "That cake was just to keep them away from this so you'd have leftovers."

"Oh, ho, I can eat that, too," Dave says.

Seren points at the fridge door, and I realize she really did tape a cropped photo up there.

"Oh, gross." Ardath's shaking her head. "Why are we all staring at a naked picture of Dad right now?"

Seren laughs. "It's inspirational. That Dave got a lot more hot women than this one does."

Before I can even get my slice of cheesecake, Dave's crossed the room, wrapped his arms around Seren, and he's dipping and kissing her. We all groan and shout our protests right on cue, but like the cake gag, it feels different this time. It feels. . .corny, yes, but also good.

On the plane the next morning, Octavia takes my hand. "Thank you," she says.

"For what?"

"Last night—actually, the whole day yesterday was one of the best days I've ever had. Your family's kind of my dream."

"Your dream? I don't understand."

"They're so. . ." She sighs. "They're just, I don't know. Yes, they're a little cheesy, and they can be loud, and Killian's a mess. Ardath is a little. . .different. But they all love each other so much, and it feels like you've stepped into some kind of hokey Christmas film when you sit down in Seren's kitchen."

I actually get it. "I think that's what I didn't like about it when I was growing up."

"The Christmas movie thing?"

I shake my head. "It felt unreal. Sometimes it felt like they were all acting, like they were trying to deliver lines or something."

"Are you sure you weren't the one who felt like he had to deliver lines?" Her eyes are soft.

I lean over as people pass us in the aisle, and I kiss her right on the mouth. "You are brilliant," I whisper against her mouth. "That's exactly true. This weekend, for maybe the first time, I felt like I fit right in, and it's because of you. You brought me into the warm, happy, bright circle."

After I drop her off, I can't help thinking that *this* is the goal. My whole life, I've loved Bea. She makes me a better version of the person I already was, but she and I didn't *fit*. Octavia's different. She's as shiny and warm as Bea, but she *fits*. She gets me without even trying. It's like she has the key to unlocking my brain. Or maybe it's my heart.

She makes me the best version of Jake.

When I open my own front door, I'm still smiling. It was a very quick trip, and I have to report back on set in two hours, on a Sunday afternoon, but it was totally worth it.

"So you *do* come back here occasionally." Dad's lying on the sofa, but he sits up. "Thank goodness." He swings his legs over the edge and drops his elbows on them. "I'm ready, finally, to repay Dave and Seren for their heroic efforts over a decade ago, and you're going to help me."

CHAPTER 19

JAKE

I drop my bag and toss my coat on the chair, and then I smile. "Not this time, *Dad*. You're on your own, and you should know, we won't be easy to break."

Dad stands. "So you and the Fansees are a 'we' now?" His eyebrows rise.

"We are." I fold my arms. "I talked to Dave this weekend, and it turns out, that stupid photo you sent was from *before he ever met* Seren." I drop into the chair. "So that's not going to do a thing. Seren actually laughed about it."

His face falls, and he sits silently for a moment. Then he starts to laugh.

It's a scary laugh.

Unhinged.

"After fifteen years locked away, that's what you thought I was going to use?" He finally stops laughing. "Oh, Jake, you never cease to amuse me." He sighs. "No, no, I didn't expect that to fool you this long." He shakes his head. "You were living with those idiots, and you didn't figure out that he's entirely besotted?"

I frown.

"Marriage is the oldest, the original con, and Dave got tricked years and years ago."

Trust my dad to turn loving devotion in marriage into a grift. "Then what are you going to do?"

"Maybe I shouldn't tell you," Dad says, dropping back to his seat on the sofa, but perching on the very edge this time, his hands steepled. "You might run right over and tell them my plan."

"I will," I say. "Whether you tell me up front, or I have to figure it out, I'll tell them it's you. I'll tell the police it's you, too. That's why you should just give up now."

Dad's laugh this time is downright maniacal. "Jake, Jake, what did I teach you? Have you forgotten everything?" He points at the ottoman. "Shift closer so I can show you a few things."

I hate that I listen to him. "Just show me already."

"You know, babies imprint so easily." He clucks. "You were just a little guy when they took you away from me. They thought they got to you *just* in time, but they didn't know that I had an ace-in-the-hole. I always do. Don't you remember that?"

I'm annoyed now. "Is that why you wound up imprisoned for fifteen years?"

"I'm a patient man." He doesn't look the least bit ruffled. It's irritating.

And a little nerve-wracking.

"I'm going to tell you up front that I'm going to destroy them with your help or without it, so if you're smart, you'll help me. It's the right play." He drops a file on the ottoman. "Your *perfect,* wannabe-stepfather has been sexually harassing maids and support staff in that hotel for years."

"That's clearly a lie," I say.

"Look at the file."

I flip through the statements. It's a bunch of signed affidavits of women, which Dad easily could have paid for, but when I'm about to toss them at him, I realize I recognize one of the photos.

Yvonne.

She had just gotten to New York, and she was desperate for work. I wasn't sure why she just didn't show up for work her third week. She took one paycheck and left. It felt strange at the time. I read her statement, my certainty slowly eroded word by word.

But then, I think about Octavia. If she was here, what would she tell me? She'd tell me to believe in Dave. She'd tell me that I *know* him. And she's right. I also know my dad. He's a master at hiding things, but when I look at him, there's an almost undetectable nervousness beneath his polished calm.

"You made this up," I say. "They're all fake."

Dad smiles. "You're not such a moron after all." He snorts. "Of course I did. Those idiots who raised you are as boring as they look."

"It won't stand," I say.

"It doesn't have to hold up in court," Dad says. "The lawsuits, and the way they keep popping up over and over. . ." He shrugs. "It'll destroy their company. People will believe that where there's smoke, there's fire. Their hotel will go under—collateral damage of my smear campaign."

"You didn't even ask the women to lie—you *planted* the women."

Dad points at me, his finger wagging, and his smile widening. "That's the first time I've been proud of you in a long time. Normally I'd never have been stupid enough to run a con with that idiot warden in a place I couldn't escape, but I needed money to pay the women I was using, because the Fansees were too *good*. By the time I realized the warden's greed was going to expose us, it was too late. But one good thing came of that whole debacle. I paid enough women to put together my revenge."

"You really do need to stop obsessing," I say. "Do you realize that you spent the last fifteen years of your life trying to prepare for one single job?" I scoff. "A job without an upside."

"Oh, I beg to differ." Dad leans closer. "Some jobs pay in more than cash. Revenge is going to feel very, very good. It's their fault I partnered with that idiot warden, which makes the second round of time I spent their fault, too."

"Okay, but now I know what you're doing." I shrug. "I'll just testify against you, and they'll believe me." I smirk. "I am your son, after all."

"Actually, about that." He pulls another folder out and drops it on top of the other. "You're not."

"What?" He's not making sense.

"Ace in the hole, remember?" Dad pats the top of the folder. "I know you were never a very good student, so I'll summarize." He leans closer and drops his voice. "You're not my son. Your mother was, however, my whore of a sister. She fell in love with the single most famous serial killer in North America, and then she got pregnant with you on a disturbing conjugal visit that wasn't even supposed to be allowed." He shudders. "Your birth made headlines across the entire country. You can look it up. Your real name's Kimball Frankfurter."

"But. . ." I frown. "That can't be true. I've seen my birth certificate."

"It gets better. In addition to spreading her legs for that disgusting man, my sister was actually taking orders from him. They found out about two weeks after you were born that she'd killed three people under his direction. She was living in Texas, sadly, so that was enough to get her lethal injection."

"She—you said you didn't know where my mom went after she dumped me on you."

He shrugs. "That much was true. Heaven? Hell? Who knows?"

"But I don't see how—"

Dad smacks me, his open hand making a loud slap against my cheek. "Think, idiot. How much do you think the American public will like hearing that their little golden darling was the son of two murderers?" He can't seem to stop gloating. "You'll lose it all. Public support, fame, money, and the ridiculous little family you seem so grateful for."

I shake my head.

"You don't think so?" Dad snatches the folder. "Let's see what happens, then."

"Wait," I say.

"You just realized your girlfriend wouldn't look at you the same ever again, didn't you?" He cackles.

"Shut up."

His laughing just gets louder. "Ah, Jake." He shakes his head and wipes his tears. "You thought you were a baddie, but you're such a baby, still. Now, you can choose to help me, or I can go ahead and give all the paperwork about your true parentage to the media. They'll know just what to do with it." He pats my knee. "What'll it be?"

CHAPTER 20
JAKE

I thought I was pretty awesome. Dad was right about that.

In school, no one dared mess with me. I gathered information and kept records of everything I found. I used it whenever necessary, just as Dad taught me. By high school, I started to feel a little bad about it doing it, because I'd started to see another way.

Kindness.

Loyalty.

Sacrifice.

I wanted it, and I was fascinated by it, but I never trusted it.

Until two days ago, I never felt like I fit in with my foster family. I wasn't sure why. I thought it might have been because I still had a father. I told myself it was, like my dad always said, because the Fansees were unbearable do-gooders.

Victims.

I was born to be a warrior, a taker, not a patsy.

Imagine my surprise to discover that I really *am* the son of two infamous murderers. At least warriors and invaders like Vikings or Saracens were honest about their violent intentions and proclivities. They were raised in a culture that celebrated their barbarity.

No one celebrates murder.

There's no narrative where I'm the child of anyone good.

After I manage to film the scene I agreed to do today, barely, I stumble back to my apartment. Blessedly, my dad—er, my uncle—is gone. I spend more than half of the nine hours I could have slept digging around for and reading articles on my parents.

My disgusting, horrible, awful parents.

They were every bit as terrible as my uncle described. In fact, I'd have said few people were as bad as my dad, but it turns out my dad was closer to the pope than he was to my real biological father.

And my crackpot mother might be worse yet.

She fell in love with him via *email* after he'd already been convicted.

No wonder I don't fit in with the Fansees. No wonder helping my 'dad' came so easily to me. I was a monster all along, from the very most basic level of my DNA on both sides.

When Octavia calls the next morning, it wakes me up with *just* enough time I can shower before showing up for my scene. I look like death when I roll up, but the makeup people are miracle workers.

I should be relieved that I'm able to work, but I'm not. A Viking wouldn't struggle with their true nature, so why should I? But that night, when I'm finally done, and Jane sends me home, I text Octavia.

Dinner?

She likes the text, so I tell her I'll pick her up in twenty minutes.

Before I can leave, May jogs up, waving her arms. "Hey, any chance I can grab a ride?"

"Oh, shoot," I say. "I'm about to go pick up Octavia, and I have a two -seater car." I point.

"Where are you picking her up?"

I rattle off her hotel.

"That's where they have me staying." She beams. "If you can just drop me off there, that would be amazing."

"Sure."

I jerk my thumb at the passenger door. She must be able to read my mood, because she spends the whole ride texting on her phone, probably with her boyfriend.

My mind works frantically the entire ride. I've worked out one way out of this mess—one—but it's a nasty one. Sadly, any way I look at it, this is the only way. When I get to the hotel, I wait for May to get out, and then I press my head against the steering wheel and think it all through one last time.

There's a tapping on the glass.

I whip up my head, prepared to chew May out, but it's not her.

It's Octavia.

She's even more breathtaking than I remembered. It's like every time I see her—fragile and strong, smooth and raw, brave and scared, fury and forgiveness, all in one—it breaks me all over again. Tears actually well up in my eyes, and I have to shove them back down.

When I get out, she hugs me. "I know it's only been a day since we saw each other last, and I know this is kind of silly, but I *missed you*." She looks up at me with a half-smile. "And I know I shouldn't say this, but the thing is, I always wondered how people could possibly know stuff like this, and now, for the first time, I get it."

Huh?

"Jake Priest, I've been a fangirl for a long time, and I knew you had a gorgeous body, and I knew your dimples were amazing and your sparkling eyes made women swoon. I knew I could stare at your poster for an hour, but now that I know *you*, you're not what I thought you were." She rests a hand against my cheek. "I realized in the past day, while I was missing you, while everything reminded me of you, that I *love you*, Jake Priest."

She giggles, and it's not annoying at all. It's light and bubbly and joyful.

"Why do I keep saying your first and last name?" She shrugs. "I don't know, and maybe this is way too soon, but I—"

"We need to break up," I blurt. I hate myself for using what she just said to do what I need to do, but it will make things easier and more believable, and this has to happen. For her sake.

She freezes.

Then she laughs. "Ha." She slaps my chest. "Good one. You almost got me."

I shake my head. "It's not a joke."

She stiffens.

"I really like you, and you're all the things I said, but this is just too much." I step backward. "I just. . .can't. I can't do this anymore."

Her lower lip trembles, and I scramble around in my brain for *any* other way, but there isn't one.

"I'm truly sorry."

Before I can say anything else, she nods once, tightly, spins on her heel, and marches woodenly toward the lobby.

It feels. . .too easy. I know it's awful, but I sort of hoped she'd argue with me about it. I thought. . .I really am the devil. I just dumped her and I'm sore that she didn't push harder to keep me around?

Ugh.

"That was. . ." May's baring her teeth on the other side of the car. "Really, really brutal."

I glare. "What are you doing here? That was private."

"I'm so sorry," she says. "But I took my backpack and left my purse." She points. "I didn't realize it until I got to my room and. . .no swipe card."

I try to release some of my anger, but I can't seem to do it. "Well, grab it." I hit the unlock button. "And get out of here."

"Jake—"

I throw up my hand. "Don't." I do not have the patience to deal with anything else right now.

"But, Jake—"

"I said *don't.*"

"I lied," she whispers.

"Huh?" What's she talking about?

"I don't have a boyfriend." Her eyes are darting all over, from me to the car, and back to me. "I told you that, because I knew you had a girlfriend, and I was desperate to do the movie with you."

"You were that desperate to launch your career?" I practically spit the words out. "You shouldn't have lied about it. It's not like I can't work with someone if they are single."

"I wasn't desperate to get the part," she says. "I've just been obsessed with you for *so* long. I knew if I didn't fake having a boyfriend, you'd realize how I felt about you immediately." She circles the car. "I'm sure dealing with a breakup is hard, so let me just say that I'm here." She touches my arm.

"And there's nothing you could want that I wouldn't be happy to do."

I leap backward, my eyes hard. "Good, then do this." I lean down, the bitter words coming easily. "Go away. If I see you for one single minute when we aren't working, I'll never talk to you again, not a word that isn't a line."

She flinches, like I'm a monster, and it feels like the first *right* thing in my life right now. She should flinch—she senses that I'm telling the truth. But her reaction's also kind of a joke. She's nearly as bad as I am, coming on to me eight seconds after I've dumped my girlfriend. What kind of person does that?

Maybe we deserve each other, but I'm too wrecked to even consider torturing myself with someone like her. She *is* a good actress. I thought she was the girl-next-door in all but location.

Why does everyone lie, even people who seem so nice? When I get back to my place, my uncle's waiting for me, outside the door as I requested.

"You didn't go in," I say.

"I couldn't." He glares. "You changed the locks."

I smile. "I sure did." The one good thing that happened today.

"And you told me to come an hour ago, so I've been waiting up here this whole time."

My smile broadens. "You told me who I was yourself." I pause. "So now I'll tell you who you're trying to bully." I step closer, our faces inches apart. "You told me your plan yesterday, but today you can hear my terms. I've dumped the burned girl." I manage to say that without flinching. "You thought my feelings for her were a weakness." I scoff. "I used her, just like you used me."

"Bravo," my uncle says. "I really thought you liked her."

My nostrils flare. "You said it yourself. I'm an excellent actor."

"Perhaps the student has surpassed the master," he says. "Go on. Tell me what you want now."

"I'll hire you as my manager—but you're not my father. To the whole world, you'll be Mr. Kingsley. No one will know you're my uncle, and if you follow that stipulation, telling people you've already told that it was a joke, then you'll get your twenty percent of my cut."

"Okay," he says. "And?"

"And then you'll have skin in the game." I smile. "Because I make a *lot* of money."

He frowns.

"You want revenge on the Fansees, but that bores me." I shake my head. "You'll drop that, or I'll release the information about my parentage to the media myself, and you'll lose your gravy train." I fold my arms. "Those are my terms. You can work for me, but you'll remember that *you work for me.*"

I expect an outburst, or maybe another slap.

He smiles. "It's taken twenty years, but son, I'm finally proud of you."

Even though I just beat the devil himself, I've never been more depressed in my life.

CHAPTER 21
OCTAVIA

Cinderella's fairy godmother offered her one fabulous night.

She knew going into the evening that her carriage was made of pumpkins. She knew her clothing wasn't going to last. She knew it was all beautifully temporary.

What the movie doesn't show is how devastating it is to get a glimpse of your heart's desire. It makes losing it so much harder than never having had it.

But I'd do it all over again.

When someone flinches at the sight of me, I close my eyes and imagine Jake barging into my apartment and telling my mother off. When I read a nasty comment online, I remember him telling me over and over that I'm the most beautiful person he ever met.

He said he'd tell me every day, and he has.

Because I remember how he sounded when he said it. He may have been my boyfriend for less time than milk can sit on your fridge shelf without souring, but it was enough to change me.

Bea comes out in her lacy dress. "You ready?"

I force a smile. "I love that."

Bea rolls her eyes. "No one really loves what they settle for. This was our second choice, and we both know it. There's no reason to pretend, not with me."

"He's still not answering?"

She sighs. "He dumped you, okay. It made no sense, but then why would he cut us all off? What's going on that we don't understand?" Bea starts pacing again. "We have our album shoot today, and then we have to go back home. I hate this, because he has weeks left, and I just can't disappear and hope he'll come to his senses. Jake's not smart with stuff like that. You have to shove him the right direction or he gets confused."

I hate this almost as much as the moment Jake dumped me.

Even though I felt *so* stupid in that fragment of time. What kind of idiot confesses her *love* to someone who's about to dump her? Read the room, Octavia, geez. To make matters worse, I realized as I walked back inside that his stupid co-star May was standing on the other side of the car the whole time.

She heard my pathetic confession and his breakup soliloquy.

I'm sure they've laughed about it together.

Heck, I've laughed about it, bitterly, but still. I was truly delusional to think that I'd fit into his shiny life. I get it. No hard feelings. But it could have gone down in about two thousand and three less embarrassing ways.

I push that futile thought out of my mind, and I throw my lace-overlay mini dress on, and I force myself to at least glance in the mirror. I touch up my makeup and hair, and then I'm as ready as I'll ever be. By the time Bea and I reach the location they chose for our shoot, we're raring to share our ideas.

But when we get to the pin, it looks *nothing* like we expected.

"The Walt Disney Concert Hall?" I ask.

"It's pretty, at least," Bea says. "But what are they going to do with us here? We talked about fountains, town squares, and open spaces."

By the time we park, we're already late, and the heels we chose aren't exactly jogging friendly. I nearly twist my ankle, but we manage to shoot inside less than five minutes late.

We're both panting like labradors on a summer's day, though.

Which, in LA, November *almost* is.

"Finally," a woman in all black says. "Hurry back. We still have to get you dressed."

I frown. "We are dressed. Who are you?"

"Yeah," Bea says. "We used the approved costume budget for these. We have artistic approval over the album cover. It's in our contract."

The woman shrugs. "I answer to Eddy. You can follow me and argue with him."

But when she finally stops walking and we barge through the double doors into the dressing area, Bea and I both freeze. I can't even form words.

"What is that?" I whisper.

Bea shakes her head.

"This is what you're going to wear." The woman points. "Eddy's insisting."

It's *the* gown.

I walk toward it slowly, terrified and delighted. Afraid and excited. I lift my hand toward it, preparing to brush the back of my hand on the chiffon. That's when I notice there's a small card pinned to the top of the dress form.

I pull out the stick pin and pluck out the card.

My name's clear on the front, and it's handwriting I know. Small caps—only the first letter of each word is larger, but everything is caps.

It's from Jake.

My hand trembles.

I force myself to open the card anyway.

Dear Octavia,

I know we didn't work out, but that doesn't change the fact that you *belong* in this dress. It was designed for you, and it *has* to be the album cover. Wear it, and don't turn to the left. Smile so that the whole world sees your beauty the same way I do.

They'll be transfixed.

Shine for them, even when it's hard. The world needs your light.

-Jake

The shoot ends up being *way* delayed. They have to redo my makeup entirely, because I cry so much that it runs down my face. But when the photographer shows up, and when everyone else in the band—including Bea—has changed into all black, they won't listen to a word of protest.

"You'll all disappear," I say.

"We should." Now Morgan's crying. "We all should."

"I think the cover should just be her," Q says.

"Yes." Bea nods. "I wrote every song for you." She smiles. "Please?"

In the end, they do take some photos of just me, but I make them take photos with the whole band as well.

"We can let editorial decide what's best," Bea says. "If they want us there, we'll all be on it. But the shots of just you are powerful."

"I think they kind of frown on us peering over the photographer's shoulder," Morgan says.

Bea laughs. "Frowning doesn't scare me. Jake Priest's my brother."

We all laugh, but it hurts just a little.

When I try to leave, the shoot director insists I take the gown with me. "I can't," I say. "You have to return it."

"The studio didn't pay for it," the director says. "Jake paid for it himself, and he was very adamant that it was meant for you."

It barely fits in the van—shipping it is a complete ordeal. Even so, I'm secretly delighted.

Bea and I both try going by Jake's apartment several times, but if he's there, he never answers the door. Eventually, we board our flights home. The movie catches up on the filming, because within a week or two of getting home, we start seeing ads for it.

I ignore them, mostly.

Though it's nice to hear our music. A few weeks later, our album launches with just me on the cover. Well, me and The Dress. It feels like it needs its own zip code. I brace myself for the nasty comments, the cruel criticisms, and the rude digs. A few do pop up, but way, way fewer than I expected. The beauty of the dress works its magic, because the vast majority of the comments actually say they finally understand why Jake's with me.

That hurts worse than digs about my face, honestly.

Two weeks later, we see the first official trailer for the movie, and that's the first time I hear rumors connecting May with Jake. It's worse than the comments about us being together after he dumped me, because I know they're a better fit.

And fans go wild.

Rumors circulate like wildfire, some of them portraying me as a horrible shrew, while others maintain I was wronged. Plenty of others paint me as a tragic figure who made too many demands, or the femme fatale that broke Jake's poor, battered heart.

In those, May's the heroine who nursed him back to health, basically.

Since I know how ridiculous they all are, I should know that it's even odds whether he's actually dating May. But he did like her, and she is adorable, and they did work together. They kissed each other, too.

If I'm being completely realistic, I have to assume they are together.

And I need to get over it.

I try.

I really try.

At least I don't mope around and stop living. Quite the contrary. Bea and I start working on new songs. I work with her on wedding details. We go to lunch. We make appearances, and we talk with the other members of the band.

To my surprise, they all opt to stay with us, moving to New York to work with us on the next album. Sales are better than anyone had any hope they'd be, with the movie not releasing for another six weeks yet.

Life's truly good.

Which makes it harder, knowing how much better it

could have been, if only I hadn't badgered or irritated or weighed Jake down. I spend way too much time running through the possible areas I could have gotten things wrong. It's a little embarrassing, or it would be if anyone else knew. I have lists all over my place.

But one week before Bea's wedding, I wake up, I gather up all the lists, and I throw them out. "It's time," I tell myself. "Time to move on."

I refuse to think about Jake. Every time I do, I sing *Yankee Doodle Dandy*. At least, for the first day. The next morning, I decide I should get something useful out of it, and I switch to pushups. Five pushups every time I think about him.

My arms are going to look *amazing* in another week or so.

It's not like I can do anything truly stupid like drive past his apartment. Bea's living there alone now—he had someone pick up all his stuff within a few days of our arrival back home—but it bummed me out, knowing there wasn't even much chance of us inadvertently bumping into each other.

That didn't stop me from coming up with other, more implausible ways we might meet by chance, not that it would matter if we did. It's just what happens in all the movies.

I'm just hoping it's more of a *Sex and the City* encounter, and less of *The Way We Were*.

Once Bea and I get our list of songs pulled together, I have to go into the agency office and sign the agreement. Just in case Jake might be there—we are agency siblings, after all—I get dressed in my favorite sweater, and I pull on my fur-trimmed jacket, imported from Amsterdam.

No harm in being prepared.

I've been doing the pushups, and I've been doing much better about not just randomly thinking of Jake, but I know this is the moment in the movie that I'd meet him, so I can't help it. I look around from the moment we enter the building, until we're escorted downstairs. Pathetically, I even make a stop at the coffee cart, desperate for a few more moments before we have to exit the building.

Bea sighs. "I kind of—"

"Hoped we'd run into Jake?" I hate how disappointed I sound. "I'm sorry."

"He was supposed to be my best man," she whispers. "But he hasn't even RSVPed."

I'm filled with such sorrow, and frankly, embarrassment. "I'm so sorry." I take Bea's hand. "I've only been thinking about myself. He's your *brother,* and he hasn't RSVPed to the wedding yet." I wince. "I'm so very sorry if it's my fault—"

She shakes my hand. "Don't you ever say that. It's not you —his stupid father is messing with him. Nothing else." She hugs me tightly, which makes me feel way better.

Unfortunately, it also makes me spill my coffee. Blessedly, it's an iced coffee, and it only dumps on me.

Unluckily, it's an ivory blouse.

"Shoot," I say.

"I'm such an idiot," Bea says. "I can go get you a shirt, and you can go hide in the bathroom until I come back." She points at the restroom sign. "I'll be right back."

Before I can argue with her, she sprints for the exit. She's such a good friend. I drag myself to the back of the building, and I find myself sort of stuck. If I want to have any decent chance of cleaning my blouse, I have to take it off, but then I'm standing in the middle of the bathroom nearly naked.

There's a pretty steady run of people coming and going, and they're all talking about someone's speech, so I'm guessing it's people at a conference or a presentation of some kind that's brought all these people to the building. I wind up compromising by dousing paper towels and using them to try and dilute and blot the unsightly stain.

It doesn't really work. Mostly it just spreads it.

Thankfully, Bea should be here with my new shirt soon, and the flow of people has almost stopped. A moment later, there's just one person in the bathroom, when I hear her call out, "Is there any toilet paper out there?"

"Oh, no." I say. "Hang on, I'll check." I examine all three of the other stalls, and find a total of three squares. Clearly the building wasn't prepared for this kind of traffic today. "Um, I can't find much more, but I can get you a paper towel." Only, I fail at that, too. I used so many trying to blot my blouse that the last woman to dry her hands finished them off.

"Actually." I cringe a little, but I forge ahead. "It looks like those are gone, too. I'm so sorry. I can run out and get you some."

"Thank you," the woman says. "I really appreciate it. I have to go pick up my kid from school. I can't hide in here all day."

I glance down at my blouse, which is now half-covered by a brown blob, and has the notable addition of tiny, soggy flecks of paper towel that have stuck all over it.

Ugh.

I'm brushing them off as I walk out of the bathroom and run—SMACK—right into some man's back. When he turns around, I realize our movie's a rom com. Or at least a comedy. The man I just smashed into is Jake, and I can't think of a time in the last month that I've looked more pathetic than I do right now.

"Hey," I say lamely.

His eyes widen as he glances down at my shirt.

"I can explain," I say.

He smirks. "I'm sure it has something to do with Bea. This has her name written all over it."

Just then, my phone starts ringing. "Speaking of." I show him the screen and hit talk. "Oh my word, you're never going to believe this."

"What?" I ask.

"While I was inside the store buying your shirt, some huge delivery truck totaled my car."

Jake's eyes widen, so I know he's listening. "Are you alright?"

"I'm fine, but my car looks like it needs to go in a recycling bin." She moans. "And you're stuck there, waiting, and I have no idea how long this will take."

"I can help," Jake says.

"Hey!" Bea sounds desperate. "Is that Jake, or am I hallucinating his voice now?"

He laughs.

"It is," I say. "I just rammed into him by mistake."

"Oh, thank goodness. The cop just got here. I have to go. I'll call you back!" She hangs up.

"Erm, did you want me to take you home, or to a store? Or you can hide in the bathroom and I'll—"

"Oh, no!" I grab his arm. "The bathroom!" I point. "I left a woman in there with no toilet paper." I close my eyes and sigh. "See, I'd used all the paper towels, and then these women used all the toilet paper, and I was the only person in there, and she has to pick up her kid."

"So you want me to. . .what?"

"Can you go get a roll of toilet paper from the men's bathroom?" I make prayer hands.

"The rolls are encased in plastic and they're huge."

"You can press a button and they come open." I mime doing it.

Jake snorts and shakes his head. "Only you." But he ducks into the bathroom and comes out a moment later. "I had to wrestle this out of the arms of a very beefy man."

"I'm so impressed." I assume he's kidding until I hear shouting. "Wait, did you really?"

"We should go."

I'm still pretty sure he's kidding, but I hear some grumbling, so I grab Jake's arm and yank him into the ladies' room. "Were you serious?" I look up at him.

He shrugs. "Maybe a little bit."

"You left some man without toilet paper?"

"I asked him nicely to share, and he told me—you know what? I don't feel bad about it. They have paper towels. With a little creativity. . ."

"You could have grabbed the paper towels!" I smack my head.

"I should have thought of that." Jake bites his lip.

I'm laughing when I hand the woman the roll the size of a pumpkin. "Good luck," I say.

"You ready to go home yet?" Jake arches one eyebrow.

Just then, I hear a man shouting outside about someone stealing his toilet paper.

Jake shrugs. "Or, we could stay in here a little longer."

The woman shoots out, runs her hands under the water for a *very* short time, and ducks out. We listen for a moment, but she doesn't say a word about us to anyone.

"Probably didn't want to be implicated," Jake says. "Coward."

I giggle.

"I've missed you," he whispers so quietly that I'm not entirely positive I heard it.

"How's May?" I ask.

"Huh?" Jake turns toward me, and I realize I'm crouched

against the wall with him on my left side. That *never* happens. I'm always aware of my good side, and I always position people there. Even after he dumped me, there's just something about Jake that makes me feel safe around him, even when we're hiding in a bathroom together as a result of noble criminal activity.

"You know, when you think about it, we should be getting praise," he says. "We did a good deed."

"You could have let the guy use it before you snatched it," I say.

"He wasn't even in the stall yet, and although I hid it behind my back, he should have checked that the stall had paper before going in."

I snort. "We're the Robin Hood of restrooms."

"Exactly," Jake says. "That was my favorite Disney movie."

"It would be." I shake my head. "Bunch of thieves."

He smiles. "Precisely why I liked it. Some of us do what we do for good reasons."

"Were your reasons for cutting the Fansees out good?" I ask. "Because Bea's really hurting."

Jake's face falls.

"What's going on?" I ask. "Can't you tell me?"

A muscle in his jaw works, but he shakes his head.

"You stole from them and your dad's threatening to tell them?" I ask. "Because if you did take money from the Fansees, and your dad's holding that over you, I think they'd forgive you."

"He's not my dad," he snaps.

I blink. "What?"

He turns away.

"Jake, at least explain that. Do you just mean that you don't like him, so you don't consider him your father anymore? Because the Fansees are your real family, and I swear, they would—"

He's glaring at one tile on the floor, as if it punched his sister. "I'm doing this for them."

"I knew it." I grab his hand. "And May? Are you two really dating?"

He rounds on me so fast, I almost fall backward on my butt. "No way."

I can't help my smile. "No?"

He exhales loudly. "How could you even think that?"

I can't help it. I burst into tears.

"Oh, no, don't." He reaches for me, and then he yanks his hand back. "It's—I'm bad, Octavia. I don't deserve you, believe me. If you knew. . ." The next breath he drags in is ragged. "You would run."

"Try me," I say.

"What?" He's frowning.

I wipe at my tears. "I've spent every single day since we broke up thinking of what I might have done wrong. I've analyzed and re-analyzed, and I swear I'll do better this time, if you give me another chance. I'll be so breezy, and so easy-going that you would barely know we were dating."

"It wasn't you." His eyes are sad. "I swear."

"I've also gone over and over what might have made you dump me if it wasn't my fault, and I haven't been able to think of a single thing I couldn't forgive." I pause. "Well, mostly."

"Mostly?" His eyebrows rise. "What does that mean?"

"Have you molested children?" I can't help wrinkling my nose. "Or really committed any kind of sexual assault."

"Absolutely not," he says.

"Have you murdered anyone?"

He exhales slowly. "No."

"What about stealing? Did you go back to that? Because you have all that money, and you said you don't really spend it, but maybe when you bought my dress—"

"Octavia."

I turn to face him, my bad side still turned his way. "What?"

"You have to stop. I can't tell you why, but believe me when I say this is for the best."

"No." I shake my head. "I don't believe you. I never will. I think, just like you finally did with Dave's photo, you should tell me the truth and let *me* decide. And if you don't, I may never forgive you for that, for not trusting me."

He swallows. "That's not. . ." But then he frowns, and he seems to be thinking about it.

I strike while I have the chance, remembering that Bea said he had to be shoved. "Your family loves you, too. They deserve to know what's keeping you away. If it's something that makes them cut you off, well, then you'll be exactly where you are now. If it's not, then you're being a real idiot." I quirk one eyebrow. "I still love you, so I'm definitely an idiot, and they say it takes one to know one."

"You still. . ." He drops one hand over mine. "That's what scares me. When you hear the truth, you won't."

"Then out with it," I say. "Because I've been trying everything to get over you, so if this truth will really help, if it does what you say, then great. I welcome it."

He stares.

"Come on."

"My dad's not my dad," he says. "He's my uncle. My real dad's a serial killer, and my mom fell in love with him while they corresponded back and forth. She got pregnant with me on a conjugal visit, and then—"

"Wait, you're saying your dad's the—"

"Yes." It looks like he just swallowed a mouthful of vinegar.

"And?" I peer at him. "Get to the bad part."

"Stop."

"Stop what?" I'm confused. "Unless. . . Do you think that *is* the bad part?" I shake my head. "Jake, Adam and Eve had Cain. The frivolous, idiotic parents in *Pride and Prejudice* had Kitty and Lydia, and they also had two amazing daughters." I poke his arm. "Do you know what these people all have in common?"

He shakes his head.

"Every person born has one thing in common—we only own one single thing in this world."

"What are you talking about?" But his face already looks lighter. He looks almost hopeful.

"We all have one thing when we're born that only we own, and that's our *choices*. So stop making such stupid ones. The Fansees won't care any more than I do who your biological parents are. You could be the son of the devil himself, and I'd still love you."

He swallows, and then he brushes himself off, and he offers me his hand. "I haven't heard any yelling or banging in a while."

At that very moment, a janitorial cart rolls in, a very large woman pushing it. She shrieks when she sees Jake.

"Sorry," he says. "So sorry."

Of course, then she realizes who he is, and she shrieks for another reason. It takes his signature and smiling through a few moments of gushing in broken English, but we do finally escape. As we walk out of the building, I'm still lamenting my spoiled shirt. "This is so not how I wanted to see you again."

"You could have been wearing an orange trash bag." He takes my hand in his and interlaces our fingers. "And I'd still have said this meeting was perfect." He jerks his finger at the coffee cart. "You thirsty?" But his eyes are sparkling, and I know he's teasing me about the stain.

"Shut it, jerk."

I get a few glares as we exit the building, but I can't tell whether it's my face, the awful coffee stain, or our joined hands.

"Thanks for the dress, by the way," I say. "It was beyond my expectations, and—"

"And it *made* that album cover. I hear the sales have been phenomenal."

"You heard that?" I ask. "Or you illegally logged in and checked?"

He stops walking and spins me around until I thunk into him. My hands spread out across his chest. "I love you, Octavia Rothschild. I love you in an orange trash bag. I love you in a fabulous ball gown. I love you when you're contemplating stealing toilet paper."

"To be clear, I proposed that you *ask* for it. I never condoned stealing."

He winces. "You knew who I was when you picked me up."

I laugh. He's right. I did. "But go on."

He smiles. "I love everything about you, but even if you aren't scared about who my parents are, I worry that in the future, you'll get sick of always having to redirect my little boat before it crashes into rocks."

"As long as we're talking about a metaphorical boat, I'll be fine. I hate real boats. I get sick as a dog."

"Do dogs get sick on boats?" he asks.

"Oh my word, get back to the point."

"I love you," he says. "I have for a long time, I think, and I won't run away again, I promise."

I jab him. "You better not. And you need to RSVP to your sister's wedding."

"Can't I just go as your plus one and freak everyone out?"

I roll my eyes.

"Is that eyeroll a yes or a no?"

"Definitely a no. You have to at least talk to Dave and Seren first, or you'll be too scared to go, even with me as your shield."

"Fine," he says. "But you have to come with me."

I smile, because I was hoping he'd ask.

CHAPTER 22
JAKE

On the day I came to live with the Fansees, they sat me down. The other kids had already gone to bed. Emerson was always a total nerd, so one word sent him away. Bea initially argued to stay with me, but she disappeared after *the look*. Seren still has the power to make all of us listen, at least while we think she's close enough that she could come after us. I'm not sure what I think she might do, but that look still promises something very, very bad.

Sitting alone, across from the people I'd tried to steal from, and whom I was now through a bizarre twist of fate living with, I remember thinking that I would never believe a single thing they told me. I had a lot of guesses about what they'd say now that everyone else wasn't watching.

No social workers.

No friends.

No semi-siblings.

No one would believe a word I said, but I knew how to handle that. One of the first things my dad taught me to do was record a conversation without the people who were listening knowing. Then, whatever they said—or did—I could prove it. If I had to, I could use it to get a new home placement. Better yet, I could use it to blackmail them into doing what I wanted in the future.

"I'm sure you're scared," Seren said. "I'm sure you're hurting. I'm so sorry that your father had to go to prison." She was actually crying. I was very impressed. Legitimate con artists sometimes have trouble summoning believable tears without a lot of irritating histrionics first.

Dave patted her shoulder.

She shook her head and swiped at her eyes. "Tonight, I'm going to tell you a few things, things you might be horrified to hear. I'm going to tell *you* my deepest fears and my deepest secrets, because you're family now."

Was she serious? I thought they were sly, but I was beginning to think they were idiots. Revealing secrets to people they barely knew? Dad would, at least, be pleased.

"A few years ago, before I ever met Dave, I was married." She sniffed. "I was the one who rented the car for a family trip we went on. I was married, and my husband and my parents, my grandparents and my siblings all went on a trip with me." She bit her lip. "And I knew my dad had been drinking. Not much, and I thought he was fine, but I should have asked."

I blinked. "Asked what?"

"He had back pain," she said. "Chronic back pain. I should've asked whether he'd taken a pain pill that morning and exactly how much he'd had to drink. But he was my dad. It might have embarrassed him in front of my husband, so I kept quiet." Her tears are quietly rolling down her cheeks now.

Dave's eyes welled with tears, too. Those two were a real pair.

She looked up at the ceiling for a moment, and then she

sniffed again. When she looked back at me, she nodded slowly. "If I had said something, my dad might not have gotten in a wreck. Because I kept my mouth shut, everyone in our van died, and everyone in the car we hit died too. Everyone except me." Her voice dropped to a whisper. "Including my unborn child." Her hands went to her belly.

In that moment, I realized she was serious. This wasn't made up.

"I—" She dropped her face in her hands for a moment.

"When we met, Seren thought she'd never have kids, and that was all she'd ever wanted," Dave said, taking over while she calmed down.

I could see her having 'mother' as her highest goal in life. Kind of sad, I thought.

"Because of the surgery they did to save me, doctors told me I could never have children in the future either. I had done it to myself—I had killed everyone I ever loved." Seren leaned toward me, her face puffy, and her lip trembling. "When I tell you this, know I mean it, Jake. You're going to make mistakes. You might even do bad things on purpose to see whether we really mean what we're saying."

"I thought it sounded nuts at first," Dave said, "when Seren told me she loved Emerson. She'd just met the kid, but she knew."

"I felt the same way about Bea," she said. "And also, when we met you and realized what you'd be dealing with."

I can't help my snort. There's no way these people could love me. They might hate me, but we just met. You can't love someone you just met.

"I know love sounds like a big word," Dave said. "And believe me, I was as skeptical as you, but I've learned to trust this woman and her big heart. The moment she saw Emerson, her heart said *mine*. I thought she was a little crazy then, but she was right. God has given her children, and even if she didn't give birth to them, when she sees them, her heart knows."

She scooted toward the edge of the sofa. "Jake, I know you have a dad." She frowned. "And I know this might seem strange to you, but you *are* my son. No matter what you do, no matter what happens in your life, no matter who else may show up, *you will always be my son*. You can test it however you want, and you can make any mistakes you need to make, and there will be consequences for your actions, but I will be here for you through it all, always. No matter what."

Sometimes when I get really depressed, I listen to that conversation.

I was glad I recorded it for a very different reason than I expected. And I did test them, over and over. But today's test feels harder somehow. They've always known my dad was a criminal, but they didn't know how bad it was. They didn't know anything about my real parents.

Will it change things? Will Seren's face fall? Will she give up on me, once she knows where I really came from? Octavia insists I text them on our way over, telling them the two of us are coming and asking if they're around.

Within two minutes, they've both texted back.

Yes. Please come.

Even so, when we show up, I'm nervous. I ball my hands into fists and release them. I fidget with the gear knob on my car. I button the top button on my shirt and then unbutton it. When I put the car into park, Octavia drops her hand on mine. "Jake."

I turn toward her.

"They aren't going to care. They know and love *you*."

"But I don't have a plan yet for how to deal with my dad. How do you think they'll feel when the news is released and the public hates me, and maybe also the people who took me in? What if it ruins their hotel business?"

Octavia laughs, and it's a high and melodic sound. "Oh, Jake. You're worrying about things that won't happen, I promise."

"But they could. My dad's a bad person."

"Your uncle's not a great person," she says, "but he was never your dad. Dave is, and you take after him."

I frown.

She wipes the wrinkles from my forehead and tosses her head. "Let's go."

It's good I brought her, because she has to drag me to the house. Thanks to the stupid Ring, they open the door the second we arrive.

"Hey," Seren says. "Come on in." She's smiling, but it's a sad smile, like she knows it's going to be a hard visit.

"I'm happy to see that you're with Octavia again," Dave says. "I'm still hoping you'll come through that door soon to tell me you're getting married."

"Maybe we get through Bea's wedding before we start talking about another one," Seren says. For the first time ever, I notice wrinkles on the corners of her eyes and a few faint lines on her forehead. I wonder what kind of toll my actions have taken on her.

I feel bad about it.

"Jake here was trained from an early age to run away after doing something he shouldn't have done," Octavia says. "It's just what he does naturally, but today, he's here, and he has something to tell you guys."

"Is this about the funnel?" Dave arches his eyebrow. "Because Killian finally came clean about it last week."

I'm going to kill him. "Uh, no."

"Alright," Seren says. "Let's sit."

"Is it about the jar that—"

Seren grabs his arm. "Stop, Dave. Let him talk."

Octavia's laughing for some reason. "By all means, let's focus, but I also want to come back to these other things when we're done. I have some questions of my own about what Jake was like when he was small."

"Exactly the same, but the dimples looked bigger because he was smaller, and his stories were slightly less outrageous back then."

Seren whaps Dave. "Stop."

Dave shrugs. "Fine, I'm stopping."

"I—" I'm not sure where to start. I glance at Octavia helplessly.

"Jake found out recently that his dad wasn't his dad." She arches one eyebrow. "I'm a little sore about it, because instead of telling me what he learned, he dumped me." She folds her arms. "But when you love someone, you come help them even when you're annoyed by something."

Seren grins at me.

"So he's just as stupid now as he was then." Dave shakes his head. "What a shame." But he's smiling.

"My real birth father was—"

"The most notorious serial killer in North America," Dave says. "We know."

A chill runs up my entire body, and for the first time in my entire life I burst into spontaneous tears without forcing it. "You—you knew?"

Seren's lips compress and her head tilts. "Oh, Jake." She lunges at me and hugs me. From right next to me, her voice is very, very clear. "You were never really his kid. You've always been my baby."

My tears turn into sobs, but she never lets go. She pats my back. "I told you that on the first day you came to live with us, and I meant it then."

"We found all that out before we took you on," Dave says. "The social workers had your file—it came out in the investigation. Your dad thought he'd covered it up, but they fingerprint people who are born into the system. Before they took you from your mother, you were printed, and it was a pretty easy connection for them to make."

My voice comes out a little strangled, even as I'm choking back my emotion to try and get ahold of myself. Men do *not* sob like idiots, and Octavia's right there. "You knew *before* you took me in?"

Seren finally releases me, but she doesn't sit down. Her hand cups my cheek. "I was trying to tell you that first day— no matter what you think, no matter what the world says, no matter what you do, you're mine, and I love you, and I don't care about anything else."

"I love your mom. She's the best," Octavia whispers. Then she turns toward Seren and raises her voice. "In fact, do you feel anything from your heart when you look at me? Because I could definitely go for a trade-in on my mother."

Dave and Seren's faces look horrified at first, and then they realize she's kidding. The laughter's uproarious, from all of us.

"We'll always be here for you too," Seren says, "but I think if we tried to adopt you, Jake might never talk to us again."

"Yeah, I'm not dating my sister."

"I heard a rumor that you actually tried to confess your feelings to Bea." Dave's clearly trying *really* hard not to laugh.

"I'm a smart guy," I say, "but I've had my share of damage. I got confused, and Bea slapped me upside the head, mostly metaphorically."

"She told me," Octavia says. "She said you don't share well, so in spite of never once making any advances or moves, when Easton came along, you got jealous of her time and wanted to keep your favorite toy for yourself."

Dave and Seren are actually laughing harder. "I actually did *not* hear that part, but boy is she smart."

"All our kids are," Seren says.

"Well, Killian's cute, at least," Dave says.

Seren smacks him, but I notice she doesn't argue. Poor Killie. "Alright. Well."

I try to stand up, but Octavia and Seren each yank me back down. "You can't just leave," Octavia says. "Not unless you're ditching me. I demand another game of Settlers."

"Oh, ho, ho," Dave says, "but you can't possibly win now. We're onto your wily ways."

Boy is he wrong. The game is almost a repeat of the last time.

"Maybe she just has a real, genuine talent for Settlers." Seren's frowning at the board, clearly counting the points. "When did she buy those cards? And why were they all victory points? All I ever get are stupid cards that move the robber."

Dave laughs. "Some people are just blessed." He leans back in his chair. "And although we've lost to Octavia twice now, I think it might be us."

Seren smiles. "Yes, I think you're right."

"But what are we going to do about my dad?" I ask.

"We need a new name for him," Octavia says. "Because I'm not calling him that anymore."

"We can call him my uncle," I say. "That's what I usually do, when I remember."

"He doesn't deserve that," Octavia mutters.

"I think he cared about me in his own twisted way," I say. "I'm not sure he knew how to do any better."

"He's a good looking, smart guy, but he's a manipulative and vengeful one, too," Seren says. "I say we call him your uncle. It'll honor that he tried, possibly, but that he's not your dad and he was never honest in the way he treated you or the things he told you."

"Sure." I nod. "He can be my crazy uncle."

"Wait," Dave says. "You already have a few of those."

"Bentley," Seren says, "is definitely already your crazy uncle."

"I don't think he likes me much," I admit.

Dave shakes his head, but he's smiling. "For an intuitive guy, you struggle at reading honest people. Bentley loves you for just who you are."

"You should hear him brag about you," Seren says. "He's always going on about his famous nephew."

"Actually, that gives me an idea," Dave says, "of how we can deal with your uncle."

His smile makes me nervous, but not as nervous as Octavia's. "I wonder if we have the same idea."

CHAPTER 23
JAKE

If you poll a kindergarten classroom, most kids want to be the President, or a movie star, or a rock singer. Not me. All I wanted to be was a dad. I thought my dad knew *everything*. He was the closest thing I'd ever met to a real superhero.

Of course, that was largely because of all the lies he told me.

I thought, obviously, about reporting my dad's past crimes and plans to defame the Fansees and getting him sent back to prison. At the end of the day, I don't feel good about it. It's using my dad's own playbook against him, and I'd rather throw it away.

The problem is that I *do* actually like my job, and the only other way I can think to defuse the situation is to drop a bomb on my career and walk away. If I didn't care about acting ever again, that would be fine. That was what I did for years and years—walked away.

But I don't want to do that anymore.

Thankfully, it turns out Dave and Octavia *did* have the same idea.

While risky, their idea was intended to try and preserve my ability to work as an actor. Their suggestion sent me to the internet, researching extensively. It turns out, the key to managing bad information if you're a celebrity is twofold.

First, it's important to be honest. When it came out that Hugh Grant had hired a prostitute, he didn't prevaricate. He didn't make up excuses. He apologized on primetime television, and he said he'd made a terrible mistake. No excuses. No story. Just a confession and an apology. I found countless other examples of celebrities who actually fessed up to bad things they'd done, and the public outcry was cut much shorter.

But secondly, when you can control the narrative, you can often almost eliminate the pushback. Not all the bad things a celebrity deals with are scandalous. Sometimes, our biggest hurdle is choosing a film or series that bombs. When Ryan Reynolds did the *Green Lantern*, one of the most epic flops ever, it could have spelled disaster for him, but he didn't let it. He mocked himself and the franchise freely, and he used it to push his other stuff.

Most relevant to me, David Letterman was being blackmailed by someone just like my uncle for having an affair. Instead of paying the blackmailers off, he went on his own late-night show to confess to what he'd done. He apologized to everyone involved and to the public for what he'd done and begged for forgiveness. Another similar incident happened in 1991, when Magic Johnson chose not to hide his HIV diagnosis. He announced it right away and asked people to support him.

Which is why I've called a press conference for this morning.

"Why, hello." I force a smile, but I really miss facing something bad without Octavia's hand on my knee. "Thank you for coming to hear me out today."

"What's going on?" one reporter shouts. "Did you have an affair with a married woman?"

"I wish," I say.

They freeze, and then they laugh.

"What is it then?" a woman shouts.

I hold up my hand. "I have a statement, so if you can hold questions until I'm done, that would be great."

They do settle down, thankfully.

"Today's news may be unsettling to some of you. When I say it was unsettling to me, you will understand why. Something most people don't know, because I've largely kept it quiet, is that the man who raised me for the first ten years of my life has been in prison for the last fifteen or so years for theft. He was the consummate conman, and now he's out of prison on parole."

That's definitely not what they were expecting me to say. When they start clamoring, I shake my head.

"I'm not quite done yet. Bear with me."

Lots of flash bulbs keep blinding me, but I plow ahead.

"The thing is, when he got released, he came to find me. He planned to use some information he had hidden about me to force me to harm people I cared about. He threatened that if I didn't let him manage my career, he'd expose the truth about my past, a truth I didn't know until that night. At first, I let him." I don't have to fake my remorse. "I thought I was protecting the people I loved by living a lie, but one very special lady cornered me, and she forced me to fess up."

I wish she was here with me.

"Octavia Rothschild has always been way too good for me, but she helped me find my way here today. She's probably the reason my so-called father had to finally threaten me with the truth about my past."

When I confess who my real biological father and mother are, every single reporter looks appalled.

"I think I can safely say that none of you would have welcomed that kind of news about yourself, and all I can say is that it shook me. I knew that if he leaked this information to all of you, you'd no longer want to come to movies I made, and I wouldn't blame you for it."

The murmuring returns. That's a good sign, maybe.

"I dumped the one girl I've ever loved, to try and keep her away from me. At that point, I didn't think I was worth much at all, and I just didn't want anyone else to discover it. I hope none of you have ever felt the way I felt, but if you have, then maybe you'll be able to understand. I pushed people away *because* I loved them. But when I bumped into my darling Octavia in. . .let's just say it was under strange circumstances, she pulled the truth out of me, and to my shock, she said she didn't care who my parents were."

Thanks to a ridiculous swell of emotions, I stop for a moment.

I bang on my chest with my closed fist. "Sorry, thinking about that moment, about my total shock when Octavia loved me anyway, in spite of what I'd found out I was. . ." I cough. "It still wrecks me. But she gave me the courage to tell my foster parents, and I found out that they'd known all along, and they loved me just the same, too."

I don't cry, but it's a near thing.

"They gave me the courage to tell you what that conman who claimed to have raised me was holding over my head, to take away his power. I've also reported the crimes he's committed that I knew about to the authorities, and I've fired him from the job he extorted me into giving him. I'm sorry that I kept this information from all of you for so many weeks, and I'll understand if you're less understanding about all of it than my foster parents and girlfriend have been."

Oh, boy. Now they have questions.

"I think I should ask the first one." A voice—a *gorgeous* voice—from the back rises above the others. "As your girlfriend, I'd like to ask what you would like to do if the public, like me, doesn't care at all what your parents are like. If they choose to place their value on what you do and who you are, and not what your parents did."

I can't help my smile. "Oh, man, I really love you."

Now the flashes really are blinding. "I love you, too," she says, "but that's not an answer."

"Well, isn't this where I'm supposed to say, 'I am Ironman'?"

I do not expect everyone gathered to clap.

"Clearly I'm not Ironman," I say. "He never wept like a pathetic little baby. But I will say that I'm very grateful for the support I've received, and I'd like to encourage everyone who still supports me to let the former fans express themselves without criticism. I've been lied to most of my life, and I know it feels lousy. I'm sorry to have done that to you."

I answer questions for twenty minutes, but then I close it down.

"I will just say one last thing. On the horrible night my uncle—who claimed to be my father until recently—told me about my true father, I recorded our conversation. So, for those of you who still feel like I might not be telling the truth, I'm releasing the recording to the media outlets who request it."

My uncle calls me moments after I walk out of the conference. More accurately, he'd already called a dozen times, since it was being live-streamed, but I finally answer.

"Why hello, Uncle."

"What the h—"

"Ah, ah," I say. "I'm recording this call, too. Let's keep it polite."

"Have you lost your mind?"

"No," I say, "but I'm pretty sure you've lost your leverage. And in case you get any bizarre ideas, let me just tell you that with the help of your old friend Vincenzo, I emptied out your Cayman account. I'm happy to release that money, as I believe you'll need it for your legal defense, but only if I find that you don't make any public statements or try to make this worse in any way over the next month. You can take the money after that, and you can slink into a corner so deep and so far that I never hear from you again. And if you don't do that, I'll find a new way to deal with you. That's a promise."

"You think you can do this to me?" He snorts.

"I think you forgot who my real parents are," I say. "They're two very good people and two murderers, and I got something from each of them. You better not ever push me hard enough that you discover which set I favor more."

He definitely doesn't stay polite, so I go ahead and hang up.

Then I block his number.

He'll find another way to reach me, but it might take him a few days, and I won't release his money until I'm sure he hasn't tried to sell a conflicting story to anyone. Ironically, he's the one who taught me to always have a failsafe. Now that the police have the dossier of information on his past that I compiled, I doubt he'll be brave enough to come after me publicly.

I actually feel a little guilty about how I forced my uncle into a corner—at least, I do until I see Octavia. She's coming around the corner, and when she sees me, she smiles.

It's my favorite thing in the entire world.

"Hey," I say. "You weren't supposed to be there."

"Are you kidding me?" She shakes her head. "With as hot as you are, I needed you to say you loved me on air, or you'd be hounded for the next few months. Women *love* a man who's willing to say he's sorry. It's like finding a unicorn."

"Maybe not so much with the crying."

She brushes my cheek with her thumb. "A good solid cry is fine, as long as you man back up and don't make it a habit."

I laugh. "I'll try."

"Good." She stands on her tiptoes and kisses me then, and I stop caring about how things are going. Even if my career is over, at least I'm not standing in the shadow of any threats, and the truth is out there.

I didn't realize until this moment what a freeing thing the truth can be. But as it turns out, I have nothing to worry about. People are overwhelmingly forgiving of my hiding who I was, and no one particularly seems to care about my birth parents.

Over the next few days, I hear from quite a few people who also want nothing to do with their parents. They may not be as bad as mine, but they're close enough that they get it.

I actually have quite a few speaking requests for schools. I turn them down—I'd be a horrible role model for children— but it's nice all the same. And when I get dressed up for my sister's wedding, and I pick up my plus one, it feels really nice that I'm not going with a secret.

"You're not wearing the dress," I complain.

Octavia rolls her eyes. "I told you, that's not a dress you wear on someone else's wedding day."

"But no matter what day it is, when you're with me, it's

your day," I say. She slaps me, but I grab her hand. "I mean that."

"Yes, well, that can be true every day *but* today. I love Bea, and nothing's going to happen today that's going to take the attention off her."

I can't help my smile then, because poor Octavia doesn't have a clue.

CHAPTER 24

OCTAVIA

My dad has always been all the things my mom isn't. The second he hears about Jake's press release, he calls, but it's a whirlwind for a few days, especially with my connection as both his girlfriend and a friend of his sister who did the soundtrack for his movie.

I finally make time for him the morning of Bea's wedding.

"I brought bagels," he says, when I open the door.

"Dad, I said I'd be making waffles."

He shrugs. "I didn't get them toasted or sliced, so if you don't want them, you can pop them in the fridge and eat them later." He walks through the door with an abashed smile. "My mom would kill me if she ever found out I showed up somewhere empty-handed."

"She's dead," I say.

"That makes it scarier," Dad says.

I can't help my laugh.

Once we get our waffles ready, mine covered in fruit, Dad's drowning in syrup and chocolate chips, I tell Dad about Mom crashing at my place without telling me.

"Of course she did," he says. "I swear, most things—like

wine—get better with age." He lifts his eyebrows, leaving me to intuit his meaning. Dad's always been a big fan of not saying the mean thing, but making it clear with subtext.

"Yeah, Mom looks pretty good, but otherwise she's not aging well at all."

"You said it," he says.

I can't help my laugh this time either. "Dad, agreeing with me is just as bad."

"Tell that to your grandmother," he says. "She was the master of never saying a rude thing but still making her meaning clear."

My dad clearly adores his mother, even now. I think that's why my mother's shortcomings upset him so much. He knew how much better a mother could be.

"How did you ever get her out of here?" Dad glances around, and then he whispers, "Or is she still staying with you?"

"Jake tossed her out," I say.

He straightens. "I really like this kid."

"Dad, he's almost twenty-seven," I say. "He's not a kid."

"Agree to disagree," he says.

I laugh.

By the time we finish our waffles, I know my dad has something to say. I thought maybe he just came to check on the Jake thing, but it's more than that. Dad hates blueberries, but he picked one up, dropped it in the syrup puddle on his plate, and now he's chasing it down like it owes him a car payment or two.

"Dad."

His head snaps up. "Yeah?"

"What's up?" I stare pointedly at the blueberry. "That poor thing didn't do anything to you. Put it out of its misery already."

"Oh." He smooshes it and shoves it to the side of the plate. "So, I actually came here to say something."

"No kidding." I can't help loving this poor man. In fact, with his trouble saying things that he cares a great deal about, he reminds me of someone else I like. Maybe he's what prepared me to understand Jake so well.

"Your mother—" He sighs. "I know it's my fault. I married her, and that's why you got stuck with her too."

Wow. He said something plainly. "That must have been hard for you to say." I actually appreciate that my dad almost never said anything bad about my mother. He left all the vitriol and pettiness to her. It made my life better, because I was always smart enough to see it for myself. I didn't need to hash and rehash it constantly.

He plows along as if he didn't hear me. He's focused enough he might not have. "Your mother has been jealous of you her whole life."

I didn't realize he'd noticed that, too.

"Today I'm here to beg your forgiveness." He drops to his knees in front of me, tugging his ball cap off his head. Bowed like that, I'm just staring at his shiny, round head.

"Dad, get up."

He shakes his head. "I knew she was, and I should have fought her on it. I should have protected you better, but I didn't. I failed you, because I'm a coward."

I stand and pull him upright. "Dad, sit down. You did just fine. I'm safe, believe me."

He doesn't meet my eye, but he does sit. "From the moment you started singing, as early as three years old, it was clear you were special. I wanted to put you in piano and voice lessons. You loved it too, but your mom got angry. She wanted them for herself instead, and she said she'd always been denied as a kid. She was angry her child would have what she never got.”

She really is a pretty lousy mother, but that doesn’t mean her life wasn’t hard.

“Like a petulant child, she cried and complained until I gave in. I’d come home from work early so I could watch you while she got the lessons I wanted for you.”

“Dad, I don’t care.” I touch his wrist. “I really don’t.”

“It gets worse,” he says. “Just listen for a minute.”

I think about how hard it was for Jake to tell his parents things they already knew, and I nod and wait.

“As you got older, it got worse. You’d go to auditions and they’d turn her down, but they’d ask about you when you hadn’t even tried out. You were such a beautiful child and so gifted. The more it happened, the more she resented you for living her dream.”

I knew that part, too, maybe better than my dad did.

“I think she was relieved when you got burned.”

“Dad.” I shake my head. “That’s too harsh. She was there at the hospital.” Off and on. “I remember her distress. She didn’t fake that.”

“You didn’t hear her at home,” he mutters. “But regardless, you know we did surgeries at the start, but do you remember when we went back? It was a few years after the initial attempts, when your doc said they had a new technique.”

I remembered meeting with someone. “But they said I wasn’t a candidate. I was a little disappointed, but I didn’t have high hopes to begin with, and the idea of more painful surgery wasn’t ever a good one.”

“That’s the thing, though. You were a candidate, a *perfect* candidate, and we meant to tell you as your sixteenth birthday. . ." Dad squishes his hat into a very small ball, and I worry the brim won't ever recover.

Distracted by the hat, it takes a few seconds for his words to register. "What? You never told me that."

"Because your mom put the money we had in savings down on that three month acting camp in California when she realized we'd need it all for your surgeries. That was the last straw for me. Her selfish decision caused our divorce. I'd been looking the other way with her affairs for years. They never lasted long, but her selfishness never changed. She wanted your party to be perfect because she'd stolen your surgery money for herself. Again."

My parents hid their dysfunction way better than I realized. "But that means *I* really did break you up."

He shakes his head. "Not at all. I was staying with her *for* you. I'd have left her way earlier if you hadn't been born. The only reason I'm telling you now is to warn you. As you find happiness, expect her to become uglier to you. She's not someone who can overcome her jealousy. She'll never be the mother you deserve."

I tell him about how Jake cut her off and threatened her. Dad actually starts to bawl, and he says, "I'm glad you've found someone who can be the man I wasn't able to be for you."

It takes me half an hour to compose myself after all that, but when Jake shows up, I'm as ready as I'll be. I'm wearing a strappy black sheath dress that really hugs my figure.

I honored Bea's one request: no sleeves. The burn on my arm's bare.

Other than the album photoshoot, I've never gone out in public like this. I expect Jake to comment on it, but he doesn't even seem to notice.

"You're not wearing the dress." Jake frowns.

I can't help rolling my eyes. "I told you, that's not a dress you wear on someone else's wedding day."

"But no matter what day it is, when you're with me, it's your day."

I slap him playfully but he uses it as an excuse to grab my hand. Then he lowers his face to my level. "I mean that," he says softly.

He really does seem to. Every single day he shows up, and he never looks at me with anything but adoration, even today with my bare shoulder exposed.

"Yes, well, that can be true every day *but* today," I say. "I love Bea, and nothing's going to happen today that's going to take the attention off her."

"Shoot, but what about Easton?" he asks.

"Huh?"

"How's he going to feel when I show up with a way prettier girlfriend, looking so much better than he does?"

"I swear, the biggest risk in dating you is that my eyes will get stuck up inside my head one of these days."

When we get to the Serendipity Inn, it's transformed. I've been to Dave and Seren's a few times now, and the old house always looks gorgeous. But this is next level. It's clear that someone paid a lot for the fresh flowers. It's December tenth, and the place still looks like a hothouse.

"You know," I say, "I was pretty worried about a mostly outdoor wedding in December."

"You shouldn't have been," Jake says. "My parents know how to entertain."

It warms my soul to hear him call Dave and Seren his parents. "Alright." I walk up to Seren. "I'm ready to be put to work. Give me any task."

Seren frowns. "We don't need help. Everything's ready.

We're all here early to watch the full-length trailer for you, Bea, and Jake's movie."

"What?" I turn toward Jake. "You said we had to come early to help get last-minute things ready."

"We have all our employees doing that stuff," Seren says. "Weddings should be magical days, not grueling and miserable."

"Are we going to stand around, or are we going to watch the new trailer?" Jake asks. "It drops tomorrow."

"I have it set up in the wedding hall." Bea's not in her dress yet, but that makes sense. It's several hours before the wedding starts. She still looks every inch the bride, with her hair already curled, and a little A-line white sheath dress. "Let's go."

Bea jogs over to where I'm walking. "Are you excited? The movie comes out in a few days."

"Should you really be worried about that?" I ask. "It's your *wedding*."

She shrugs. "It's important, yes, but I'm not Bridezilla. The most important thing is celebrating the love Easton and I share, and you and Jake got together *because* of Easton investing in the movie and us doing the music." She opens the door and gestures us inside. "I'm almost as excited about the movie as the wedding, but don't tell Easton that."

I suppress what would have been a very unladylike laugh.

Jake's fiddling with some kind of electronic thing, but Bea ushers us all into seats. When Killian tries to sit next to me, Ardath makes a buzzer noise. "No way, kid. That's Jake's seat."

He tries to sit on the other side, and she acts like she's going to kick him.

"And that one's mine." Ardath drops into the chair next to me. "Other than knowing you have great skills with board games, I feel like I don't know you yet." She smiles. "But I have a feeling I'll be getting to know you much better soon."

Is she saying I'll get sick? Gosh, I hope not.

"Okay, we're ready." Jake glares at Ardath. "Hush up everyone, until this is done."

Seren glances right at me before finally dropping into the seat on the other side of Ardath.

"Have you guys all seen this already?" I ask. "Did they use a clip from the music video or something?"

Jake's smiling. "Just watch."

It does actually start with a scene from the music video, and then it cuts to still shots from the album shoot. But that's where it starts to fall apart. Instead of clips from the movie, it starts showing clips of me and Jake.

In one, he's defending me from Patrice. In another he's tucking hair behind my ear—on the left side of my face. Then it's our kiss from the set. And then it cuts off, and I'm very confused. "That's a terrible movie trailer," I say lamely.

Seren, Ardath, and Bea laugh.

"I mean, she's kinda right," Killian says. "I wouldn't go see that movie if they paid me."

"Well, I liked it," Easton says.

"Shut up," Jake says. "All of you." He walks toward me, and he crouches down on the chair in front of me, so he's on level with me, or close enough. "I didn't realize it for a long time, but for most of my life, I've acted based on fear. I didn't really commit to the Fansee family, because I was afraid it would fall apart. Then I dumped you, Octavia, because I was afraid I'd hurt you, or that the closer I got to you, the worse it would hurt if you left me."

He stands, and he pulls something out from under the chair in front of me. At first, I think maybe he's proposing, because it's a box. But it's a *large* one. When he removes the lid, what he pulls out is a tall, thin vase. "This is the very first piece of raku pottery that I ever fired in America. I gave it to Seren, but when I was talking to her yesterday, she agreed you should have it." He offers it to me.

I take it, and the closer it gets, the more breathtaking it is. "This was your first?"

He laughs. "Sadly, yes. The very first attempt I ever made has by far been my best, because with raku, you can know everything, and you can have perfect technique, but you can fail more than you succeed. Similarly, sometimes everything comes together perfectly when you have no idea what you're doing. That's what happened there, and I believe it's what happened when you were born. You are, in every single way that matters, my perfect woman. You're bright, caring, generous, forgiving—"

"That's an important one if you want to be with Jake," Killian mutters. "Get ready to forgive a lot."

Everyone laughs.

Jake glares, but then he smiles and tilts his head. "The kid's right." He kneels on the chair in front of me, and he leans closer. "Octavia Rothschild, you are the most divine, the most gorgeous woman I have ever seen in my entire life. You bring me nothing but joy and peace."

"And anxiety, fear, and stress," Dave says. Then he pats Seren's arms. "All the best ones do."

"I knew I should've done this without the audience," Jake mutters.

I can't help my smile. "No, this is perfect."

"I only invited them because you told me that my family was the most perfect thing you could imagine—what you'd always wanted. Since my biggest fear is that you'll one day wake up and realize what a loser I am, I figured I should go ahead and face that fear right away. I'm such a coward, I wanted to do everything I could to show you that betting on me isn't a bad call. See the family you get if you say yes when I ask you. . ." He snatches the vase out of my hands, inverts it, and catches the ring that drops out of the interior. "Will you marry me, Octavia?"

Before I can even respond, Bea says, "Please say yes. It would be a real bummer if you said no."

I laugh. "You people have to give me the chance."

"So that's a no?" Killian asks. "Because if you've realized what an idiot my brother is, I'll just mention that I graduate in a few short months."

Jake actually lunges for him.

"Yes," I whisper. "Yes, Jake Priest Fansee, I will marry you."

My fiancé freezes, and then he changes direction and plows through the chairs to yank me to my feet.

Everyone's chanting, "Kiss her, kiss her, kiss her" and he finally does.

Oh, he does.

CHAPTER 25
ARDATH

My mother was the single best human ever to walk the earth. Since my dad bailed before she even knew she was pregnant, it was always her and me against the world. Mom worked two jobs, but she only took positions that allowed her to bring her child along with her. She homeschooled me, and she never let me leave her side. I'm convinced she never would have let me leave her side if she had a choice, but sometimes your body doesn't care what you want.

She told me that only two things mattered: family and smarts.

When she died in my arms, minutes before the ambulance arrived, I decided that I'd become a doctor one day, and I'd make sure as few little girls as possible lost their mothers. I was planning to become a surgeon, but during training, I changed paths and went into emergency medicine. It was so visceral.

I still like riding with the ambulance from time to time. There's something therapeutic for me about being there, with my boots on the ground, using my two hands to save the people I couldn't have saved when I was a kid.

But I didn't get here overnight.

It was a very long road, and it started when I was barely in middle school. I had no money, I had no mother, and I was living in a group home. That meant I had to try twice as hard as everyone else, and I didn't have a safe place to do things like science fair projects.

That's why I set mine up in the back, near the dumpsters behind the school. Although my idea was a basic one—grow plants, and see which ones do better with various additives—I was determined to make mine stand out. After quite a bit of research, I settled on using the top fertilizers, ranked by brand and cost, and meticulously measuring my yield. I also thought I'd be able to set my project apart by doing five samples of each plant, to account for natural variation based on location or other variables outside of my control.

It took me days and days of research to set things up.

I had to skip lunch for three weeks to save up the money to buy my supplies. Then I had to lug them to school over a period of days so the group home director didn't notice. I found a way to sneak out before school, during lunch, and after school so I could monitor and chart the growth.

It wasn't like I was a criminal, I reasoned. I just didn't have the permission to use the premises because the school couldn't extend the same courtesy to everyone. I felt a little guilty, and I was scared I'd get caught, but I'd heard the winner for the whole school district got an interview for a scholarship to the best private school in Scarsdale. I was determined to win. I knew college was hard to get into, much less pay for, and I planned to get there any way I could.

The first two weeks went perfectly.

I measured the fertilizer carefully, using the same cup for each brand so they wouldn't become cross contaminated, and feeding each plant with a funnel to make sure the water and fertilizer were evenly distributed. I'd chosen snow peas, because the crop should be easy to objectively measure, plus it was a good growing season for peas in the spring in New York. Not that many things can be sown directly in March here.

I covered them before a storm. I put up a barrier to keep stray animals away. I limited every variable I could think of.

By the third week, I had a very respectable start to my experiment. I was optimistic. But then, at the beginning of the fourth week, without any reason or warning, a whole row of my plants started to die. I was frantic. It made no sense. I cradled the tiny, wilted yellow leaves carefully. I spoke to them. I sang to them—then I realized they'd probably die faster if I continued.

By Thursday, when the plants on the second row started dying too, I decided it was time for drastic measures. I skipped school the next day to get eyes on my plants, so I could figure out what was going on.

I'd chosen my spot for its inaccessibility, and I felt reasonably confident no one would stumble upon me. They had to go around the dumpsters and then behind a half wall, and there wasn't anything else back here. It was a real stroke of luck for me that the district had installed a water spigot. Otherwise, I'd have had to haul water out here three times a day.

For hours and hours, I waited, but nothing happened. Lunch came and went, and I started to doze off. Then voices woke me—unfamiliar voices.

"I think I can make it to the third row today," a boy said. "It's all about the angle of your hip."

"No way," a younger boy with a bit of a lisp said. "There's no way you can."

I crept forward until I could peer around the corner of the trash cans to where the boys were standing.

"I can. I know it." Older kid.

"You have to hit the funnel or it doesn't count," the little boy said.

Then, before I had the time to figure out what to do, the biggest boy unzipped his pants, pulled out his. . .

I gulped.

And he *peed* up, up, up and over in an impressive arc that ended right into the funnel that he had stuck in the perfect, bright green snow-pea plant of the third row. I was so shocked, I had no idea how to react.

The little boy did the same thing next, only he aimed for the funnels in the front row, hitting them all in sequence.

I didn't think it through. I didn't consider my options. Watching all that ammonia poisoning my plants, I acted entirely on instinct. I burst around the corner, my arms waving, my face frozen in a rictus of rage. "Stop it right now, you miscreants! I'll report you to the police."

The bigger boy turned around, so shocked he didn't stop what he was doing, and he peed all over my shoes.

I burst into tears.

"There you are." A small girl shot around the edge of the school, freezing, clearly horrified, when she saw us. "Jake, what in the world are you doing?"

The little boy turned around then, still mid-stream, and coated the other girl's shoes. He swore, *loudly*.

"Who are you?" the girl asked, clearly addressing the smaller boy.

"I'm Killian." He put his business away, and then ducked his head. "I'm Jake's little brother."

"Excuse me?" the girl asked.

"My assignment," Jake said. "You know, because of *the thing*, I had to do community service." He widened his eyes and tossed his head at me.

"What were you two doing?"

"Skipping class," Killian said. "And learning to pee sooo far."

"I'm going to kill you," the girl said, "but that would be redundant, because Dave's going to *bury* you already."

"Please don't tell him," Jake said.

"Hello?" I asked. "I'm standing right here, the scientist whose experiment they've been wrecking while they skipped class and exposed themselves in public."

"Public?" Jake sneered at me. "Please."

"I need this experiment to go well," I said. "It's my only hope of getting an interview for a scholarship to Harvey."

Jake rolled his eyes. "Harvard from a bunch of peas? Yeah, right."

"You idiot," I said. "HAR*VEY*." I scoff. "It's a private school for smart kids, so definitely not you. You can't even *hear* right." I grabbed my bag. "I'm going to report you for this."

"What happens to your experiment if you do?" the girl asked.

"Just let her do it, Bea. Who cares what the nerd says?" Jake shrugged. "It won't be the first time I get in trouble."

"You *peed* on her stuff," Bea said. "That's pretty bad. It's also public exposure." She spun around. "Even if this isn't exactly public, it's not private."

"Right?" I pointed at him. "You're cooked."

But Bea wasn't done. "You—why do you need a scholarship? Most of the parents around here would die to send their kids there."

I frowned.

"Your parents can't afford it?" She didn't look like she was trying to be rude.

"I don't have parents," I muttered. "My mom died."

Bea's face softened. "A scholarship would be good, but. . ." She glanced at the peas. "What if I could offer you something better?"

I wasn't sure what she was saying.

"The boys will apologize, and they'll promise never to come here again, and *never* to pee anywhere but in the toilet."

"Hey," Jake says. "You're not my—"

"What was that, exactly?" Bea frowned. "I'm not *what*, exactly?" She dropped her hand on her hips, and a flare of jealousy surged up inside me.

This girl was everything I wasn't.

She had a family.

She was brave.

She was unapologetic about her demands.

"Go," she said. "And if you ever argue with me again I'll tell everyone you're perverts."

To my shock, they ran.

She turned back to me. "Now, let's talk about this scholarship." She smirked. "As good as it would be, and maybe you can salvage. . ." She frowned. "Whatever experiment this is."

"Maybe," I said.

My one hope was that I could still use the three mostly unharmed rows of plants. I ran over and watered the ones Jake just hit, hoping to wash away any damage. Three sets of plants wouldn't be as impressive, but it might do alright. "You'll keep them away, and I keep my mouth shut?" She's right that if I handed them in, I'd also have to out myself for using school property without permission. They might not do anything to me, but they'd definitely throw the plants away, ruining my whole project.

But she didn't threaten me like I expected. "I have some people I'd like you to meet. How'd you feel about sitting next to me for lunch tomorrow?" Her smile was kind, one of the kindest things I'd seen.

"Alright," I said. "I guess."

And then, I did. She was right. Meeting Dave and Seren was way better than a scholarship in every single way. It changed my life forever.

All I had to do was keep my mouth shut about the funnels. In a way, what Jake and Killian did was the best thing that happened to me after my mom died.

The funnels made me a Fansee.

**I hope you have loved reading about Octavia and Jake's story, and I hope you'll be excited to join me when I write Ardath's story, Old Money. It'll be out by April of 2026 at the latest. I'm always hopeful I can move things up, and I'm sorry you have to wait! I always have too many projects and not nearly enough time. If you can, preordering it now helps me gauge interest and make decisions about series in the future. (Like how many books to write for the series and which series to prioritize!) Thank you!

If you haven't tried my (women's fiction) Birch Creek Ranch series yet, I think you'd probably really like it if you like this one. You can grab a whole series bundle here for a big discount (almost 40% off.) You can also check out my Finding Home series for a significant bundled discount. It's a series of nine standalone but connected romances just like these.

Thanks again for the support! You can also join my newsletter on my website. I'd love to be able to keep up with you on my new releases and promos/discounts. XO, Bridget

Acknowledgments

Thanks to my cousin Katie for sharing her personal stories and experiences with me. Your bravery and buoyant spirit have inspired me my entire life.

Thanks to my husband and kids for being so supportive of my writing, always. Thanks to my mom for the exact same. I'm blessed to have only the best of family in the past, present, and hopefully forever in the future.

And a huge thanks as ever to my editor Carrie, my cover artist Shaela, and my ALL STAR ARC team. You guys are the very best. I love you so much.

To my readers, I couldn't do this without you. I'm so very grateful for your support each and every day.

About the Author

Bridget's a lawyer, but does as little legal work as possible. She has five kids and soooo many animals that she loses count.

Horses, dogs, cats, rabbits, and so many chickens. Animals are her great love, after the hubby, the kids, and the books.

She makes cookies waaaaay too often and believes they should be their own food group. In a (possibly misguided) attempt at balancing the scales, she kickboxes daily. So if you don't like her books, maybe don't tell her in person.

Bridget is active on social media, and has a facebook

group she comments in often. (Her husband even gets on there sometimes.) Please feel free to join her there: https://www.facebook.com/groups/750807222376182

You can also sign up for her newsletter and get a free book at www.Bridgetebakerwrites.com

ALSO BY B. E. BAKER

I write women's fiction and clean romance under B. E. Baker (so it's kind of strange that I wrote a Donner Party book, but here we are.)

The Irish Escape (women's fiction with romance):

The Crumbly Old Castle

The Creaky Old Barn

The Scarsdale Fosters Series (romance with women's fiction!):

Seed Money (1)

Nouveau Riche (2)

Minted (3)

Loaded (4)

Filthy Rich (5)

Old Money (6)

The Finding Home Series (romance with women's fiction):

Finding Grace (1)

Finding Faith (2)

Finding Cupid (3)

Finding Spring (4)

Finding Liberty (5)

Finding Holly (6)

Finding Home (7)

Finding Balance (8)

Finding Peace (9)

The Finding Home Series Boxset Books 1-3

The Finding Home Series Boxset Books 4-6

The Finding Home Series Boxset Books 7-9

The Birch Creek Ranch Series (women's fiction with romance):

The Bequest

The Vow

The Ranch

The Retreat

The Reboot

The Surprise

The Setback

The Lookback

A standalone historical fiction:

Hungry: The Inspiring Tale of Three Donner Party Survivors

Children's Picture Book

Yuck! What's for Dinner?

I also write romantasy and end-of-the-world fiction under Bridget E. Baker.

The Dragon Captured Series: (dragon shifter romance!)

Ensnared

Entwined

Embroiled

Embattled

The Russian Witch's Curse: (horse shifter romance!)

My Queendom for a Horse

My Dark Horse Prince

My High Horse Czar

My Wild Horse King

My Trojan Horse Majesty

My Death Horse Overlord

The Magical Misfits Series: (paranormal humor!)

My Pigeon Familiar

My Mongrel Pack

My Itching Scales

The Birthright Series:

Displaced (1)

unForgiven (2)

Disillusioned (3)

misUnderstood (4)

Disavowed (5)

unRepentant (6)

Destroyed (7)

The Birthright Series Collection, Books 1-3

The Anchored Series:

Anchored (1)

Adrift (2)

Awoken (3)

Capsized (4)

The Sins of Our Ancestors Series:

Marked (1)

Suppressed (2)

Redeemed (3)

Renounced (4)

Reclaimed (5) a novella!

A stand alone YA romantic suspense:

Already Gone